Other Books by Daniel Paisner

FICTION
Mourning Wood
Obit

NONFICTION
The Ball
Horizontal Hold
Heartlands: An American Odyssey (photographs by Jane Sobel and Arthur Klonsky)
The Imperfect Mirror

COLLABORATIONS

Game 7, 1986 (with Ron Darling)
The Power of Broke (with Daymond John)
The Way Around (with David Good)
I Feel Like Going On (with Ray Lewis)
The Fixer (with Ira Judelson)
Qaddafi's Point Guard (with Alex Owumi)
Chasing Perfect (with Bob Hurley)
Scratching the Horizon (with Izzy Paskowitz)
Nobody's Perfect
(with Armando Galarraga and Jim Joyce)
Rubber Balls and Liquor (with Gilbert Gottfried)
Every Other Monday (with John Kasich)
My Father, the Captain
(with Jean-Michel Cousteau)
The Brand Within (with Daymond John)
All Things at Once (with Mika Brzezinski)
The Trump Card (with Ivanka Trump)
On the Line (with Serena Williams)
The Complete Game (with Ron Darling)
The Girl in the Green Sweater
(with Krystyna Chiger)
Sex, Science, and Stem Cells
(with Diana DeGette)
Change in the Weather (with Mark McEwen)
The Game of My Life
(with Jason "J-Mac" McElwain)
Display of Power (with Daymond John)
A Hand to Guide Me (with Denzel Washington)
Facing Down Evil (with Clint Van Zandt)
Stand For Something (with John Kasich)
Morning Has Broken
(with Emme and Phillip Aronson)
Get Your Own Damn Beer, I'm Watching the Game! (with Holly Robinson Peete)
Moneymaker (with Chris Moneymaker)
You're Hired (with Bill Rancic)
The Price of Their Blood (with Jesse Brown)
Say What You Mean and Mean What You Say!
(with Judge Glenda Hatchett)
Winners Make It Happen
(with Leonard H. Lavin)
Last Man Down (with Richard Picciotto)
A Dozen Ways to Sunday (with Montel Williams)
The Hill (with Ed Hommer)
I'm Not Done Yet! (with Edward I. Koch)
You Have to Stand For Something or You'll Fall for Anything (with Star Jones)
Pataki: Where I Come From (with George Pataki)
Book (with Whoopi Goldberg)
True Beauty (with Emme)
Mountain, Get Out of My Way
(with Montel Williams)
One Man Tango (with Anthony Quinn)
Citizen Koch: An Autobiography
(with Edward I. Koch)
Exposing Myself (with Geraldo Rivera)
First Father, First Daughter
(with Maureen Reagan)
Theo and Me: Growing Up Okay
(with Malcolm-Jamal Warner)
America Is My Neighborhood
(with Willard Scott)

A SINGLE HAPPENED THING

A NOVEL

BY

DANIEL PAISNER

Relegation Books, USA

This book is a work of fiction. Names, characters, places, and incidents are the product of the author's imagination or are used fictitiously. Any resemblance to actual events, locales, or persons, living or dead, is entirely coincidental.

Copyright 2016 by Daniel Paisner

All rights reserved.

Cover Photograph of Fred Dunlap courtesy of Library of Congress Prints and Photographs Division (Reproduction Number LC-DIG-bbc-0351f)

Book Design: Zach Dodson
Set in Caslon

ISBN: 978-0-9847648-3-9
Library of Congress Control Number: 2015958932

A SINGLE HAPPENED THING

A NOVEL

BY

DANIEL PAISNER

RELEGATIONBOOKS
2016

FOR ROSIE BUD

Contents

PART ONE
August 1998

1. Throwback
2. A Little Thrilling
3. Catch the Train
4. And Then What?
5. The Line on Dunlap
6. Gone

PART TWO
April–October 1999

7. Plain as Day
8. Calling
9. Beaneater
10. Grand Single

PART THREE
March 2000

11. Turn Back the Clock

"What looks large from a distance, close up ain't never that big..."

—**Bob Dylan**
"Tight Connection to My Heart
(Has Anybody Seen My Love)"

PART ONE

AUGUST 1998

One
THROWBACK

I am not, by nurture or nature, an extraordinary man. I have not lived an extraordinary life. I have slept with just one woman, left the country only five times (including three trips to Canada!), and held gradations of the same job since college. There are no premium channels on my cable box, no custom calling features on my home telephone, no redeemable miles in my frequent-flyer accounts. I am not pierced, tattooed or even contact-lensed.

Such full-bodied indistinction, I feel compelled to note, did not begin with me. My grandfathers did not invent anything worth patenting or mass-producing. They did not expand any territories or collect any bootlegged fortunes, and there's not a dime accumulating interest that either one of them had a thing to do with earning. My father was a salesman, my mother a homemaker, and we siblings were all solidly in the middle of the height and weight charts throughout our growings up.

About the only extraordinary aspect of my circumstance to which I can lay any claim are the times in which I've chanced to live—although in this, too, there is nothing to set me apart from the six billion or so other ordinaries in my swirl. We, all of us, stand alike in our extra-*ordinariness* and a world apart from the couple thousand golden souls who occupy our shared attentions. We live in our sheer commonplaceness to refract the light that flows from those who make the money, the headlines, the really, really important decisions; we are dulled so they might shine.

An introduction is in order. My name is David Felb, a name I have done my best to hide behind for the nearly half-century it has been mine. Actually, the name I was given at birth was Felber, but my father thought to shorten it. He did this on the possibly confused theory that a doll-hair salesman from Queens would have a better shot at moving merch if his calling card didn't advertise his Eastern European roots, at least not quite so loudly. He got this idea from his own father—our founding ordinary!—who had earlier trimmed the family name from Felberstein on something resembling the same notion. The running joke, which I parse over family dinners, is that I just might take this genetic name-shortening one step further and change my name to Fe, which I add is often reflective of my mood.

And yet I'm not changing a thing—mostly because there's not much of the family name left to snip, and also because there's no good reason to do so. Too, I don't have it in me to make such a proactive move. I'm more the type to take things as they come, to roll with the punches, to grin and bear it . . . basically, to string together a long list of clichés to reinforce a point I seem to have made despite myself. Besides, we're already down to a lone syllable, and any remaining half-syllable might look more like a symbol from the Periodic Table than a discernable surname. David Fe is no more effective a handle for a low-level publishing type than David Felb, except in the way it suggests something exotic and Far Eastern and, well . . . out of the ordinary.

In practice, I suppose it doesn't matter what we book publicists call ourselves, because we are judged by the authors we represent and the money we have to spend on our attention-getting campaigns, and certainly not by the effort we make on ourselves. If we have the goods, and the goodies to accompany them, our calls will be returned, our jobs secure for another week. If we have a pet psychologist making the rounds on a twelve-city book tour (as has happened!), our success will owe less to our pitch or our name than it will to the whims of certain small-market talk-show producers, the alignment of the stars, the promotionally distressed leather feed bag with the book's title—*Bark Once for a Hug*—discreetly branded to a luggage tag at the zipper. It is a silly job, undertaken by silly people whose career paths will forever be charted by the silly, seat-of-the-pants decisions of others. By me: David Felb, an ordinary Jewish boy raised beneath the flight path to LaGuardia Airport in a two-family row house in Rego Park, Queens; husband to the also-ordinary (and also Jewish) Nellie, an emergency-room nurse with a great baseball name; father to three beautiful daughters (and not a doll-collector among them, despite their grandfather's constant giftings from his sample case); keeper of a strange, uncertain flame I did not seek and could not at first understand.

Okay, then. Enough with the pre-ambling. Here's what happened—how it started, anyway. It was the summer of Monica Lewinsky and Mark McGwire and *Armageddon*. I was on a short business trip to Philadelphia—a handholding, as it is known in the office. I was sent, via Amtrak, to coddle one of our midlist writers, a frighteningly serious young man who had written a frighteningly serious biography of Benjamin Franklin in which the author claimed to have uncovered letters and papers confirming the latent homosexuality of this particular founding father. In every other respect, his was a good, thorough, scholarly account, the first reappraisal of Franklin's life in more than a decade, and yet the only piece people seemed to want to talk about was this homosexuality business. I might have known, but that would have painted me a shade brighter at book publicity than I actually was. This was just as well with me, whose job it was to attract attention of any kind, on a nothing budget, and it didn't take too many brain cells to think a trip to Philadelphia might increase our profile exponentially, at no significant cost. I'd arranged a couple book signings, a reading at Penn, a lunch with a feature writer from the *Inquirer*, half an hour on the local talk-radio station, afternoon drive. This was all for a Thursday. There was also an early Friday appearance on *Wake Up, Philadelphia* or *Hey, How's It Goin', Philadelphia?* or whatever they'd taken to calling their local morning show. *Yo, Philadelphia!* Something derivatively fresh.

The plan, originally, was for me to escort the author to his interviews and appearances, and to be available to accompany him to dinner that evening, but he begged off on dinner. I understood; it must not have been an easy thing to spread such salacious information about a favorite son like Benjamin Franklin, especially to an audience of Mummers and Brotherly Lovers. To have to spend an awkward night on the town with his lowly publicist was perhaps more than he might have thought contractually expected of him.

So there I was, blessed with an evening alone. No Nellie. No girls. No social obligations. Happily, the Phillies were in town, so I taxied out to Veterans Stadium for what was left of a rare midweek doubleheader—the by-product of a tropical hurricane that had downgraded its way up the eastern coast. I was not alone in this. The resurgent Phillies were suddenly respectable, sitting unobtrusively in the vicinity of .500, and 25,000 fans would head out to the park on their own version of the same idea. The Phillies' ace, Schilling, was scheduled to pitch the first game against the strangely uniformed Arizona Diamondbacks, and the forecast called for a clear night sky, with temperatures in the low sixties and the clean scent of recent rain all around.

My first impulse was to call the front office and arrange for a house seat at field level. People in publishing do this sort of thing, whenever they can manage it, and here I might have, had I been more like most people in publishing. Some years earlier, we'd published the musings of Hall of Fame pitcher Steve Carlton: *Telling All*, a title meant to tweak the prevailing impression that the author was a tight-lipped sonofabitch who never spoke to the press. This may, in fact, have been true, but it was not an impression we could let stand if we hoped to sell a meaningful number of books, and so we prevailed on the tight-lipped sonofabitch to loosen up a bit. Helping us with the prevailing was a kind soul in the Phillies press office who had promised to set me up with tickets the next time I was in town, as I am sure he would have gladly done if I had thought to remember his name. Regrettably, a series of increasingly half-hearted inquiries revealed no such person matching my description, and I was left to make my own arrangements, and I remember thinking (also increasingly) that this was just as well, to be sent to the cheap seats with the other ordinaries, to have to pay my way in and sit where I belonged, after all.

It was a tremendous August night for baseball. Even my second-choice seating turned out just right, for I told myself it was from these heights that night baseball was meant to be seen. As I strode through the tunnel leading to my section of upper deck, I was hit once again by the bright green of the stadium carpet, the soft-tilled reddish brown of the dirt around the bases, the too-soon klieg of the pre-dusk lights overhead, the miniature sameness of the ballplayers below. One misstep brought the familiar feel of a squeezed pack of Gulden's underfoot, flattened to the concrete floor—and, now, smushedstuck to the bottom of my shoe.

I kept score. Or I meant to. The first game was nearly wrapped when I arrived, with Schilling putting the flourish on a four-hit, fourteen-strikeout performance. There was no sense doubling back to fill in my program, but I used the time between games to record the starting lineups for the nightcap and to consider that the only missing ingredient was a pennant race, some sort of final accounting for these late-summer games. The Phillies were a good young team on the come, but they were well off the pace, and the D-Backs (or Snakes, as the desperate-for-a-nickname sportswriters had quickly taken to calling the already nicknamed upstarts) were at the caboose end of the National League. It would have been nice if these games *meant* something in the larger sense of the phrase, although in truth the insignificance added a loose, meandering quality to the action.

In any case, the games seemed to mean something to the couple dozen fans in my section, approaching the right-field foul pole. We'd sprinkled ourselves among the few hundred seats as if we were contagious, splaying our legs across the empty rows in front, spanning our arms across the seatbacks at our sides. We were, a lot of us, alone, and I wondered at that, but then I realized, of course we were alone, for who but the lonely take in a meaningless late-season doubleheader, midweek, in the cheapest seats in the house? Without our children or our friends as props, we showed ourselves as we truly were: baseball fans, middle-aged, with little to amuse us beyond these ritual doings on the fake grass of an obsolete stadium.

(Aw, hell . . . we were very nearly obsolete ourselves.)

And then, second game, bottom of the third, two outs, Glanville on second and the purposeful young slugger Rolen at the plate, the skies opened up and swallowed my world whole. I don't mean to overstate, but I can't think how to tell what happened next without some sort of drumroll. (Cue the man in the lighting booth!) It happened before I could realize it. Rolen kept fouling off Arizona's kid pitcher, Sodowsky, and the count held at two balls and two strikes for the longest time. Understand, those words, *the longest time*, are carefully chosen, for the count held at two strikes as if it were freeze-framed. It is difficult to recreate here the tension of those long moments, the feeling that we were all being led down a path never before taken. It was a palpable, edge-of-the-seat sort of feeling. It was, I have no doubt, the single longest turn at bat in the history of the game. At some midpoint in the duel, I made a note to kick myself for not keeping a pitch count or setting my stopwatch at the outset, for it soon enough seemed to be some kind of record stalemate. There must have been ten foul balls by the time I sparked to what was happening, and another ten before the half-full ballpark began to recognize the tension, and another ten after that before the scattered few of us in our section of upper deck were standing with every pitch.

I was counting now. We were all counting now, and Rolen's hot bat only added to the drama. He had gone three for four in the first game, with a home run and five runs batted in, and he would go on to drive in another four runs in the second, and he had us cheering. Oh, did he have us cheering! The bat was like a magic wand in the young slugger's hands, an extension both of his meaty forearms and his very will. With each swing, I couldn't shake the feeling that Rolen knew exactly what he was doing, working the pitcher until he found *precisely* the pitch he was looking for. Whatever Sodowsky threw at him, Rolen was ready. A fought-off pitch down the third baseline, a looping slice just out of the first baseman's reach, a nothing nubber beyond the batter's box. It was a moment hasped by time and put on pause—or, better, a series of such moments, and if it weren't for the now rhythmic movements of pitcher and batter, the scampering of ball boys to retrieve the foul balls, the sleight-of-hand soft-toss of a new ball from the bottomless pockets of the home-plate umpire back to the pitcher . . . well, if it weren't for the odd, monotonous choreography of the dance, the place might have seemed pretty much still. There was movement and no movement, progress and no progress, haste and calm. We stood and cheered, sat and waited, stood and cheered.

Counting now, and slashing off another tally of five in my scorebook, I thought: Isn't it just like the world, to stop spinning and leave me reeling?

Ten minutes, things went on in this way. Fifteen. We fans flashed each other looks, as if to confirm that we were all in on some quiet piece of history. Instinctively, we sought out our ticket stubs, fisted into the tight pockets of our jeans, and thought they might now be worth something. In this, the second game of an otherwise inconsequential doubleheader, in a sport bounded not at all by time and hardly at all by space, we were caught inside the longest stretch of time between a single happened thing and the next happened thing. It was like stepping into a strange fold in the universe... and we were desperate for proof of our being there. We indicated our watches, our programs. We shrugged as if to say, "Damned if I know." We took each other in, for there weren't so many of us in the upper reaches of the right-field stands that we couldn't imprint the faces around us in the midst of such an uncommon unfolding. We wondered how this moment would be recorded, if it would be recorded at all, if we weren't perhaps imagining it.

One guy in a tight-fitting "Cubs Fever: Catch It and Die!" T-shirt pointed frantically to his radio headset, which I understood to mean a kind of confirmation. After all, a not-happening thing such as this not-happening thing could not possibly *not* happen without someone in our ears to offer the play-by-play. Otherwise, where's the context? How could we ordinaries ever hope to grab the importance of what we were experiencing without the express written consent of the Philadelphia Phillies and Major League Baseball? Who were we to judge, on our own?

A halter-topped young woman with a pierced eyebrow caught my eye and began twirling her index finger alongside her ear, as if to indicate that we were all in a shared bit of plain craziness.

Finally, twenty-two minutes in, and thirty-seven pitches into my late-in-the-game count, Rolen connected on a screaming rope down the right-field line. Actually, to set off what happened next with a qualifier like *finally* is to cut it short, for Rolen would take another swing before doubling to the gap in left-center. But it was this penultimate foul ball, the thirty-eighth (by my count), that put my story into play—and those of us in the upper reaches of the right-field stands on alert.

Truly, amazingly, the ball could not have left Rolen's bat fast enough. We have all, by now, seen McGwire's record-wounding sixty-second later that same summer, a soon-to-be-fabled drilling that made the left-field fence at Busch about a heartbeat after it left the bat. This bullet off Rolen's wand reached our section of upper deck in the same rush, and I barely had time to think it was a good thing we were all still standing. I would have had no chance at it if I had been stretched out in my seat, as I had been just a few beats before. As it was, I had a good few rows to myself, and I quick-stepped over the row in front of me to the railing and extended my bare right hand into the coolwet night air. Reaching, I thought of the dozens of nights I'd spent out at Shea, Iona in tow, willing a foul ball our way so I could see the smile on my daughter's face when I made an athletic grab and presented her with the souvenir.

(Or, more likely, so she could barehand the ball herself—and then of course I'd be the one left beaming.)

Man, was that Rolen ball hit! I might have even closed my eyes to it, I can't recall, but it was my play to make, my moment to step from these other lonely upper-deckers and take my bow. In that one protracted instant, I allowed myself to regard my catching this one foul ball as a sure thing, and I fast-forwarded to the other side of what might happen. I could see the ball in my hands, the fans below cheering my surprising agility in catching it, the players themselves looking skyward in admiration. In a flash, I could see myself shaking off the sting in an exaggerated pantomime, wanting to let the rest of the world know that it *hurt* to make such a dramatic catch, but not so much that I couldn't laugh it off. Not so much that I couldn't roll with it and collect the *attaboys!* of my upper-deck brethren like we were all in on some small, secret triumph, like this sort of thing happened to me, near me, in relation to me pretty much all the time. There I'd be, magnified on the Diamond Vision scoreboard, pumping my fists in excitement. (Hell, I could even see a highlight on *SportsCenter*, possibly to open the program.) I could see Rolen, pleasantly agreeing to sign the ball to my baseball-mad daughter Iona, after I remembered the name of the guy in the Phillies press office and arranged for a trip to the locker room after the game. I'd present the real ball to Iona, and buy a couple souvenir balls for her sisters, Sally and Patsy, and all would be right with us Felbs for the next while.

It was all so *right there*.

And then it was gone, for just as I stretched and leaned over the railing as far as I could stretch and lean over the railing, just as I relaxed my hand and waited for the ball to find it, just as I allowed the rest of the scene to write itself in my head, another arm outstretched my own and caught the ball.

My ball. My one chance to shine.

From nowhere, it seemed, a tweed-coated forearm hauled in my prize. I thought, Damn! Nothing's ever *mine*. My disappointment was perhaps more than it should have been, to have lost out on a five-dollar souvenir. And yet I was overwhelmed by a deep, suffocating regret. If you must know, I was devastated. There had been no one around, certainly no one in arm's reach, and yet somehow I was beaten, for that is how these moments left me feeling. Beaten. Duped. (Stunned!) There had been, I gathered, a remarkable catch, judging from the ovation the gentleman to my left was apparently receiving for making it. I couldn't say firsthand, because as I've suggested, I might have closed my eyes to it, or looked away at just the wrong instant, or blotted the entire business from specific memory, because the next moments remain a muddle. Soon, though, I could see there were backslaps and colorful congratulations and even an awkward high five, received by the strange interloper with the kind of graceless unfamiliarity that belied the athleticism of his great grab.

I turned and considered the man with the ball. I'd spent all that time taking in the few faces around me in the stands, but I'd never seen this man before. He was about my age and height and weight, although he carried himself as if from someplace other than the middle of the height and weight charts. He wore his medium size as if it mattered. He seemed to be about five-eight, but he had a powerhouse of a body. (There were muscles, I could swear it, in his small hands!) Surely, I would have noticed his clothes. He was dressed like a throwback—a tight-knit tweed suit (three-piece, far too heavy for August), a felt bowler, spats. And if not for the clothes, the rest of the package might have stood out on its own. The man's face was dominated by a smartly handlebarred moustache and framed by the kind of sideburns Neil Young used to wear, back when he was singing about how everybody knew this was nowhere, trimmed into an arrow shape at the end, pointing to a small mouth and an unusually bad set of teeth. He tossed the ball up and down in his remarkably small right hand, like he was looking for a game, and then he stopped to reflect on the weight and heft of his prize, the hand-sewn stitching, the official markings. It was as if he had never seen a baseball before.

"That young fellow from the Philadelphias," the man said pleasantly, looking up from the ball and indicating the batter's box, which now seemed about a hundred years away. "He swings the hickory like all creation."

The words hung in the night air, as if from a different time.

I wondered at this remark, at the unusual phrasing, and as I tried to place the accompanying unusual mannerisms I marveled once more at the clothes—indeed, at the man himself. I couldn't figure what to make of him, with his carefully groomed moustache and hair, middle-parted, slicked down with a substance that seemed to shimmer in the harsh stadium lighting. The ivory-handled cane he rested on the railing in front of him. The tailored clothes. A maroon silk waistcoat that nicely contrasted with the muted tones and the rough texture of the suit vest atop it. The well shined shoes.

He was, in every respect, a dandy.

◆

There is a reason for this account, I must state in the early going. On one level, I'll admit, it will tell the story of my undoing—my unmooring, at least. This would be my Nellie's take, although lately I've come to a different view, a more hopeful view, and so on another level it will tell a different story entirely. In my unpracticed hands, these musings will set out for anyone who has considered what it takes to accept the unacceptable, to know the unknowable, to think the unthinkable, how it is I have been lifted from the hardly moving sidewalk of my life and set down on a whole other plane. I imagine my Elder & Gold colleagues reading over my shoulder, critiquing my style—or the lack of it—but as I start in on the retelling, I must acknowledge the matter of perspective. There is the way the story I am about to share unfolded for me, the way it is unfolding still, and there is the way it can be seen by almost everyone else. There is what happened, up against what others choose to believe.

Basically, there is the not-so-plain, not-so-simple truth, and then there are its many layered consequences, and somewhere in the fine middle there is a lesson on life and love and legacy.

It is a lesson I am still trying to understand.

I suppose I should clarify. The *others* I mention here, the *everyone else*: I am referring quite specifically to only one other someone. To my one and only other someone. I am referring to my wife, Nellie, who collected the details of these events in a once-removed sort of way—and, in so doing, came to the conclusion that I was slipping away from her.

How's that for a neat little euphemism to slick-package my wife's agonizing concern? I suppose I should come right out and say it: She thought I'd gone bat-shit crazy, and along with what may or may not have been my bat-shit craziness a kind of firewall went up inside my Nellie, one I could no longer see my way over or through or otherwise past. As my days began to fill with mystery and faith and abstract wonder, hers began to fill with concern. With dread, even. For on the back of my hard-to-figure experiences, she found reasons to worry— while I, correspondingly, found reasons to wonder. And cheer. She saw the sureness of her life, of the life we'd built together, begin to unravel; I saw the fullness of our lives, in vibrant colors I'd never even imagined. In time, her perspective no longer matched my own. In time, she came to believe that the man she had married was just out of reach. More and more, just out of reach.

And maybe I was. Maybe I *have* slipped away from her. My Nellie has always been right, about most things, so maybe she has me pegged.

◆

Think of it: For an ordinary life such as mine to be touched in ways such as this was fairly preposterous. And what ways were these, exactly? If I told it straight, if I downloaded onto these pages what I now *know* to be true, you might think me a fool, or a blowhard, or—worse!—a romantic who needs to adjust his medications. Better to kind of ease you into it, as I was eased into it, as I attempted to ease Nellie into it, as Iona eased herself alongside, so that what under different circumstances might seem far-fetched will hopefully appear as merely . . . well, fetched. I have come to realize we human animals reach our various truths by degrees. A conclusion reached by leaps offers less haven than one reached by reason; wouldn't you agree? So I'll lay it out as it came to me, beginning with that unfathomable encounter in the upper reaches of Veterans Stadium.

"That young fellow from the Philadelphias," the well-dressed interloper said—I repeat myself, I know—"he swings the hickory like all creation."

"Ash, actually," I finally, stupidly remarked, after pausing again to take in the man's appearance. I had just read that the majority of Major League Baseball bats were now being made from northern ash lumber, and for some reason I felt it necessary to correct the record.

"I'm afraid I don't understand," the ball-catcher said pleasantly. He spoke with the kind of swallowed-up vowels and rolled consonants I now place as coming from the Baltimore area.

"Ash," I explained. "The kind of wood they use. For the bats."

He nodded. "It's a funny expression, then," he offered. "I suppose at one time, they were made from hickory."

"I suppose," I supposed.

He paused to reflect on this revelation. "Old wagon tongue," he eventually added, smiling in such a way that his moustache appeared to do a small dance. It curled and dipped and would not sit still. "Never understood that one either."

"Now it's me you've lost," I said. Old wagon tongue? I wrote the words in the margin of my scorecard, thinking I could look up the phrase. There was a lot to consider all at once. I was still marveling at the sudden appearance of this gentleman to my left, at losing out on Rolen's foul ball, at the marvelous, unimaginable turn at bat we'd all just witnessed, at the odd, unspoken fraternity that seemed to rise among us in those outfield stands . . . while underneath I was being made to small-talk my way toward an inevitable introduction. If we weren't careful, we'd back right into a nice, fat handshake, and then where would we be?

The awkward silence stretched between us as if it might become another Rolen at-bat—another fold in time into which this unusual fellow could exit just as swiftly as he had entered—but I could not wait it out.

"David Felb," I eventually said, extending my hand, not knowing what else to do but make this man's acquaintance.

He clutched my hand in his and I was right away taken by the gentleness of the gesture. He had a mighty grip, I'd been right about that, but oh, were his hands small! And yet, just a moment before, I had seen him reach out and barehand a rope off Rolen's bat without flinching.

"My card," he said in introduction, fishing in his suit vest for an ivory-topped card case that matched the detailing on his cane, and pulling from it a linen-white business card about a half-inch shorter on all sides than most conventional styles, closer to square than rectangular. The edges of the card were fancily frayed in the manner of the pages of the more high-minded books we publish at Elder & Gold. "An honor to meet you, Mr. Felb," he said, handing over the card. "My apologies for upstaging you on the ball."

He held the ball out again—whether to show it to me or to study it once more, I could not be sure. He turned it in the light and considered the stitching, the weight of it, the feel in his small, powerful hand.

"'S'okay," I stammered. "It's just, you know, I didn't see you. I didn't think there was anybody else nearby."

At this, he merely smiled amiably.

I looked at the card. There was no address. No telephone number. No e-mail, cell phone, or fax. Just a simple inscription in raised letters: *Fred Dunlap, Pittsburgh Nationals*. It seemed to hardly announce the man's arrival, much less offer a clue how to subsequently contact him.

I stood there gracelessly for a beat or two, perhaps longer, not knowing what was called for in a social situation such as this. I had nothing to go on except to follow this other man's lead, so I fisted my wallet from my rear pocket and located a card of my own—this one entirely not linen and not at all fancily frayed. I handed it over and the man took it gladly, as if he had some sort of collection going.

Having never heard of Fred Dunlap, or the Pittsburgh Nationals, which I later deciphered as accepted shorthand for the Pittsburgh baseball club of the National League, once dubbed the Alleghenys and then the Innocents but soon and widely and still known as the Pirates, I simply pocketed the card and returned my attention to the game. At least, that was my intention. The stranger kept his place to my left—directly to my left, in the seat next to mine, notwithstanding the empty seats all around. He was hungry for talk of baseball, wanted to know the names of the players, their tendencies, the arcs of their careers. Or maybe what he wanted was the company—and in all modesty, at a baseball game, I'm not a hard guy to be around. (I don't mean to talk big, but this is what I've been told.) He was particularly amused at the way the scoreboard announced updated batting averages before each turn at bat, remarking how in his day such numbers were usually compiled at the close of each week of play.

"And what day was that, Mr. Dunlap?" I tried, bemused, having assumed by the lines on his face that we were about the same age.

He ignored the question and moved instead to the next item on his open list of fascinations. "You have children, Mr. Felb?"

"David," I said. "We're at a ball game. You can call me David."

"Alright, David. And you can call me Fred. Dunny, if you'd prefer."

"Okay, Fred," I said, reaching under my seat for the beer I'd left behind a half-inning before. "What is it you want to know?"

"I was wondering if you had any children."

"Three," I said. "Girls."

"They are fans of the Philadelphias?"

"Actually, they're partial to the Mets. The oldest has a thing for Mike Piazza."

He smiled in a way that suggested he did not know Mike Piazza from Hoss Radbourn.

"Catcher," I explained. "Hits a ton."

"A ton of what?" my new friend wanted to know, but with this the inning came to an end—the Phillies having managed just one run, stranding Rolen at second—and as the Arizona Diamondbacks left the field the strange man sitting next to me stood and did the strangest thing. He seemed to do it without thinking, for I saw no notion of it alight on his face. It was as if he'd been waiting for the inning to end, so he could do what was expected of him, what he'd meant to do all along. He whistled, presumably to catch the attention of someone a long distance away, perhaps someone down on the field. And it was no ordinary whistle. It was the kind of full-throated trill that would win prizes in calling contests for whatever farm animals are known to respond to whistling. The man pulled back his face, and as the handlebars on his moustache tucked in over his bared teeth, he let forth a shrill, high-pitched warble that might have pierced the night sky. I would not have guessed such a sound existed in nature if I hadn't heard it myself—up-close enough that my left ear rang for the next while.

Realize, we were in the upper reaches of the right-field upper deck, in the shadow of the foul pole, with the ballpark only half full, but the sound carried as if it were amplified over the public address system. And it might as well have been, for it seemed as if everyone in Veterans Stadium stopped what they were doing and turned skyward in our direction. Vendors, box-seated fans, ball boys, umpires, even the Arizona Diamondbacks returning to their dugout from their positions in the field: No one could guess what had made such a noise.

Somehow, my interloper made eye contact with Devon White, the fleet Arizona center fielder, just beyond second base. He cemented this eye contact with some furious hand-waving of the sort I had not seen since the cancellation of a children's television show called

Wonderama, to which I was unreasonably devoted as a small child. In all this attention-getting and -holding, White actually stopped, directly astride the second-base bag, facing the right-field foul pole, and crossed his arms to consider what this unusual fan in the sky seats might do next. From the vast distance that separated us, it was possible to confuse the ballplayer (at least in posture and affect) with Yul Brynner, for surely these developments were a puzzlement to us all.

White's teammates left the field, but he stood still. He appeared to want to play this out, whatever it was. Yes, there was a game to be completed, and a commercial break to be gotten through; yes, it was August, both teams playing out the string; yes, it was the second game of a midweek doubleheader, but the center fielder seemed to have all the time in the world.

The Phillies, too, held their spots in the first-base dugout, not wanting to take the field until White had finished making his stand. The guy had been around the league; he'd been an All-Star. If he wanted to stand at second base and have a moment to himself, they weren't about to take it from him. Plus, they wanted to see what would happen—ballplayers, at bottom, being as ordinary as lowly book publicists and everyone else in the too-calm stadium, fixed as we all appeared to be on this remarkable exchange.

After a long moment of this, the man to my left held up one finger to White down on the playing field. White offered a slight nod in receipt of the gesture, and in a swift, effortless motion the man next to me managed to remove his waistcoat, hand it to me for safekeeping, step into the aisle to allow himself more leg room, reach back, kick, and throw with a somewhat constrained version of the unusual sidearm motion I would later read about and attempt to replicate. He sent Rolen's foul ball rocketing back to the playing field in the kind of straight line usually reserved for architectural drawings, in the kind of hurry usually claimed by sound. Devon White, it turned out happily, had been the recipient of several Gold Glove awards for his slick center-fielding, which left him more than qualified to lift his glove in time to grab the throw. He didn't have to wait for the ball, or move toward it, or do much of anything but open his glove to it and absorb its surprising impact, right around his midsection. Really, the ball *thopped* into White's mitt with the kind of purpose I remembered from those snap-cords you used to see on vacuum cleaners before concerned parents decided those whipped-around plugs were a danger to their two-eyed children.

And you could hear it! All the way up in our section, you could hear the *thop*, like a thunderclap. The place was so otherwise silent that the plush smack of pill against mitt echoed all around, and in the flash of time we fans had to consider if we had in fact seen what we all thought we had seen and heard what we all thought we had heard, we had time to also consider the circumstances. We'd all seen this same man make a remarkable catch of this same ball. We'd all stood to cheer—all of us except at first for me, who could not climb from my crestfallenhood in time to offer congratulations. We'd all marveled at Rolen's monumentally long turn at the plate and wondered at its history-making implications. And we'd all returned our attentions to the rest of the inning, and the run it produced, and its place on the string of this long season. It all came together, in a rush of clarity, to where those of us whose attentions were caught by this peculiar display were able to make a kind of sense of it. Yes, we had time to think. This is not so unusual. This is a man who caught a ball and is simply returning it to the field of play. This happens, sometimes. In Chicago, in the Wrigley Field bleachers, it happens every time a visiting player clears the ivy. And from these heights, who knows how a ball is meant to travel? Maybe the line and pace of the ball are unavoidable, when thrown from these upper reaches, a couple hundred feet from field level, and another couple hundred from Devo's place at second to the corresponding point beneath our seats. Maybe this is how things are supposed to go, when they go in just this way.

At the other end of this unexpected business, there followed a sustained and genuine applause, and the kind of head-scratching you could actually see from where this gentleman and I looked down on the confused and delighted faces all around. A great many fans had been milling about or moving toward the concession areas and were unaware of any between-innings excitement, but they quickly returned to their seats or repositioned themselves to understand the fuss. As a result, I managed to detect two giant, separate waves of recognition following this stunning throw: one from those of us who had seen and heard it all, and the other from those who had momentarily looked away and been pulled back in time to worry over what rare thing they'd just missed. And at the cross-currents of these two waves, there was Devon White, alone now on the field, the ball fairly suctioned to his glove. There was nothing for him to do but remove the ball and hold it skyward in his bare hand, and point with the index finger of that bare hand toward our spot in the right-field upper deck. Then he dropped to his knees and offered a bow of supplication, also in our direction, which I guessed was a play on the "We're not worthy!" catch-gesture from one of those *Saturday Night Live* sketches that refuse to go away.

It was, as moments go, grand.

And, as ballpark moments go, it was so far off the map of our shared experience that I didn't quite know how to react. None of us did, I now imagine, and we simply rode whichever of those giant waves had to do with us and let it take us where it might. I found myself cheering, along with everyone else, and disbelieving, but then I turned to my new acquaintance and crinkled up my face in a look of such utter confusion that he must have felt the need to explain himself.

"In case they run out," he said, clapping too, caught in the same strangeness that gripped us all. He must have seen from my expression that this last was no explanation, and so continued: "It's a two-gamer. They'll need the ball back before too long."

Two
A LITTLE THRILLING

There was everything to say, and no place to begin.

Returning to my hotel room, decompressing, moving instinctively to call home . . . my one clear thought was that I couldn't get the words out fast enough. A thing like this (and it was a relatively small thing at first), it overtakes you until there's nothing else.

There is what you know and what you can only imagine—and then, in the vast, uncertain middle, there is something perilously in between.

I'll offer this: It doesn't take much to get me going once I stray from the familiar, which for its part was combusting on the other end of the phone, waiting for me to tap back into it. It was like I was merely downtown, and running late, instead of out of town and running out of ways to explain the inexplicable. There was Nellie's day, and whatever was going on with the kids at school, and various logistical details such as when my train was due at Penn Station the next afternoon and whether I would have time to stop at the apartment for lunch before heading to the office. The *so on* and *so forth* of the life we had cobbled together. (The *lives* we had cobbled together!) There was a report on what the exterminator had found that might explain the profusion of water bugs in and around our bathtub drain, and another unreturned phone call from the guy we'd supposedly hired to remodel our kitchen. Oh, and a new draft of a will for Nellie and me to jointly consider, prepared for us by an estate-lawyer friend of one of Nellie's cousins who'd taken the time at a family wedding to press the notion of mortality onto our otherwise preoccupied spirits. And yet all of these regular distractions would have to wait for this astonishment to pass.

Ah, yes . . . *that*!

But what, exactly, was the extent of my astonishment, as I closeted myself in my Suisse Chalet economy suite after a short cab ride from Veterans Stadium and hurriedly called home? Whatever it was, there was too much for just me, just then, and Nellie—sweet Nellie, sweet-tolerant-willing-to-get-caught-in-my-excitement Nellie—had been a mere phone call away. See, at just that moment, I knew nothing of Fred Dunlap beyond the fancily frilled and oddly dimensioned business card I now held gingerly in my pocketed right hand. I knew nothing of his triumphs, his holdout, his sad passing. Indeed, I couldn't imagine that I would ever again set eyes on the strange gentleman who had alighted in my section of upper deck like particles of moonbeam, that I would ever have cause to consider him, again and again and again.

"It'll be on television, Nellie," I said, wanting her to taste what I had just tasted. "You'll see."

"And what is it I'll be looking for, my baby boy?" Nellie sang back, teasing.

"The throw to second base," I said. "The catch. Everything."

"The spats?" she pushed. "Will they make it on *SportsCenter*, do you think?"

With this, I suspected Nellie's sweet tolerance had morphed into impatience, and I realized I had been filling her ear with more than she cared to know. Or, more than she could process without having been there at my side. She was home with our three children, her out-of-town husband had nearly caught a foul ball and met a fairly unusual somebody, and my, wasn't it the longest at-bat she could remember? Of course, even Nellie had her limits.

"Too much?" I said, slowing suddenly.

"Like, a couple pounds over."

"Sorry, but—"

"No sorries, Felb," she said, cutting me off. (I not-so-secretly love it when she calls me Felb.) "You had a nice time. Something a little weird happened, a little thrilling. You want to share it. It won't kill me to listen."

"True," I allowed, "and it won't kill me to wait. I'll be home tomorrow."

"I'm working night shift," she said, which meant I'd have the girls for the evening. Baths. Reading. Maybe catch a couple innings of the

Mets game on television with Iona after Sally and Patsy go to bed, maybe fill Iona in on the strange doings in the right-field stands out at the Vet and hope she'd understand.

"But lunch?" I said. "You're around?"

"I'm around. Love you."

That she does, my Nellie. Since 1981. Russian Tea Room. Elder & Gold Christmas party—my first at the venerable second-tier publishing house. She was riding EMT detail out of Columbia Presbyterian and caught the call when our marketing director went down with a massive coronary. I was on a more dubious assignment, riding junior flack detail, trying for the sixth or seventh time that holiday season to make a good first impression on my various superiors—one of whom, in fact, had been the felled marketing director, who looked at me, after some insipid, first-impressionless remark, turned an autumnal shade of orange-yellow, and slumped to the floor. The poor guy was dead by the time the ambulance arrived, after which, for some reason, there was a lot of waiting around—which, for some other reason, didn't manage to quite kill the party. Apparently, there were two ambulance crews dispatched to the scene, and some confusion over which was to take the body back to the hospital, and no good reason to send everybody else home, with all that food and drink and Russian elegance already paid for. Nellie and I spent the too-long wait making goofy eyes at each other, and soon enough some goofy small talk, and by the time the two crew chiefs sorted out their responsibilities we were planning to meet later for coffee.

Some people meet cute; we met hairy.

Turned out Nellie was right about *SportsCenter*, because I watched the same show twice, wrapped around half an hour of *Baseball Tonight*, looking for my highlight, and there were no spats, no sure shots to Devo a-huggin' second.

Watching, hungry for small-screen validation, I started to wonder: What is it about our public events—baseball games, presidential inaugurals, riots—that leaves us racing for the television to place ourselves in context? It is as if we haven't been until we can relive our having been on television, until others can place us at the epicenter of public attention. Absolutely, the having been has supplanted the being there as a kind of currency, and television's role has become to confirm our place in the cultural firmament. Yes? Or is it that I'm merely weighing one odd, hazy experience against the also-odd, also-hazy experience of absorbing an endless loop of inconsequential mid-August sports highlights, trolling for confirmation?

Nellie again, this time electronically—and, rather miraculously, after an inability to sleep tossed me to the dormant laptop on the slab of pressed wood that passed for a desk in my Suisse Chalet economy suite. I'd carted the thing along to pass the time on the long train ride, to polish a couple press releases I'd needed to finish to keep up with the fall list, to sort what insignificant e-mail might come my way. (Mostly, though, to keep my string of consecutive wins going in the FreeCell game that had come bundled with my purchase—this before I'd figured out I could simply abort a game if it wasn't going well and still convince the computer my streak was intact.)

Checking in, I'd seen a lobby card with a photo of Dick Cavett, or Dick Clark (some Dick), trumpeting the motel chain's commitment to "multi-task preparedness," which among other conveniences promised a modem jack in every room. And so, hardly thinking but nevertheless multi-task prepped, I rolled out of bed, crawled around on the not-too-filthy carpet looking for the promised jack, flipped open the screen on my Dell Inspiron notebook and commanded the thing to start dialing local America Online access numbers, all with the kind of fluid motion that belied my otherwise technophobic nature.

It was as if I did this sort of thing all the time.

Bummer, Felb, Nellie had written behind her neat NURSENEL screen name that always left me thinking of the too-white Tretorn tennis shoes she wore to work each shift, her baby-blue scrubs. *Nothing on ESPN, CNN or MSG. Possible you're hallucinating?*

How about that? I marveled to myself. I didn't just think it; I marveled. The distinction is important because, to just me, just then, it was a truly remarkable revelation, that my Nellie would e-razz me for expecting to see such a small event as my nearly catching a foul ball replayed for a national cable audience, and yet would also stay up late to see for herself. She's a fan, as I believe I have written, although perhaps fanatic is too worked-up a description for her muted brand of zeal. She appreciates baseball, understands its history and its place on our shared landscape. She's certainly watched enough of it these days, thanks to Iona, our little phenom. Nellie knows the game and its nuances, although she's more aesthete than fan. She follows the doings of her favorite players (lately, the dazzling young Cuban shortstop Rey Ordonez of the hometown Mets), but what she can't abide is the endless going over of nothing much at all that tends to fill the hour-long *SportsCenter*-type shows that have metastasized on late-night television. She can't even suffer the seconds-long bits I sometimes smuggle in during commercial breaks of the syndicated sitcoms she likes to consume when the house is finally quiet. And so, absolutely, that Nellie Beane Felb had apparently abandoned *Taxi* or *Cheers* or whatever retread she'd been watching these nights to join her pathetic-seeming husband in his pathetic-seeming enthusiasms was a marvelous thing indeed.

Trust me, I quickly wrote back behind my own PRGUY37 handle, which proudly advertised that I had been the thirty-seventh male (at least!) to toil in at least the appearance of some capacity in the public-relations field to live down to the creative challenge of coining an AOL screen name.

Nellie, as if from the next room: *Riddle me this, doughboy...*

Riddle her what? I wondered. *???* I shot back.

(I not-so-secretly hated it when she called me doughboy, a thing she rarely did in public, but I chose to let it pass electronically. It's tough to start an argument online, and I knew she was just being playful. I am, after all, her baby doughboy. Her baby doughboy public relations guy.)

What's a wee publicist like you doing up at such a wee hour?

Hmmm, I thought. A riddle. A tease. Or perhaps it was just the familiar blather that sometimes passes between husband and wife, even electronically. *Wee Willie Winkie*, I wrote back, intending to hold up my end of the blather, but instead sending only this first bit before doubling back and completing the opening refrain: *Running through the forest.*

Missing you, I got back, meaning we had now sidled into that corner of the space-time-instant-messaging cosmos that allows otherwise intelligent people to step on each other's lines as if two-way communication had not yet been invented. Experience warned that if one of us didn't hold our IM tongues for an extra couple beats, we'd be talking over ourselves for the rest of the evening.

I waited a shade longer in my response before typing back. *U 2,* I finally tried, meaning in the shorthand I'd picked up from our girls that I was missing her too.

Running through the town, I got back, suggesting Nellie had waited half a shade shorter than her impatient, creatively challenged baby doughboy of a husband. *There are no forests in London.*

Sherwood Forest, I tried. *Where's that?*

U 2???

As in, you too.

Remember that ski hill, lower Catskills, Sherwood Forest?

I uses TT4N, to sign off. The "I" referred to our oldest, Iona, who resented her name except for the fact that it left the rest of us referring to her in her first person, which was unwittingly appropriate, and just about the way a just-about-fourteen-year-old figures she fits into the rest of the world.

Nell's turn: *Upstairs, downstairs, in his night gown.*

Sterling Forest, I think.

Remind me to tell you what the vet said.

Pataki's in the news. New York State is buying up all that land. Our own private Idaho.

Are we going round and round here, or is it me?

River Phoenix, yes? Our own private Idaho.

That's where we used to ski?

Tough Titty For Nellie?

Ta Ta For Now.

This time, I waited a good long while, wondering if my last message might stand as explanation and signoff. Yes, it was a sweet, intimate thrill to find my Nellie online—at this late hour, over this not-so-very-long distance—but it wasn't enough of a sweet, intimate thrill to keep us amused indefinitely.

That it, then? I finally got back.

That it.

TT4N.

XXX.

I logged off before Nellie had another chance at a signoff, and as I slipped between the well-tucked sheets of my too-pillowed bed I realized that the two of us had been so momentarily charmed by a recent innovation we'd forgotten the more fulfilling charms of a previous one. I might have called her again. Nellie might have called. Think of it: We'd been enslaved by the technology more than we'd been liberated by it, and I found time to wonder in that space between sleep and racing imagination how we are sometimes trapped by the moment, our various indecisions mapped by technology, or custom, or some confluence of circumstances outside our own experience. We make our progress by degrees, I sleepily reminded myself, but rarely on a direct line forward. We plow ahead because we can and double back because we must, and in the balance we might find we've inched somewhat forward, or to the side, or shifted our positions so subtly we can't recognize the change.

I must tell you, these ramblings made enormous sense to me that night in my Suisse Chalet economy suite as I struggled to nod off. In half-consciousness, they seemed to fairly crystallize the whole of our human condition—at least, the whole of *my* human condition—but as I set them to paper now they seem ... well, rambling. Unsophisticated. Without focus. The product of a lazy, acquiescent mind, reluctant to drift off for fear it might miss something.

There was also this: As I tossed and turned a final time or two, my right hand brushed lazily across my pillowed brow in a way that nearly shook me from half-sleep to full alert. There was a sharp, throbbing pain pushing back against my hand that seemed to arise on its own. And yet there it was—a knot, a bruise, a swelling of some kind, at just about my hairline. Whatever it was, I touched it again, and another pain shot through me, only this time I was braced for it. This time, it was just something to notice, and as I did I thought what to make of it, but I'm afraid I didn't get too far in this because that's the last thing I remember from that fateful evening.

I closed my eyes and I was gone.

◆

My Iona, she's the writer in the family. She's the one who can sit down in front of a computer and have the words flow from her fingertips like nothing at all. I look on and wonder if she even stops to think when she writes, or if the stuff just comes. Her latest efforts are on behalf of her school newspaper, *The Quartermaster*, in which she's been given a sports column and the freedom to fill it as she pleases. School sports, professional sports, the karmic implications of serving flash-frozen sushi in the right-field stands at Shea Stadium... whatever catches her attention.

But this is meant to be about my frustrations, not Iona's accomplishments. These sustained musings are a first for me—no doubt because until that bizarrely missed opportunity in Veterans Stadium I never had anything to say. Nothing had ever happened to me or in any way remotely connected to me that seemed worth sharing in any public way. I had never been the type to regale friends and family with stories, to hold someone's attention as if I had some insight to offer or a special flair for the dramatic. I'd long supposed, though, that if a head-scratching dilemma or significant epiphany or unlikely piece of excitement should have somehow alighted in my path, I would have the tools at my disposal to make a note of it. Every hack would-be writer who's ever signed up for a writing workshop has been told by his hack would-be instructor that a writer must write what he knows, but what did I know, after all? All I knew, really, was what it took to settle, how to get by, how to ensure that my reach would never exceed my grasp. Oh, I loved my wife and my three beautiful daughters, and I knew they loved me, for reasons that by now had reached beyond blood and proximity, but in every other respect, my life had been a disappointment. I'd made a living out of coming up short, succeeding merely in extending the ordinary string of affairs begun by my grandparents and sustained by my parents, accomplishing nothing less than what was expected of me, and nothing more.

Christ, I was a book publicist—and not a particularly good one at that. In the social pecking order of the Upper West Side of Manhattan, I fell somewhere between the guy who orchestrates the sweepstakes mailings for Publishers Clearing House and the office manager at a small accounting firm. It killed me to admit it, but I had the kind of job that would somehow get done without me—and if it didn't, it wouldn't much matter. Once, during an ill-advised Career Day appearance before Sally's second-grade class, I made the mistake of suggesting that one of the "neat" parts of my job was the chance it gave me to meet famous people. Actually, the admission contained two mistakes for the price of one: I used the word "neat" in front of my daughter's friends, and I failed to name any celebrity authors of my personal acquaintance other than the Rice University historian who'd just completed the second volume of a lifelong work on Estes Kefauver.

Stasis.

If I'd somehow taken up the guitar and thrown in with a motley crew of middle-aged lazies who had also become suddenly and mysteriously proficient on drums and keyboards, that'd be the name of our heavy-metal cover band. *Stasis.* No new songs, no new arrangements...just the same old material, sounding slightly *off*, played by going-nowhere guys like me who needed an outlet for their regret. And yet even such as this was beyond me. I would never do anything that interesting. I would never go anywhere interesting. I would never witness anything interesting. I would never write anything beyond memos and flap copy and travel itineraries. I would simply love my wife and my daughters and hold them close and continue to take in meaningless midweek doubleheaders and mismanage the selling strategies of our midlist titles and ride along whatever middling currents I could manage until I washed up on some predictable shore.

At least, that was where I was before this chance collision between everything I knew and everything I imagined. Before this odd confluence of wonder and fear and disillusionment and just about every emotion that had ever registered in my limited range. It may have been nothing, and at this early point that's all it amounted to, but it may have been everything, as well. Something like this—losing out on an historic foul ball to a man who appeared as a specter, a trick of the mind—it doesn't just *happen*, does it?

Three
CATCH THE TRAIN

Next morning, seven or so, I wrapped a towel around my waist and poked my head through my triple-locked and oddly chained hotel-room door, hoping to find a complimentary copy of *USA Today* at my feet.

Regrettably—and, perhaps, predictably—there was none. The length of maroon-based paisley carpeting stretching from my room to the corner by the third-floor ice machine was dotted every here and there by the rectangles of colored newspapers, only the here and there did not happen to overlap with where I was at the time. This troubled me initially, being without my own freshly folded set of complimentary news, until I realized it was not meant as some sort of slight, or nod to my modest station, as much as it was more likely a lapse in the Suisse Chalet's internal procedures. It was, I knew, nothing personal, even as I took it personally. And it continued to trouble me as I considered my next moves. I could have retreated into my room uninformed of the colorful events of the day before—and, as ever, a step behind the rest of the world. I could, perhaps, have pinched a copy from one of my unfortunate neighbors. (Who but a peep-holing guest in one of the adjacent rooms would have known?) Or, I could have merely stolen a look at the sports section of the paper nearest my feet—which, after all, was all I was after. I didn't need to actually *own* a complimentary copy of *USA Today*; I just needed to borrow one, and I folded the odd tuning-fork of a door latch so it faced flat across the open doorway, making sure not to inadvertently lock myself out of my room. And so there I stood, barefoot and toweled, off on some barely illicit and hardly shameful mission, prevented from further indignity by a safety lock shaped like a Jew's harp and deployed in a manner wholly counter to its design. This deep into the enterprise, I reverted to the less time-consuming option of swiping the paper outright. Let another of my fellow travelers go overlooked, I rethought as I set off. There's nothing that says it always has to be me.

I must admit, the feel of the Suisse Chalet's mostly maroon industrial weave underfoot was like a summons. Those same bare feet had only steps earlier been atop a similar weave, no doubt woven in the same mill, and purchased on the same order, only here, now, beyond the comfort of my own room, it felt like I was walking over hot coals. With one step, I belonged; with the next, I did not.

I've searched my Microsoft Word thesaurus for a verb to adequately convey my swift early-morning movements down a quiet hotel hallway wearing only a towel, and about the best I've come up with is *scurried*. *Scooted* doesn't quite do it, suggesting some sort of motor I did not, at that moment, possess, and *scampered* strikes me as somehow too catlike and playful. So, I scurried. And, being forty-six at the time and not having scurried in a too-long while, I think I also pulled something, some muscle where my energies hadn't reached since I started sitting mostly still for a living. Bending, too, was its own bother, constricted as I was first by the wrapped-around towel, and now by the pulled something or other, and I found myself hoping no one was looking down the 301-to-319 room corridor at just that moment. I didn't exactly cut a graceful figure. I couldn't even stoop to pick up the paper. What I actually did, I think, was curtsy.

To be clear: It had been some time since I'd been called upon to scurry and curtsy in very nearly the same motion—in all probability, it was a Felb first!—but I pulled it off with the towel in place and skulked back to my room with my prize, hopefully unseen. I let the door find the jamb behind me, rested my back against it, and allowed myself the small actorly sigh I'd seen mostly in bad television movies when the main character narrowly escapes some predicament or other.

Just then, there was a knock on my door. It wasn't a thundering *hey-you-in-there!* sort of knock, although it did startle me from my tiny sigh. I've since figured it was a rather tentative, unobtrusive sort of knock, the kind you might attempt when you're not wanting to disturb the person on the other side of the door unless that person happened to have his head resting against it.

I thought: room service? Hotel security? The guy in 311, looking for his pinched *USA Today*?

"Yes?" I said, a little too loudly, reconsidering the soft knock.

"Mr. Felb?" I heard back in the kind of whisper you might expect from a person not wanting to awaken the entire third floor at seven in the morning. "I'm sorry to trouble you at this hour, but I noticed you were up. I thought we might speak."

I couldn't place the voice—although, to be honest, my racing mind was well ahead of this small point and focused on the somewhat larger issue of what the hell was going on. "Who is it?" I tried.

"Mr. Dunlap," came the measured reply. "From last night. I feared I left you in a pucker over that baseball."

Naturally, with the name now attached to voice and circumstance, I knew who it was in a flash, and as I made the connection I had time to think it was rather presumptuous of this Mr. Dunlap to assume I'd know what he was talking about. But then, how could I not know? It was all I could think about—the one that got away! What I didn't know was what a pucker was, but I didn't see that it much mattered, and what I couldn't figure was how the man had traced me here, but if I dwelled on this last for any length of time I might have shit.

"It's early, Mr. Dunlap," I said, wanting instinctively to put him off. "Maybe we could meet in the coffee shop downstairs. Say, in about an hour?"

"Ah," he said, "you fellows and your coffee." There was a too-long pause, then: "An hour would be fine."

I stepped from the door thinking I was out of my mind to meet with this curious stranger, in a strange city, at this strange hour of the morning. At that point, I confess, I didn't know that I would. It was one thing to set a vague appointment, and another to keep it. See, one of the basic agreements Nellie and I have with each other is not to die foolishly. We've discussed this. If one of us is hit by a car or a falling safe, so be it. Malaria. Toxic shock. Embolism. The deal is, if it's out of our hands, it's out of our hands, but if I suddenly determined to take up skydiving, or drunk driving, or consorting with gang-bangers,

I'd be in violation. I even ignore my cholesterol levels at my own peril. Neither of us wants to be left behind with the notion that our partner had been a complete ass where his or her wellbeing had been concerned. It's basic. Surely, inviting this Fred Dunlap person into my hotel room at seven in the morning would have qualified as foolish on top of foolish.

Still, I was torn. I leaned this way and that. Should I stay, rooted in my unremarkable sameness, or should I take what I had quickly begun thinking of as the biggest leap of faith in the history of leaps of faith? There were arguments both ways, and I used the good portion of my hour to offer voice to each side. Yes, I actually spoke these thoughts aloud—to myself, to whatever gods or fates had conspired to leave me in such a predicament, to unimagined electronic surveillance devices that might have been planted in any number of nooks or crannies of my so-called suite.

The man could crush an eagle with his bare hand, I thought—somewhat unreasonably, I should add, save for the fact that I was in Philadelphia, with the penumbra of team sports on the brain and the somewhat more salient recollection of the man's unusually firm grip.

Really, I couldn't think how to explain this man's sudden appearance the night before at the stadium. That he was here, now, left the realm of the reasonable and the expected and entered into another dimension entirely. You have to understand, we in publishing are often the purveyors of all manner of unorthodox thought. Actually, you don't *have* to understand this, but I believe it helps. It goes to state of mind, as I've too often heard said by scripted defense attorneys deflecting the knee-jerk challenges of scripted prosecutors. It goes to how an otherwise educated, literate, professional-type person can find room in his thinking for possibility. For an out-of-the-ordinary thing to collide headfirst into an ordinary existence. Here is my armchair philosophy: I read, therefore I think. And, relatedly: I think, therefore I am. Up until these hard-to-figure moments in Philadelphia, unchallenged at work and grooved into routine at home, I had far too much time for both, reading and thinking, therefore I was far too inclined toward chance, and so I was leaned all the way out the window and kept from falling by my heels. Out of nowhere, and for no good reason, I justified what had happened, and what was about to happen, and what was likely happening without my knowing as having to do with fate. Mine. Fred Dunlap's. Someone's. This . . . *thing* was far bigger than any other *thing* I'd ever been called upon to consider. I didn't have the tools to explain it any other way.

I *knew*. And yet I wasn't sure, so I started talking to myself.

"You're out of your mind, Felb," I said.

"Play it out a little longer, see where it goes."

"Order room service."

"Catch the train."

"Order room service."

"Catch the train."

(This last was like a mantra.)

As I spoke, I continued showering, dressing, and going through a series of general leave-taking motions that would allow me to keep the appointment. It was as if the decision to meet this oddly out-of-place man in the coffee shop of the Suisse Chalet was not an issue so much as a fascination. My descending to the lobby had developed its own head of steam, and I was powerless against it. I went through the motions of withstanding, but they were motions, just.

It was at this moment I remembered the knot on my forehead from the night before. As I finished in the bathroom, I caught a glimpse of myself in the big-screen mirror atop the sink, and it occurred to me there had been a small concern as my head hit the pillow and I fell off to sleep. It came to me like a flash-memory. There had been a tenderness, a sharp pain against the slight touch of my hand, but now as I studied my face in the mirror I could find no bruise or discoloration. There was no swelling of any kind, nothing to suggest what may or may not have been the source of my dreamy pain.

There was only my plain face, staring back at me with a look of crinkled-up confusion and wonder.

◆

I headed for the coffee shop about ten minutes early. I paused to imagine how the encounter might go, what I was expecting, and I realized I expected nothing and everything all at once. I worked the equation in my head: Nothing plus everything equals anything.

Anything . . .

There was no cap on my imagination, no end to where things might lead. It smelled more than a little like buying one of those scratch-off lottery tickets at the newsstand. When the notion hits and the loose change in your pocket makes the argument against long odds and rational thought, there is no holding back, and in the tug and pull between impulse and reason there is a small, sweet voice: *What if?* That's all I ever need to hear. *What if?* What if the ticket I am meant to buy, the one at the top of the pile, or the one at the in-use end of the roll, or however it is they dispense these things . . . what if that's the one? What if the road not taken turns out to have been the path to glory? Yes, absolutely, the next one could always be mine. It's always someone's, and it might as well be mine. Anyway, you never know, right? You never expect the stars to truly align and smile on your affairs, but you are ever mindful that they might, they just might, and you don't want to be caught not believing. *What if?* Stay open, or keep closed. One day, and soon, your number will be called, and you will be pulled from the not-so-swift currents of your existence and set down upon the unbelievably treacherous whitewaters of uncertainty. Or not . . . but that's not the point. That's never the point. The point, always, is to step to the plate and take your cuts. Expect nothing and everything all at once. Believe.

Anything can happen.

And so, have me committed, I stepped warily into the aggressively lit coffee shop off the Suisse Chalet lobby with my overnight bag and sought my fate. Of course, at just that moment, I was still blissfully unaware of Fred Dunlap's place in baseball history. I didn't even know he had a place in baseball history beyond the previous night's game. All he was, at just that moment, was an oddly overdressed man sitting silently in a booth by a far window, overlooking the parking lot, struggling with a menu. There was a working coffee cup on a saucer within reach of his left elbow and crumbs of some kind on a bread plate to his right. I imagined, from his settled-in appearance, that he had come straight downstairs after our encounter at my doorway, not wanting to trust our meeting to such a thing as an appointed time, or not having any place else to go.

The menu-struggling seemed to have to do with the pictures, which in turn seemed to have to do with a certain style of menu found in the coffee shops of moderately priced hotel chains. Pictures of food. A pancake with whipped cream and chocolate chips, done up in an eerie smiley face that would surely scare the appetite from any child. A double-decker turkey club with strips of bacon that appeared to glisten with painted-on fat. A serious slice of apple pie.

"These daguerreotypes," he said, standing and extending his right hand in greeting, indicating the menu in his left. "It will take some time getting used to these."

I fumbled for a look or phrase to politely report my confusion, and apparently stumbled across just the right response without saying a word.

"The bill of fare," he meant to clarify. "With the photographs. Tell me, they prepare the food, they take a photograph, they record it onto the page so we might know what to expect, but what happens to the meal after the picture has been taken?"

"I've never thought about it," I said. "Perhaps they serve it to the wait staff."

He appeared to accept this notion. "Like a bonus? A show of gratitude?"

"Like a bonus," I concurred. I would agree to anything, just to set this bizarre business aside and move to the next item on Mr. Dunlap's unannounced agenda.

I took a moment to assess my breakfast partner. He was dressed as he had been the night before: bowler, spats, waistcoat . . . altogether, he looked entirely too *all together* for this hour of the morning—or, for that matter, for any hour of any morning. His hair was combed and neatly parted, his moustache and muttonchops as carefully groomed as if he had been about to pose for a menu.

Me, I was dressed down and bordering on disheveled, at least by contrast. I wore a pair of casual slacks, the kind endorsed in magazines by groups of same-seeming young adult males out for a game of touch football in the courtyard of some trendy art museum. Also a pale-yellow button-down shirt with a knockoff coat-of-arms thingy where the Ralph Lauren Polo logo might have been, an unscuffed pair of Saucony running shoes, and the same model Timex Ironman sports watch favored by our now fully disgraced president.

"You must have some questions," Dunlap said, declaring more than asking.

"Some," I said, and now that he had mentioned it I supposed I had, although to be candid I hadn't thought to put them out there. Who knew where to start? *That catch last night, in the stands . . . where did you come from? This morning, outside my hotel room door . . . how did you know where to find me? That hat . . . who even wears hats like that anymore?* Instead, what I said was, "You've eaten?"

"You'll have to excuse me," he replied. "I was famished. I don't mean to be rude. Please understand. These pictures. The eggs, the biscuits. It all looked too wonderful. I was meaning to join you for another round."

"Coffee's it for me," I said. "I'm not much for breakfast."

He lifted his cup, as if to say he would join me in mine, and in the same motion somehow signaled our bone-skinny waitress that we were in need of another pour. She did not appear to notice my man Dunlap, but instead drifted toward our table as if her body clock had been set to do just that at just that moment. She approached, coffeepot in hand, her arms right-angled from her sides like a dormant Rock'Em, Sock'Em Robot, and immediately began to fill my cup. Her *Have a Nice Day!* nametag billed our waitress as Martha, and it struck me as noteworthy that she didn't even bother to ask if I wanted regular or decaf, on the learned truth that casually dressed travelers at Suisse Chalet coffee shops would invariably need caffeine at eight o'clock on weekday mornings—particularly casually dressed travelers sitting across the table from elegantly dressed travelers with handlebar moustaches and spats.

"So," Dunlap finally said, examining the half-and-half thimbles our Martha had plopped onto the table. "Where do we begin?"

Here I surprised myself with the forcefulness of my reply, for nowhere in the vocabulary of David Felb, publicist to the how-to psycho-babblers of the illiterate world, had there ever been words to convey the alien mix of impatience, confusion, and astonishment that was combusting in my head. "You tell me, Mr. Dunlap," I said, firmly but pleasantly, not wanting to lose whatever advantage I may have had in this peculiar social situation. "You came to me. You wanted to talk. You, not me." The words, coming from my own lips, were surprise enough, but the tone was from some private-eye movie I could not remember having seen, then or still.

He didn't respond at first, didn't even look up from the sugar substitute packets and slim ketchup packages he had arranged on the table in front of him. Apparently, these struck him as among the top three or four most extraordinary things he had ever seen (not to mention the individually wrapped salt and pepper portions), but the words came soon enough. Softly, but soon enough. "I have no one," he said, in a swallowed whisper that came to me initially as *I've a new one*. And then—sorrowfully, fitfully—he repeated himself. "I have no one."

Now, I hope I have succeeded here in placing this confession in just the right context. If not, permit me the small indulgence of going over the situation once more. I was out of town, on purported business. I found myself with a free evening, so I took in a ball game. A foul ball came my way. I thought I had it. There was no one else around. Just then, another hand outstretched my own and made the grab. The hand belonged to an unusual-looking middle-aged male, dressed as if from another century. He sent the ball careening back onto the field of play, from an unimaginable distance, with the kind of accuracy and velocity that turned heads and opened mouths. He offered me his card. On it he had printed his name and the phrase *Pittsburgh Nationals*. I thought this strange. (Even the shape and style of the card—no phone number!—was unusual.)

The next morning—*this* morning—the same man knocked on my hotel-room door at seven o'clock. How he found me, I had no idea.

He didn't state his business but seemed to want something. I wasn't fool enough to invite him in, but I agreed to meet him here, in this coffee shop, where I now found him bemused by such things as salt-and-pepper packages and pictured menus. His small talk was smaller than mine, which was no small feat. Finally, with his eyes averted, he told me he was alone. Twice.

My first thought, naturally, was that the guy was undoubtedly gay and that this was one of the more elaborate come-ons in enlightened sexual history. I don't mean to flatter myself, or to come across as a homophobe, but what *else* was there to think? The fancy Mr. Dunlap, with his fancily out-of-date but nevertheless stylish clothes, nearly weeping in a hotel coffee shop, confessing his loneliness as if it might leave me reaching across the table to offer comfort.

(As my Iona might say with her dismissive teenage swagger, "As *if*...")

For some reason, it didn't occur to me to feel afraid—although an hour or so earlier, in my hotel room, my guard had been so up that I imagined the headlines in the next morning's *New York Post*: "Flack Hacked by Foul-Ball-Wielding Fan." Here, however, in the relative public safety of the Suisse Chalet lobby, there was nothing to fear but my own response to this unexpected turn.

"Mr. Dunlap," I managed. "I'm afraid you might have misjudged me. I don't think I'm the man you're looking for."

There, I thought. It's out there. Done. Said. I was pleased with myself for having gingerly deflected such a forward pass, and leaving room in the exchange for a graceful parting.

"What man am I looking for?" he shot back, puzzled. He looked up, his eyes a slickwet red from crying, rubbing. "I merely said I was alone." With this, he reached into his waistcoat pocket and pulled out a worn leather pouch, from which he pinched what I took to be a finger of chewing tobacco. It seemed, at first, something to do with his hands, but after placing the pinched tobacco in his mouth, between his cheek and gum, he reached back for another wad. And another. (I can't swear to it, but there might have been another still.) He noticed my noticing and briefly froze; then he extended the pouch across the table, presumably to offer me a pinch of my own, which I politely declined.

By the time he was through, and well-loaded, his right cheek was so puffed he might have slipped a golf ball inside, and a goodly amount of (mostly) brown spittle was trickling down his chin. I fixed on the trickle, and caught myself wondering if the tobacco juice would come to a stop on its own—and it very nearly did, assisted by a natural catch-basin etched onto the man's face at the down-chin junction of a rather prominent dimple and the southernmost tip of right muttonchop.

Suddenly, the man seated across from me seemed almost pathetic, and my feelings toward him shifted from curiosity to empathy. "Alone, as in no wife, no children, no family?" I tried.

"No one," he reiterated, the catch now returned to his voice. "Nothing. No home, no family, no friends. I have no one. Not a soul."

Four
AND THEN WHAT?

So there it was. Me, face-first in the middle of my unshakable sameness, and this odd fellow from out of nowhere at the bull's-eye of his own drama. It was not the most comfortable mix. And yet, still, I consigned the unlikely exchanges of the past dozen hours to the place where it didn't much matter if I couldn't think what to make of them. They were unusual, nothing more. Puzzling. But not at all the kind of head-scratching turns that leave you wondering at the line between the real and the surreal, the known and the unknown. For the time being, I wasn't too terribly concerned by the display of emotion, because it wasn't really my concern. I took it in as I might have eavesdropped on a conversation at a nearby table. What troubled me was the way our absurdly binding social contracts left me feeling unsure of myself in the exchange. I hadn't the first clue how to react, or what was expected of me in such a situation, if anything was expected at all, so I quickly figured I could finesse my way from the coffee shop and leave these various uncertainties behind, and this was what I attempted to do, thinking it made way more sense to sidestep a complicated social exchange than to face it head-on.

"Mr. Dunlap," I said, standing to leave, reaching for my bag. "Fred. I'm sorry to hear of your troubles, really, but I have a train to catch." Okay, I thought, putting this out there, pushing the scene along so I might get a handle on it. This isn't too difficult. Just keep talking and get moving. Set the thing in motion and follow it where you might.

"Not at all, Mr. Felb," he said, extending his hand as he stood up. "It's me who should be apologizing to you. For troubling you at this hour of the morning. For making myself a burden."

"David," I said. "You can call me David."

"David, then. My apologies."

"Your apologies accepted."

"And your acceptance is most appreciated," he added, and in the appending I realized I was never going to disengage from this fellow, not at this rate. The thing to do, I determined, was to walk away from the table, but in this I hesitated. Always—or, I should say, not infrequently—it is these tiny moments of hesitation that cost us, for it is in that crawlspace between thought and action that we live our lives.

Caught, I fumbled for the loose change in my pocket, meaning to put something on the table for the waitress and secondarily hoping to lose myself in a leave-taking gesture that might passively announce my departure, but in this too I was derailed.

"Allow me," this Fred Dunlap person insisted, fumbling for some loose change of his own, and at this I nodded once again in appreciation and began to back away. It was in the backing away, however, that I stumbled into a Hispanic-seeming busboy, and in the stumbling there was also a good deal of dish clattering and utensil chattering. I slipped, and knocked my head against the hard edge of one of the coffee shop's straight-backed chairs, and managed somehow to open a gash above my left eye that was immediately wet to the touch. Also, I appeared to have hit my forehead in very nearly the same spot as the half-remembered bruise from the night before—although I suppose it was possible that this was just my mind playing a convenient trick. The busboy, happily, was unhurt by the collision. (In fact, he managed to keep his tray of half-drinks and milked cereal aloft without a spill, which I found time to consider impressive.) I pressed my hand to the cut above my eye and it came back a blackish red. I hadn't realized I was in any pain until I saw my own blood, but once I had I noticed an intense throbbing—and, across my forehead to my scalp above the other eye, I could now feel a welt the size of a marble shooter.

"Jesus," I managed.

"Let us leave Him out of it," I heard back in Fred Dunlap's soothing, patient voice. His tone was almost chiding—and I must say I hadn't been *chided* in a good long while, so it took some getting used to.

(Nellie, from time to time, would come close to such a tone in public dressings-down, mostly for the benefit of our girls and the solidifying of her own upper hand.)

Next, Mr. Dunlap produced a clean white piece of linen, with which he indicated I was meant to soak up the blood, and as I did so I wondered where he'd gotten it. The paper napkins on our table had been canistered and squared, diner-style, and there hadn't been time to fetch the cloth from a waitress or manager. Dabbing, I thought the appearance of the cloth was yet another magical sleight of hand, falling just short of this fellow's startling grab of Rolen's liner in the head-scratching department. Nevertheless, I was grateful for the cloth, which I pressed to my forehead.

"Thank you," I said.

"It is my pleasure, David," Dunlap replied. "In my own way, I feel responsible. If I hadn't called you to our meeting, you would never have fallen."

"Well," I tried, "if I'd thought to look where I was going, this wouldn't have happened either."

I had mentioned that I had a train to catch, and my new friend pledged to accompany me to Thirtieth Street Station to see that I boarded safely. It was, he claimed decently, the least he could do, although I might have countered that the least he could do would have in fact been nothing at all. But he persisted, and soon enough I was too beaten down by his unceasing pleasantness to stand against it. If he wanted to walk with me the several blocks to the train station, who was I to keep him from it?

And so I walked, and my interloper followed, and even in downtown Philadelphia, heart of the morning, I imagined we made a strange picture. The streets surrounding the train station were dotted with do-rags and Allen Iverson jerseys and enough goldplated jewelry to fill a bank vault, and the heat and haste of the place might have conspired to leave us pass unnoticed. But we attracted stares just the same. I had by now knotted the white cloth into a kind of bandana bandage, like some wounded citizen soldier from some ancient battlefield, and my not-quite-welcome companion matched me stride for stride with his muttonchops and his walking stick and his general state of overdress. Heads turned in our direction as if pulled by magnets, but I kept moving. Dunlap, too, refused to "dally"—his word, not mine. I thought to compare the picture we made to that long-ago movie poster advertising *Midnight Cowboy*, the one with a dapper Jon Voight and a bedraggled Dustin Hoffman slinking along a New York City sidewalk looking like hell, only I cast myself as Ratso Rizzo, wounded as I was, and ruffled by comparison. He wasn't exactly a pretty boy, my acquired shadow, but he certainly dressed the part.

With the movie poster came the theme song. Harry Nilsson. I heard it in my head and couldn't shake it, right down to the whistling bridge, or the *na-na-nas*, or *wha-wha-whas*, or whatever passed for whistling in the late 1960s. *Everybody's talkin' at me. I don't hear a word they're sayin'.* I caught our reflection in a storefront window, and underneath the imagined soundtrack it struck me as a bad remake.

(Too, that we live in a world were the dropped *g* isn't quite what it used to be.)

"We're here," I announced, perhaps unnecessarily, when we arrived at the station, after we had banked it on over the northeast wind, and sailed on a summer breeze, and undertaken a variety of hackneyed movements to suggest what might have been my carefree state of mind had it not been occupied by a jumble of other thoughts having to do mostly with my from-out-of-nowhere companion and the strange, confounding mess into which I'd allowed myself to be escorted.

I held out my hand, willing the song to fade. "Thank you for the company," I said to the man I knew as Fred Dunlap. "I'll be fine, here on."

Dunlap shook my offered hand, and I was once again startled by his brawn. "Nothing at all, David," he said. "I only wish I hadn't placed you in such a pickle."

I was off the *Midnight Cowboy* poster now and onto other matters—chiefly the loaned white cloth, which had by now come unknotted but remained pressed to my head, and the follow-up etiquette regarding the return of such a bloodied mess. Somehow, Dunlap guessed at my concern. "Keep it," he said.

At first, I considered it somewhat supernatural that the man had seemed to read my mind, but then I realized I must have worn my concern on my plain face and he wasn't being anything more than responsive. I removed the cloth from my scalp and folded it in on itself so the bloodied portion was mostly concealed. Then I held it out as I would a glass of champagne in making a toast, in what was very likely one of the lamest gestures in the history of lame gestures. (Ask Nellie, and she'll report that I've contributed quite a bit in this area.) "Thank you again," I said.

Mr. Dunlap tipped his cap. "Good day to you, David."

"Good day," I said, and here I managed mercifully to avoid any extraneous movements or overtures of any kind, and soon enough I passed through a set of smeared-stained double doors into the station plaza, hoping to put as much train track between me and the Philadelphias as Amtrak's fleet would allow.

Trouble was, in my haste to get clear of this unusual fellow, I'd neglected to consult a train schedule, and once I found my place on the arrivals and departures board in the main waiting area, I realized I'd have some time to kill. I had been hoping to keep walking until I found my seat on the train—a dramatic exit, imagined under the assumption that Dunlap's eyes would be on me the entire time—but now it appeared I'd have to reroute myself and find a way to fill these next minutes. It was about 9:15, and there was a New York-bound Acela Express scheduled to depart at 9:52.

(My Iona once wrote a school paper on the ridiculousness of the airline and railroad industries with the way they schedule their departures at not-quite-round-number times, considering that the *actual* departure times are never as advertised, and I mention this here parenthetically as a marginally relevant digression and also as a telling indication of how my daughter's mind chooses to work.)

This meant I had fifteen or twenty minutes to pass until boarding, and I surveyed the waiting area for distractions. There was the usual dotting of coffee and donut shops, high-end and low-, news and souvenir stands, five-dollar clothing shops, and so on. Also, compellingly, an inviting-looking Borders bookstore and café—not quite of the superstore variety, but done up in fine woods and aromatic blends. I wandered over to the bookstore window in the manner we publicists have of checking out the display, and I was delighted to see an unassuming stack of my author's out-of-the-closet Benjamin Franklin biography, which was of course my reason for being in Philadelphia in the first place. Apparently, this author had the forethought to stop in on his breeze through town to sign stock, because there were special Borders *Autographed Copy* stickers on the standing-up-and-fanned-open copies in my view. Good for him, I thought, admiring the placement. And, relatedly, not so good for me, because of course such placement is one of my goals, and here I'd had nothing to do with it.

I wandered in for a look around, and without fully realizing it I came to the sports section along one of the back walls—specifically, to the baseball section, where I found myself thumbing frantically through the latest edition of Macmillan's gargantuan *Baseball Encyclopedia*. The book might have doubled as a doorstop at a bank vault—too heavy, even, to page through while standing, with a single open palm for support. I found a hard wooden chair at the end of the aisle and plopped the massive volume on my lap, rifling the onion-thin pages until I came to the entry for Fred Dunlap. All of this happened without a conscious thought. I didn't seek out the book so much as it sought me, if that makes any sense. (It couldn't!) Understand, at this point along these odd, surprising exchanges with my stalking friend, there had been no mention of a one-time career in professional baseball, no clue to this strange man's backstory beyond the simple calling card he'd fisted into my hand the night before, no reason for me to be thumbing frantically through the dense pages of *The Baseball Encyclopedia*.

And yet . . .

I was going on an impulse I couldn't place. What I was looking for, I had no idea. But there I was, in hot pursuit, determined to thumb my way through these too-many pages until I came across . . . what?

And then, as if lit by neon, there it was: *Dunlap, Frederick C. (Sure Shot), 5' 8", 165 lbs.; B. May 21, 1859, Philadelphia, PA; D. Dec. 1, 1902, Philadelphia, PA.*

Man! (Or, as my father used to say in what passed for his notion of funny: "Man, oh Manischewitz!")

Now, let me place special emphasis on the sheer surprise of what I found myself doing next before fully addressing the pure astonishment and cosmic, reality-shattering implications of my discovery. To place this reaction in context, I offer the obvious: We publishing types are reluctant to buy books. We'll haunt bookstores, and collect books until we have to consider how high we can stack them before they might tumble, and stay up reading until dawn, but we'll rarely break down and *buy* a book, like we expect everyone else to do to keep our business pulsing. I've seen the numbers back at the office, realize what it costs to actually produce a single volume in purely manufacturing terms, and I know how freely we pass these things around among ourselves. The routine, at least in book publicity departments all over Manhattan, is to call our colleagues at competing houses when we notice a book we might want to read, and offer one of ours in trade. I've got my list of contacts, same as everyone else, and if I needed a copy of *The Baseball Encyclopedia*, I might have called a guy named Todd I knew over at Macmillan and he would have been happy to send one over, by messenger no less, especially if I sent the messenger back with a latex-wrapped copy of, say, *Big Dicks*, our hard-to-get (and hard-to-justify) collection of photographs of celebrity penises. But I was acting on impulse here, and my immediate need to hunt and gather and *process* these numbers and statistics that might open a door to another life overwhelmed the delayed gratification of working a good deal once I got back to the office. Of course, I wasn't about to pay sixty-five dollars for a book, either, especially one I knew cost only three or four dollars to produce, and so I quickly tore out page 874, where Dunlap's listing began, in the swift, practiced manner of someone who's made an obsession of tearing full-page Absolut Vodka ads from glossy magazines. I hated myself for doing this, didn't fully understand what had come over me, but I was powerless and thoughtless against it. Indeed, I'm ashamed of it now, especially in this nearly public confession. I wasn't quite myself, is how I've come to justify such a rash act. (I've justified it in other ways, too: The damn book was over 3,000 pages, and chances ran fairly high that the eventual book buyer would never even notice the missing page, unless of course he was settling a bet regarding the still-swinging Shawon Dunston, or Leon "Bull" Durham, a mainstay at first base for the Chicago Cubs until Mark Grace came along.) And my shame ran double once I realized the Dunlap listing reached to the adjacent page, 875, and I had to tear out that one as well. I had torn the first page on an impulse, but the second was a willful act to complete the job, and it is this follow-up moment that has stayed with me. Then, I slammed the heavy book closed and returned it to its place on the shelf, two pages lighter, and folded my booty lengthwise and stuffed it in the inside pocket of my sports jacket. And finally, wanting perhaps to compensate the Borders gods for my small theft, I stood in line at the café, where I ordered a bag full of overpriced muffins and scones and a whipped hot concoction called a "lattechino," half-expecting to be pulled aside by a transit cop or security guard but nevertheless thinking this would call it even. Then I got the hell out of there and made for the train platform.

There is no way to overstate the stress and uneasiness I felt at my own actions. To tear out the pages of a book was anathema to me. I had a friend once who told me he was in the habit of traveling with the latest hardcover epic and ripping out whole sections of the book as he completed them, to lighten his load, and it was all I could do to not report him to the literary police. I'd seen characters in old movies tear out a listing in the Yellow Pages and cringed with moral indignation, and here I was, destroying store merchandise. It wasn't me. It wasn't even remotely like me. And yet that first tear had come so naturally you'd have thought I was a career-long book-wrecking fool. It weighed so heavily on me that as soon as I'd taken my seat on the train I reached for my cell phone, thinking I'd call Nellie to see if she had any insight into the matter. Predictably, I'd neglected to recharge the damn thing the night before, and the cartoon battery indicator was telling me my power was perilously low. (The irony, here, is not lost on me, for surely my power was drained—as in, my power to think freely, to act morally and logically, to make general sense of the human condition.) Still, I thought I might sneak in one last call before the phone went out, and I punched in the preset cell number for Nell and hoped for the best.

She picked up on the first half-ring. "That you?" she said, no doubt relying on the convenience of caller ID over the wonders of intuition.

"That me," I answered.

"Something wrong?" she asked. "You sound funny."

I'd spoken two words, and already she could tell, and I thought perhaps AT&T had added a new calling feature to allow spouses to intuit their mates' moods immediately upon connection. Caller ESP, perhaps. I thought of an ad line: *We're all connected. In more ways than you know.*

"Funny how?" I asked.

"Funny shaken," she said. "Rattled."

"I don't know how to explain it," I started. "It's the weirdest thing. Freaked me out, actually." Actually, just before I could get out the word "actually," my phone made a series of otherworldly bleeps presumably meant to further indicate my low-battery status. This had happened before, and it usually meant it would happen again, and then once or twice more at regular intervals before the phone finally gave out, and so at first I talked right through it. "It's that guy," I kept on. "From last night. The one with the spats and the foul ball. I think he's been stalking me."

I spilled the day's story.

One thing you need to know about Nellie is that she is the person for whom the phrase *It's difficult to get a word in edgewise* was coined. When she's in the middle of a conversation, she's in the middle of a conversation; in the middle, on top of it, and all around. (This, I've often felt, is one of Nellie's most endearing qualities—how involved she is, how quick to engage—although I suppose it's also been her undoing in forging new friendships; naturally, this is neither here nor there, but that's Nellie.) As I spoke I slowly realized how unlike her it was to let me string together all these uninterrupted thoughts, without so much as a grunt or an "And then what?" from her end, and I finally drew the phone away from my ear and looked into the display window and realized I had been talking to myself all along. The call had been cut after just twenty-seven seconds. Who knew what she had heard before we were cut off? I worried into what state of agitation I'd whipped my sweetsuffering wife, and at the same time I worried into what state of agitation I'd now whipped myself. First there was the general anxiety over this Fred Dunlap person, and then there was that weirdness in the coffee shop when he reached out to me the way he did, and then there was that nasty business with hitting my head, and after that there was the concern over my uncharacteristic behavior in the bookstore (a Borders, no less!), and now there was the worry over which pieces of my uncertainty I'd managed to convey to Nellie before my cell phone died. If the condition of worrying could be multiplied, exponentially, then that would fairly quantify how completely, utterly, seismically freaked out I was at just that moment. Realize, too, that my frenzied thinking had yet to fully grasp the eerie, unreal implications of the encounter itself, particularly the now-and-then aspects of the thing. It would be some time before I could get my mind around the questions of who Fred Dunlap had been, all those years ago, and who he might be at present, and what precisely he might be doing alighting in my path in just this way—if, indeed, it was the self-same Dunlap doing the alighting.

All of which conspired to place me, toe-first, in one of the great social dilemmas of our information age. If we accept the theory that there is no such thing as too much information, must we also reject the inverse? Here I'd given Nellie just enough information to worry the poor pants off of her, and now I had to consider that there was no easy way to undo that damage, to download the whole of what I knew into the whole of what she knew. To set her mind at ease—or, at least, to leave it on the same setting as mine. I considered my options. For some reason, this particular car on this particular Amtrak train was not equipped with those overpriced seatback telephones, and the lone phone in the dining car, I noticed after racing back to check the situation, had been rendered out of service, apparently by a pair of wire cutters. I could hop off at Trenton and hope to find a phone on the train platform, and the time to tell Nellie not to worry before the train pulled back out again. Of course, the best, most reasonable course was to borrow the phone of one of my fellow commuters—that is, if I could bring myself to ask, which unfortunately, at just that moment, I could not.

Here was my thinking on this: Most folks, most probably, carried the kind of virtually unlimited free-long-distance, no-roaming-charges plans trumpeted by Jamie Lee Curtis and James Earl Jones and other similarly named pitchpersons, so in many ways asking to borrow a cell phone had become a lot like asking to borrow a pen. On the depth chart of human kindnesses, that was about the size of it, and yet I still couldn't push myself to ask another traveler to borrow his or her phone. I was surrounded by well-dressed, tight-lipped business people, many of them talking constantly into their handsets, some of them donning tie mikes and other newfangled add-ons that allowed them to do their talking in a hands-free mode that to a casual observer might have suggested schizophrenia. I walked from one car to the next looking for a friendly, sharing face, but I found each passenger more intimidating than the next.

Finally, after leapfrogging the dining car, I noticed a young woman, college age or thereabouts, with a dark-green Jansport backpack and a tear in her jeans that looked like it had been cultivated. Auburn hair pulled back into one of those goodness-that-must-hurt! ponytails. I wouldn't have figured her for a cell-phone-toting type, but there she was, chatting languidly on a silver version of the StarTAC flip phone I had lately carried. I took an empty seat across the aisle and couldn't help but notice the way this young woman punctuated her talking with smirks and clever asides and real-seeming belly laughs, presumably when the other end of the conversation called for them. I thought, okay, this is someone I can ask; this is an approachable someone, and I ran through my head precisely how I would make my appeal.

A couple minutes later, the young woman flipped her phone shut, and I went for it.

"Excuse me," I said, leaning over to her side of the aisle and handing across a business card I had smoothly removed from the pen pocket of my shirt. Regrettably, this was the last smooth move of the transaction, because I proceeded to talk myself hoarse and silly, too fast for any stenographer to keep up with, and too all-over-the-place for any young coed to take anything close to seriously. "I'm not a nut or a lunatic or anything," I went on, disputing my own claim, "but I am in desperate need of a phone. Here's my card. I work in publishing. I was thinking maybe I could send you a book, in exchange for the favor. We do that all the time, you know. Give out books. It's common practice. You can walk through a bookstore, see what we're publishing these days, call me up and tell me what you'd like. Or, I could just give you a dollar or two right now, to pay you back for the airtime. Whatever you think is fair. It's just, my phone went out, and I'm afraid I've just taken a spill and hit my head. That explains the blood, right? Probably, you were wondering. So that's why I need a phone. I need to call my wife, tell her about my head. She's a nurse, I guess I should mention that. She's a nurse. Anyway, I don't understand it but there's not a public phone on this train, and everybody seems so protective of their telephones, it seems like such a personal thing, and then I saw you, and you seemed like you wouldn't mind, so I thought I'd ask..."

I'd clipped each loose thought together in such tight fashion I hadn't left room for this poor person to respond, and I wasn't done just yet. For an exclamation point, I pulled my spent phone from my pocket and held it out, as if the object alone might validate my story. "See," I said, waving the phone around for emphasis. "Same phone as yours, I think."

"Sure," she said, flashing the kind of bright, welcoming smile that could either sell toothpaste or drive an otherwise happily married man to question the institution of marriage in general and the long-term viability of his own marriage in particular. "No problem."

I took the phone gratefully and dialed Nell again. "Where was I?" I said when she picked up.

"What happened to you?" she sang cheerfully, her voice revealing nothing of the whip-frenzied agitation I'd been expecting.

"Battery."

Beat. "So, where were you then?"

"My stalker," I said. "Same guy from last night, at the stadium." As I spoke, I thought: Where the hell do I start? How do I catch Nellie up to the place of utter bewilderment where I now stand?

"Mr. Spats?" she asked.

"That's him. Knocked on my door this morning, asked me down for coffee."

"Jesus, Felb," she said. "And you went with him?" At this, Nellie showed the requisite concern. She was always on the lookout for nuts and crazies, especially where our girls were concerned, and secondarily where I was concerned, and here I'd presented her with a legitimate worry.

And, indeed, it was through Nell's eyes that I was finally able to see what an idiot I had been to engage this fellow, so I scrambled to cover my butt. It was one thing to realize for yourself that your judgment might have fallen somewhere between reckless and foolhardy; it was quite another to be found out, and found wanting, in the eyes of your wife. "I didn't actually go with him," I explained. "I met him downstairs in the coffee shop. We set a time and I met him. Seemed harmless enough."

"Felb," she *tsked*, her disapproval plain.

"What can I tell you? Guy seemed harmless. It was a weird situation."

"And then what?" she pushed.

(Leave it to Nell to keep a conversation on point.)

"And then he kinda spilled his guts," I said. "Started telling me how lonely he was, started crying even, and it was the most awkward thing, this stranger, opening up like that. I couldn't think how to respond, and you'll love this, your chickenshit Felb in fine form, I found some excuse to get out of there, said I had to catch my train, but as I was leaving I tripped and fell and cut my head, and it's just a cut, nothing to worry about, but this guy went from being all bent about how lonely he was to being all concerned with helping me. He wouldn't even let me walk to the train station on my own, insisted on escorting me. And here I am."

"Here, where?"

"Here, on the train."

"And where is this stalker fellow? Your friend. What happened to him?"

"Left him out front of the station," I said.

"And you're fine?" she said, making sure.

"I'm fine."

"Your head? Where you fell?"

"Fine."

"Still bleeding?" she wanted to know.

I touched my forehead and got back nothing. "No," I answered.

"Still throbbing?"

"No."

"So it's just the weirdness, then?" she tried. "The what to make of it?"

"Spooky, don't you think? Creepy."

There was a silence while Nellie apparently thought this out. "I guess," she allowed after a while, in the absent tone she had when she was still sorting through a situation. "Although, really, it could be nothing, right? Could just be a lonely guy you met at a ball game."

"He followed me to my room, Nell," I reminded her.

"There's that, too," she said, deadpan, and in the gap between what she said and how she said it I could read her mind. In our unspoken shorthand I got that she was more concerned than she was letting on, but not so much that she couldn't joke about it. This was a good thing, I supposed.

"Anyway," she said, "it's not like he knows your name, or how to find you."

She wasn't quite asking so much as she was checking, and suddenly I remembered I'd given this man my business card the night before at the stadium. Still, I hastily determined that this wasn't a piece of information I needed to share with Nell—not cellularly, in any case. No sense worrying her while I was still out of town, and no sense digging myself any deeper into foolishness. She already thought me an ass for agreeing to meet this guy in a hotel coffee shop. There'd be time to come completely clean—time, too, to find a way to explain this strange business with *The Baseball Encyclopedia*, the siren pull I felt in this man's presence, the cloying sense I had that there was something else going on about him. Something else entirely.

"I'm on a borrowed phone," I said. "I should probably go."

"Now that you've worried the hell out of me," Nell said.

"Now that I've worried the hell out of you," I echoed.

"More to come?"

"More to come."

With this I returned the phone to the backpack-toting coed with the killer smile and the well-placed tear in her jeans, and right away I felt exposed. The girl had had an earful. She had re-ponied her hair in the minute or two I'd been on her phone, and in her effortless movements I found cause to marvel at the swift rush of youth, the comfort we find in our daily routines, the separate ways we all move about on our parallel paths.

"Trouble in paradise?" the young girl said, most likely for no good reason but to get us both past the realization that she had just listened in at close range to what surely qualified as a bizarre exchange.

He followed me to my room, Nell.

There's a thing Iona does whenever a moment turns uncomfortable, as it had quickly done here. She stacks one hand on top of the other, in such a way that her opposing thumbs are left dangling on either side of her hand sandwich. Then she wiggles her thumbs about and says, "Awkward turtle." I've got no idea where she picked up on this, but her wiggling thumbs do call to mind the dangling legs of a turtle running in place beneath its shell, and the connection always makes me laugh. Maybe that's the point, to diffuse an embarrassing situation with a silly hand gesture.

"Something like that," I allowed, thinking for a moment about holding out my hands and making one of Iona's turtles. "Thanks again for the phone."

"You wouldn't happen to publish Ann Beattie?" she asked—incongruously, I thought at first. The young woman read the confusion on my face. "Your company? Elder and whatever. You mentioned about the books. I just love Ann Beattie."

"Oh," I said, realizing. "That. Actually, I think she's at Random, but I have a friend who can get me a copy."

"She's out with a new one," the coed offered. "There was just a review. *The New Yorker*, I think." She wrote her name and address on the back of my business card, and then she wrote Ann Beattie's name, only she spelled Ann with an *e*. "If you can," she said. "If it's no trouble, like you said." She returned my card.

"No," I said, "no trouble. I wouldn't have offered."

"Otherwise, you know, no biggie. It's not like you called Guam or anything, right? Tell me you didn't call Guam."

Five
THE LINE ON DUNLAP

I found a seat as far away from my too-smiling coed as I could, but not so far that I couldn't see the back of her lovely head and keep from wondering what her auburn hair smelled like. Apricots, I imagined. Or beer and honey. Or whatever it is they're mixing into the gels and shampoos lately favored by comely college coeds.

It was, I'll confess, a delightful piece of wondering, and there was a beat or two in there during which I could not have told you who I was or where I'd been or where I was going. Just to be clear, I was and remain a contentedly married man, but I can't save myself from browsing. And visualizing. (And, in this case, *sniffing*.) Sue me—and tell me you know a man who's any different. Nellie understands this wanderlusting, says she even finds it endearing in a schoolboyish sort of way, and often she'll act as spotter when we're out, because she knows that for all my neck-craning and second-looking I will always come home to her. Always. And yet to be completely honest—and forgive me Nell and girls and unborn grandchildren—this has as much to do with my overall shyness and general feelings of inadequacy as it does with my undying devotion to my lovely wife, although I can't shake thinking the two go together. I tell myself faithfulness is a virtue, no matter the cause, but I can certainly understand the view that it is cheapened somewhat by a simple lack of opportunity; everything is a matter of perspective, even if that perspective is blemished by the flash of tight thigh beneath an artfully ripped pair of jeans.

But I never act on wonderings such as these, never even think to give them voice except in musing, so I slouched down in my high-backed, uncomfortably angled Amtrak seat, pressed my knees to the seatback in front of me, and turned my attention to the purloined pages of *The Baseball Encyclopedia*, which I was hoping might serve as pacifier for the next hour or so.

Ah, the rich wonders of history, reduced to storied code! Here's another thing to know about me, to render these next moments clear: I have always been a sucker for the fine print on the backs of baseball cards, the weights and measures of a ballplayer's worth, the elegant distillation of a career, a season, a game . . . a single turn at bat, even, onto a line of agate type so small it likely passes unnoticed by most of the rest of the world. As a kid, I could lose myself in these statistics for entire afternoons. Fielding percentages. Base-runners allowed. Total bases. The legend in my family, insofar as we Felbersteins laid any claim to any such thing, was that I owed my early prowess in mathematics to this childhood obsession with baseball statistics. By the age of ten, I could calculate the earned-run averages of my favorite Mets pitchers. (And, at ten, I was unavoidably rooting for the 1962 Mets, arguably the most hapless team in Major League Baseball history, so these calculations ran into some pretty big numbers—including Roger Craig's 4.51, against a league-leading twenty-four losses!) Batting averages? I had those nailed at seven or eight. The single-game totals I could manage in my head, but I kept a tally of the full-season records as well, and was able to recalibrate a player's batting average after each plate appearance—this back before calculators made such equations relatively easy to figure, and before computer stat services went to all the trouble for you, updated at the pause between each pitch.

Regrettably, at least according to my mother, I shot my wad early on the math front, peaking just before calculus, which had about as much to do with keeping baseball statistics as, say, a fish hatchery. In baseball, at least, the numbers stood for something—and, inevitably, there were certain numbers that stood far taller than others. They landed in my path every here and there and called legend to mind. The number sixty, for obvious example, which dotted the landscape throughout most of my childhood as the default speed limit on the open road, always reminded me of Babe Ruth's single-season home-run benchmark; relatedly, the number sixty-one, which turned up with somewhat less frequency despite the fact that it signaled the year of my sister, Marsha's, birth, always seemed to carry a phantom asterisk at its side for the way the baseball establishment only grudgingly acknowledged Roger Maris's new high-water mark.

There was 104, Maury Wills's single-season stolen-base threshold and the street address of a boy named Billy Trinko who briefly served as best friend during a stretch of fifth grade; 190, Hack Wilson's staggering RBI total and the number of wheat-backed pennies I inherited from a cousin who had lost interest in his collection; forty-one, Jack Chesbro's modern-era win standard for a pitcher in a single campaign, which later turned up as the uniform number of Tom Seaver, the face and heart (and arm!) of our 1969 Miracle Mets. Some numbers crossed my path infrequently, usually in answer to a question in math class (or, later, as a line on my tax return), but always with a wistful memory stitched to its side: 714, Babe Ruth's career home-run total; 4,191, Ty Cobb's hit mark; 511, Cy Young's win total; 3,508, Walter Johnson's strikeout total; .424, Rogers Hornsby's modern-era single-season batting average mark; 56, representing Joe DiMaggio's consecutive-game hitting streak; also, 2,130, Lou Gehrig's superhuman consecutive-games mark... the immutable standards of my boyhood and no wrecking crew of Lou Brocks, Hank Aarons, Pete Roses, Nolan Ryans, Cal Ripkens, Rickey Hendersons—or, now, Mark McGwires—could ever dim the shine on these numbers.

And these were just the common-denominator stats, the records burned into the subconscious of virtually every boy of my acquaintance. For good or ill, my obsession also ran to 257, George Sisler's standard for base hits in a single season; 110, Walter Johnson's career shutout total; 18, the number of World Series home runs that sprang from the bat of Mickey Mantle. There was no end to what I knew, no reason for my knowing it, and no place to put my knowledge to any kind of meaningful use. Whenever I called a cherished aunt in Chicago, the 312 area code had me thinking of "Wahoo Sam" Crawford's career triples mark.

(Like I said, there was no end to it!)

The numbers stood out so vividly that they left the back of the baseball card and adhered themselves to everything else. And so the prospect of staring dumbly at the densely numbered pages I'd pilfered from the Thirtieth Street Station Borders was a welcome one, to say the least. It would do more than merely pass the time; it would fill it with miracle and texture and moment. It would transport me to another century, another place. I'd lose myself in these pages with far more ease and purpose than I would, say, in the luster of that young coed's cascading hair, and I found myself regretting I hadn't pinched more than these two sheets.

Almost immediately, my trained eyes were pulled to what might have been a career-making line in Dunlap's entry—unaccustomed as they were to seeing the percentages distorted so disproportionately in a hitter's favor, but also aided by bold-faced type to indicate league leadership in a category. I offer Dunlap's astonishing record here, registered during his lone season in the upstart Union Association, bracketed by his numbers from the preceding and succeeding campaigns and punctuated by his career totals, for context:

DUNLAP, FREDERICK C. (Sure Shot) BR TR 5'8" 165 lbs.
B. May 21, 1859, Philadelphia, PA D. Dec. 1, 1902, Philadelphia, PA
Manager 1882, 1884-85, 1889

YEAR	TEAM	G	BA	SA	AB	H	2B	3B	HR	R
1883	CLE-N	93	.326	.452	396	129	34	2	4	81
1884	STL-U	101	**.412**	**.621**	449	**185**	39	8	**13**	**160**
1885	STL-N	106	.270	.333	423	114	11	5	2	70
TOTALS – 12 yrs.		965	.292	.406	3974	1159	224	53	41	759

Now, let me make certain we understand each other on this—even as I struggle to understand it myself. To average better than one run scored in every game played over a full season was and remains a spectacular achievement; to average better than one and a half runs, which even my peaked (piqued!) math skills shouted Dunlap had done, was spectacularly rare. And to do so behind a batting average of .412, well . . . that was simply jaw-dropping. Head-scratching, eye-popping . . . there was astonishment in every body part. I scanned the small print furiously, wondering how it was that in all my baseball-loving years, all my forays into the records books, I'd never heard of Frederick C. "Sure Shot" Dunlap, never stumbled across what looked at first glance to be one of the greatest seasons of professional baseball ever played, by anybody, anywhere, at any time. If I'd noticed one of his season marks on one of those all-time lists, it never registered fully—but here, now, under just these circumstances, the line on Frederick C. Dunlap appeared to hold the most remarkable details ever squirreled inside a page of baseball statistics.

Of course, I realized that the recording of baseball records prior to 1900 was a suspect business; rules were changed constantly; statistics thought meaningful one season might have been disregarded the next; teams at the bottom rungs of league standings often failed to finish out their campaigns, folding their tents on any meaningful way to compare records over such important baselines as numbers of games played, balanced schedules and level of competition. And even a casual baseball fan could tell you that the year 1884 was more suspect than most: Bases on balls were awarded on six balls and strikeouts on four strikes; grounds-rule doubles counted as home runs; and pitchers stood only fifty feet from home plate and tended to pitch all game long on little rest. It was a different game, played in a season when three professional leagues jockeyed for the best available players, no doubt thinning the talent pool, but still ... Dunlap's numbers overwhelmed these and other considerations. The Union Association was a recognized major league, after all, and Frederick C. Dunlap had run rings around it. All I had were these two tear sheets to go on, but I knew full well that this man's totals so completely eclipsed those of his peers that I felt myself in the presence of greatness. True, legendary, larger-than-life greatness. And it wasn't just the greatness that had me in thrall; it was the *presence* of it, for surely it was all around. It was with me in spirit, in nameless obsession, in fathomless proximity. It was in my bones. And it was right with me in this sardine can of an Amtrak car.

The sheer ordinariness of these abutting seasons only made Dunlap's heroic blip seem larger still. And harder to figure. Really, Frederick C. Dunlap's 1884 performance was so far off the map of his own history that it struck me as one of baseball's great untold stories, a giant helping of drama and achievement combined with the rest of a plain-seeming career at the plate to form an admixture of high hope and purpose.

Or something.

I refolded the thin pages and rested them on my legs and wondered how it was that I'd made the connection from last night's game, and this morning's strange encounter in the coffee shop, to this right here. Think of it: There was nothing logical in turning to *The Baseball Encyclopedia* to consult this particular entry, nothing to link my bizarre acquaintance with this bizarre fellow from the upper decks of Veterans Stadium to this ancient warrior of barehanded baseball. There was a calling card, and nothing more.

Well . . . that wasn't it entirely. There was also circumstance and weirdness and the kind of misplaced instinct that leaves people playing the same random lottery numbers week after week after week. And yet this combusted illogic was part of a developing revelation, for it was in this intuitive leap that I also made room for impossibility. Implausibility. Magic, of a curious kind.

The man who'd introduced himself to me as Fred Dunlap—"Dunny," if I preferred!—was a mystery in every possible sense of the term. He'd defied logic at every encounter. He had no business reaching out to grab that baseball. (Indeed, he had no discernible place in that section of stadium just a moment before!) He had no business wearing a waistcoat or muttonchops, or affecting a cane. (On Halloween, perhaps, but never on a holiday-free August night!) He had no business hurtling that pea from those upper reaches to Devon White at second base. (Man, he unleashed a bullet!) He had no business carrying a calling card announcing merely his name and some meaningless designation—*Pittsburgh Nationals*—with no address, no telephone number, no fax. He had no business knocking on my hotel-room door that morning, or shadowing me to the train station after I bumped my head. And yet there I was, finding ways to consider how to fit this man's otherworldly countenance into the only world I knew.

Also, my head hurt. More and more as my train rattled further and further from any accessible brand of over-the-counter pain reliever, until my already clouded thoughts turned downright overcast. I had told Nellie the throbbing had tapered, but this was just a white lie to keep her from worrying. In truth, my head was pounding. I did a brief calculation to determine whether it would be easier to ask a stranger for a spare ibuprofen than for a share of unlimited cellular telephone minutes, and I supposed one was no more cumbersome than the other, except of course for the roll of the dice involved in actually ingesting pills proffered from the pocket or handbag of one of the huddled masses. I thought about doubling back to my college friend and asking if I could trouble her again, this time for an aspirin, before admitting that no headache on the tolerable side of a migraine could drive me to such an indignity, not after imagining myself into a shampoo commercial with this poor unsuspecting thing.

I pressed my index fingers to my temples and applied gentle pressure in an alternating clockwise motion, as taught to me by an author who'd some years earlier published a best-selling how-to piece of nonsense with another house on something he called "Pressure Pointology," and who, by the time he reached Elder & Gold several books later, was reduced to beating his own dead horse—or, at least, applying gentle pressure to it. The move brought no relief beyond momentary distraction, along with a slice of self-consciousness, but it was in the distraction that I considered once more the simple, elegant calling card given to me the night before.

Pittsburgh Nationals.

I couldn't guess what to make of it, and once again without thinking I unfolded the pinched *Encyclopedia* pages and returned to the Dunlap entry. No, I couldn't guess, but at the same time, as it turned out, I *knew*. In my gut, in my bones, I knew. My eyes leapt across the stat lines like a mathematician reading code, seeking clues beyond the boldfaced greatness of Dunlap's 1884 season. Sure enough, working my way up and over and (finally!) down the arc of the man's career, I caught a detail that had escaped me the first time around. Or it's possible I'd noticed it but hadn't thought it worth noticing, or to put two and two together in quite this equation. There, toward the end of the line, I saw that Fred Dunlap had indeed played two nothing-special seasons (and parts of a third) with Pittsburgh's National League ball club before ending his professional career with brief stints with the New York Players League squad and the Washington club in the American Association.

Pittsburgh Nationals. Once again, for emphasis: man!

There was another detail that found me on this subsequent pass, and I mention it here for no good reason beyond the neat ribbon it placed on the entire package. Dunlap's .412 batting average standard, highlighted in bold, popped out as the area code for Pittsburgh. I didn't make the connection before, in the way "Wahoo Sam" Crawford's triples mark connected me to Chicago, but now that I had Pittsburgh on my mind, there it was. I'd called the talent coordinator at KDKA's morning talk show enough times begging for bookings that the numbers were burned into my dialing fingertips.

One more lousy hit, and our man would have been at .413, and then where would we be?

(Springfield, Massachusetts—the cradle of *basket*ball history, of all places!)

I considered the coincidence in these revelations, and added them to the coincidence in virtually everything else about this man, this eerie sequence of events, and wondered if the entire mess amounted to anything more than happenstance. The odds ran fairly strong that a journeyman ballplayer toiling in a time of instability and uncertainty in the game would eventually toil for a team based in Pittsburgh. Yes? That three-digit batting averages might occasionally align with three-digit area codes? This last was a simple oddity, but Dunlap's professional affiliation was key. Or was it? I supposed it was possible that all roads might have eventually led to Pittsburgh for a ballplayer of Dunlap's era. (It wasn't as if they were playing ball in Montreal or Tampa Bay!)

I talked myself into and out of every scenario, one moment thinking I had chanced upon some paranormal fluke and the next talking myself down from such ridiculousness and seeking to explain these turns with reason. Nothing made any sense. About the only thing I was sure of, on this second pass in the record book, was that

Dunlap's Pittsburgh totals were decidedly less impressive than his St. Louis marks, and as I took them in I realized it was no wonder these campaigns had failed to merit the same attention.

YEAR	TEAM	G	BA	SA	AB	H	2B	3B	HR	R
1888	PIT – N	82	.262	.333	321	84	12	4	1	41
1889	PIT – N	121	.235	.290	451	106	19	0	2	59

There, I thought. See! What had once been inimitable, unimaginable greatness had been swiftly reduced to mediocrity. A .235 batting average! Almost .200 points below his benchmark of just a few seasons before! Such was life, I guessed, and such were the cloying reminders that—forget Pittsburgh!—the only sure road to disappointment ran through hope.

In Dunlap, between the lines, I began to see the whole of the human experience, tucked away in the fine print of a mighty reference bible. And then I was back again on the connective tissue that bound me to this man. Every question I raised, he stood in answer. Every place I looked, there he was; every hunch I pursued, there he was; every move I made, there he was. Set my confusion to melody and it was like the inverse of that Sting song back from his days wailing for The Police. I worked to understand it, to step back from my perspective and try on another. I lost myself in the reflex memory of the song. Hell, before too terribly long I lost myself in every reflex, every memory, every impulse I'd ever had. For the time being, though, I merely drifted in thought until I somehow landed on Bernard Malamud's wondrous book *The Natural* and inserted Dunlap in the story in place of Roy Hobbs. I couldn't think why I'd made just this leap on just this line of thought, and I can't explain it now, but there it was. Then I imagined a new title, *The Supernatural*, and from there I imagined it had fallen to me at work to find a way to promote the damn thing. I imagined a press event, possibly at Sundance, with Robert Redford and some surviving Malamuds on hand to celebrate the discovery of this unknown manuscript; of the great writer's reimagining of one of his greatest works; of one of Redford's greatest screen roles, lifted from myth to cosmic spirit; of Frederick C. Dunlap recast as Roy Hobbs and put through the kinds of storied motions that would leave us all reconsidering what it meant to be alive, what it meant to dream—what it meant, in the end, to fall short; to settle. I imagined coverage of the event on *Entertainment Tonight.*

I inventoried the highs and lows of Fred Dunlap's life—he was a manager, I noticed now, at the age of only twenty-three!—and began to revisit the whole of my life as well, the fallings short I'd managed on my very own, and as I set the pages down once more and closed my eyes to the overflow of wonder and confusion, I could see the off-white linen of the calling card I believed was tucked beneath a Blockbuster Video card in my wallet, its fancily frayed edges, the curl at its middle from where it had been riding the fold in my wallet these past dozen hours.

The message at its heart: *Pittsburgh Nationals.*

It was, all of it, too, too much to consider, too, too much to believe. Too, too much. There was nothing to do but shut down.

I fisted my left hand into my back pocket seeking the card. I did this without thinking about it, and looking back I guess I wanted a confirming touch to connect me and the man I'd just met to the startling stat lines I'd just discovered. Perhaps there was something I'd missed on the man's card, I thought. A descriptive line on the back. Some sort of tell that might cancel out these mind-blowing leaps in my thinking. But as I pulled my wallet from my back pocket and poked through its meager contents, I noticed the card was gone. Disappeared! I was certain I'd placed it in the small sleeve beneath my credit cards, but there was nothing in there except a few ancient receipts and expired coupons. Could it be I took it out to admire it or study it or consider it last night in my room, only to leave it on my nightstand for the Suisse Chalet chambermaid to sweep into the trash? I supposed this was possible, but just to be sure I emptied my pockets and rummaged through my overnight bag to make sure I hadn't stowed the card any place else.

Nothing!

I sat back down beneath an exaggerated show of frustration and confusion, because it had by now occurred to me I'd made something of a scene searching so frantically for something so small, so elusive, so inconsequential, in front of a trainload of Manhattan-bound commuters. I played it like it was a big deal and no big deal, both. Like whatever it was I'd been looking for would turn up eventually, or it wouldn't. I imagined a dozen sets of eyes on me as I attempted to mask my disappointment, although in truth it's possible and possibly even *likely* that nobody on that Amtrak train had taken the slightest notice.

Soon, the soothing roll of the train had me lolling against near sleep, and it wasn't entirely clear to me that I was thinking clearly. Oh, I was thinking, make no mistake, but my thoughts were too all-over-the-place to make any kind of sense. Disjointed. Free-flowing. Half-formed. There was my distress over misplacing the man's calling card. There was this blurry business with Malamud and Redford. There was Nellie and the girls. Iona's class play, the lines of which had been burned so deeply into memory it felt as if I wore them on my brow. Sally's spelling words for her weekly quiz. The brochures, plans and related costs for Nellie's talked-about kitchen renovation—which according to the family betting line was likely to remain just talk. The prayerful grace note Cleon Jones attached to his series-ending catch out in left field, game five, 1969 World Series, the New York Mets versus the Baltimore Orioles. The slap and scratch of the low-hanging branch outside the window of my boyhood bedroom. A plate of sweetbreads I'd mistakenly ordered at Orso's during my first expense-account lunch, trying to impress an author of a book on the space program. A pair of Puma Clydes, red suede, I wore to my friend Lubie's bar mitzvah on a dare. The time, first year of college, I fell asleep in my own vomit and had to be dragged by my pant legs to the bathroom down the hall where I was showered off by a group of friends and (mostly) acquaintances who took turns reminding me of their kindness for the next million years. The noseful of must and yesteryear that seemed to seep through Fred Dunlap's too-heavy clothes. Also, an imagined tobacco card of the young Dunlap in his prime, astride second base as if turning two.

I was caught in that space between thinking every damn thing and nothing at all, beneath that long stretch of moment that catches me just before sleep and holds me in its loose grip until there's nothing to do but be swallowed up and tossed aside by a waterfall of memory . . . the first tentative steps I made across the slope of grass in our front yard—only not firsthand, but on the tired eight-millimeter film projector we used to roll out on Thanksgiving. A Brooklyn Dodgers cap I once wore to fraying. A press release that had been giving me trouble at work. A promise I failed to keep to Patsy, my youngest, who cajoled me into a skating outing at Wollman Rink that was ultimately upset by wet weather and never restored on our calendar. Malamud, again, this time offering advice on a plot point to a younger version of me. The way Nellie's wet, hot breath, in moments of passion, sometimes reaches me like something out of my own mouth. The spaces between us that seem to grow more roomy with the years, with routine. And, once more, and still: Dunlap. The weight and heft of his bowler. The power of his grip. The stuff of his days, back then, barnstorming.

I couldn't shake the man, although eventually I did drift off. Somewhere beyond Trenton, I later figured, careening north, I was jolted awake after an undetermined collection of minutes and left to reorient myself as I gazed across the aisle at the half-torsos of the Manhattan-bound commuters gathering on the platform outside. Princeton Junction. My view was such that I could see only the legs and shoes and briefcases of the people waiting for the train doors to open, framed as they were by the low-riding windows against the high platform. From the waist down, then, there were colorless pant suits set off by loud art-house belts; low-hanging leather pocketbooks that in another era might have passed for saddlebags; polished shoes in almost every shade of black and brown, now and then a pair of pressed jeans, tucking in an also-pressed Oxford shirt and topping a pair of pristine running shoes that looked as if they'd barely escaped the box; a scattering of freestanding briefcases, some of them deep and wide and monstrously big enough to hold a couple toaster ovens; manicured hands that looked as if they hadn't done any heavy lifting (beyond these briefcases!) for decades; newspapers, folded lengthwise and in on themselves and hunched forward at their spines, the flattened pile pressed firmly against the bottom edges of pinstriped suit coats and held in place by pinky rings. It was summer, still, and yet there was hardly a piece of bare skin on that train platform; the few skirts in passing view were supported by stockinged or hosed legs, and I recall thinking as the train rickety-racked to a stop, past these clusters of seriously dressed commuters, that Princeton Junction must be a seriously buttoned-down place. Pressed jeans!

And then, as we pulled finally to a complete stop, framed perfectly by the window directly across the aisle from me, I saw him. Again. From the waist down. Actually, I *thought* I saw him. I *feared* I saw him. I hoped it was someone else. I caught the spats first, and worked my way up from the pavement. The fancy cane. The tailored flannel pant legs, riding neatly toward the low, fashioned line of suit coat. I couldn't swear to it, but it struck me as the same outfit from the morning. I thought, no! It can't be! I might have been dreaming, or caught in that strange, drifting-off space between sleep and no-sleep, but I was soon enough awake. I'd left the man in Philadelphia about an hour and a half earlier!

I leaned forward in my seat trying to lengthen my view of this man through the window, but I still couldn't see his face or his upper body, and I worried if I leaned too far he'd catch my face from his end. I sat back up. I checked my watch and ran through the timetable again, just to make sure the logistics couldn't possibly add up, and sure enough, it was impossible. Even if he'd boarded the train with me in Philadelphia, which I supposed was a prospect, there was no explaining how this man might have leap-frogged ahead to meet me in Princeton Junction on arrival. Unless of course these windows were framing some other similarly dressed dandy—but then, what were the odds of *that*? It was all too incredible to consider, and yet I found myself hoping, praying that the man outside the train window was someone other than my man Dunlap.

Pleasepleaseplease, I thought. Be someone else.

Up until this moment, I'd been mostly bewildered by my strange encounters with this strange man. There was something odd about them, but nothing more. I hadn't liked that he had tracked me to my hotel room that morning, but I never once feared for my own safety. I was curious, and I was cautious, but that was the extent of it. Any concerns I had were Nellie's, once removed. The weirdness was benign, only here, now, the situation seemed to shift into a higher gear. The stakes had changed—it was obvious!—and alongside this shift I was left feeling nervous and jittery and terrified.

Be someone else, I thought again. Be someone else. And then, for emphasis, I whispered it to myself: "Be someone else."

Willing it to be so.

The man moved to board the train with the other commuters, and in his tentative steps I struggled to place his mannerisms against those I remembered from earlier that morning. From last night. His gait was indistinct, and I found myself wondering how Dunlap had walked, from the hotel to the station. Who could remember?

For a brief moment, he disappeared from view as he inched toward the double doors at the front of the car, and in that moment I thought I might have been imagining the whole scene, but before I could get too excited about this possibility, he reappeared. On board. And, next, walking back, confident, past my coed friend toward where I sat, slung low so he might miss me.

(The man had come this far, no doubt looking for me! There was no chance of him missing me!)

The train began to move, and he took a clear, straight line down the aisle, walking against the current of the forward-lurching train. There was, I took time to notice, a discomfiting effect, as the man I took to be Dunlap appeared to make no progress against the backdrop of platform outside the window, even as he drew nearer to me with each step like a man walking up a down escalator at the mall, a mime pushing against a make-believe wind. It was as if he was approaching without moving, and as he came closer I caught his bowler, his muttonchops, his bad teeth.

There was no mistaking him.

Sting's voice filled my head: *Every breath I take . . . every move I make . . . he'll be watching me . . .*

I pretended to read. I pulled an Amtrak brochure from the seatback in front of me and buried my nose in the thing, willing Dunlap to pass. What was he doing here? I wondered. More to the point, *how* was he doing here? Why? It made no sense. There wasn't a single explanation that left me feeling good about my situation.

Without realizing it, I had resumed my author's finger-to-the-temples maneuver to relieve the mounting tension in my head, and at the moment Dunlap reached the aisle at my seat, the train picking up speed as it pulled from the station, I saw out of the corner of my narrowed eyes that he had pulled up alongside and looked down upon my brochure with unusual consideration. He paused for a beat, as if to worry what sally he might toss to announce his sudden, mysterious appearance.

"David," he finally said, all too pleasantly, taking in the odd sight of me vigorously massaging my temple in an alternating clockwise motion while at the same time holding an Amtrak timetable at a reading distance favored by the legally blind. "I fear I've placed you in a pucker."

There was that *pucker* again.

◆

Once, not too long before my unsettling trip to Philadelphia, Iona had come bounding down the long hallway in our railroad-style apartment with an epiphany that rates a mention here. Apparently, she had discovered a modern-era game that managed to reach a full nine innings without a single baseball leaving the field of play—a neat little oddity, when you think about it. She'd been doing research on a probability problem for her advanced-level math class that had lately reached just beyond my skill set, and had come across this statistical aberration. St. Louis against Brooklyn—August 4, 1908—and by all accounts the game began and ended with the same ball. It's never happened before or since, according to Iona, and I set it out now as the polar enigma to the puzzle that found us in those right-field stands that night in Philly, where thirty-eight different balls were put in play during Scott Rolen's single long turn at bat.

(Actually, now that I look back on it, I'm guessing a good number of those Rolen foul balls never left the field of play and were swiftly returned to action, but I believe my point is clear.)

"Think about it, Daddy-o," Iona said. (Yes, she sometimes calls me "Daddy-o," mostly when she gets giddy-o.)

"Okay," I said, and I meant to.

"No, really. *Think* about it. Most games, they use about a hundred balls, give or take a couple dozen. Somewhere in there. Major League umpires rub up ten dozen balls before each game, so they're ready for anything."

"And you know this . . . how?" I said. Really, this child of mine is an endless riddle. She dresses like a punk rocker gone trick-or-treating, each day's look more shocking than the day before, and underneath her costuming is a curious student, a patient big sister and a rabid baseball fan. It's the strangest mix, but Nellie and I relish it. Our Iona is one of a kind, truly, just like the lone ball from this St. Louis-Brooklyn game.

"Jesus, Dad," she said. "How many games have I watched?"

"Meaning?" I pushed.

"Meaning, you know, how many games have I watched? Break it down. Most half-innings, there's what, five or six balls fouled into the stands. That sounds about right. Maybe a couple times a game, someone hits a home run, or a ball gets scuffed and has to be removed, or a pitcher just doesn't like the way a ball feels and asks the umpire for a new one."

"Have you ever actually counted?" I asked. I couldn't imagine sitting through an entire baseball game keeping a tally of the number of balls put in play by the home-plate umpire, but then as soon as I'd said it, I realized it wasn't such a strange count to keep, given all the weird totals tracked by baseball statisticians. And it wasn't so strange to imagine my Iona doing the counting, because when she gets fixed on a thing, there's no derailing her.

"A couple times," she said. "Just to get some idea. Usually comes out around a hundred."

I thought, damn, whose child is this? And then I smiled, because she was mine. I pulled her over to the couch where I was sitting and tousled up her hair, which on this night happened to be dyed a shade of indigo blue that looked almost incandescent. "You're a nut," I said, horsing around. "You're certifiable."

"Yeah," she shot back, happy to have her deep-blue hair messed by her Daddy-o. "Look who's talking."

Keep in mind: This was before the specter of Fred "Sure Shot" Dunlap, before there was any irony in being called a nut by my eldest daughter. At the time, this was just a good-natured exchange mixed with a little roughhousing, and when the moment seemed to pass, Iona stood to go back to her room to finish up her math homework, but I called her back with a question.

"This rubbing up the baseballs," I said. "Ten dozen before each game. Where'd you learn about that?"

"Come on, Dad," she said. "Everybody knows that."

"No," I said. "I watch a lot of baseball. I didn't know that."

"The ten dozen or the rubbing?"

"Both," I said.

"It's, like, baseball 101," she said. "They rub the balls with mud to take the shine and slickness from them. You can't just take the balls out of the box and start playing with them, you know."

"You can't?" I said. "Why not?"

"They're too slippery," she explained. "The pitchers don't like it. They can't get a good grip. The infielders, too."

In a beat she went from a tone of teasing and gentle condescension to one of easiness and good cheer. She launched into a short course on the art and practice of rubbing mud on baseballs, which Iona said dated to the 1920s, after Cleveland Indians shortstop Ray Chapman was killed by a wild pitch and league officials decreed that fresh balls would be put into play at regular intervals throughout the game. Turned out it took a couple kicks in the dirt for the leather on a fresh ball to lose its slickness after being tanned, so the pitchers started to complain, having to now break in so many new baseballs over the course of a game, and as a result umpires were instructed to rub dirt onto balls before they were put into play. Soon, umpires moved from grabbing fistfuls of infield dirt and wetting it down with tobacco juice to a mysterious compound known as Lena Blackburne's Baseball Rubbing Mud, which for some reason proved enormously effective at taking the slickness off a new ball without also taking the whiteness with it. The reddish-brown compound was discovered by a journeyman ballplayer named Lena Blackburne while on a fishing trip, and it's said to contain an ideal mix of silt and sand while remaining relatively free of gravel, and for the past fifty years it's been dredged from the shores of New Jersey's Pennsauken Creek, a tributary to the Delaware River, for just this purpose. The precise location of the dredging site is a closely guarded secret, maintained by the same family for all these years.

"Why couldn't that be our family business?" Iona said, tying up the loose ends on her tutorial.

"What," I said, "rubbing mud on baseballs?"

"No," she said. "Collecting it and selling it. The mud, I mean. Guarding the secret location. Way better than making doll heads."

"Doll hair," I corrected.

"Still."

"And he was just a salesman," I clarified. "Your grandfather. Wasn't like it was his business that he could pass on or anything."

She was back on the mud already. "There's just like one guy," she said, building up a new batch of enthusiasm. "He goes out at night, by flashlight, and fills up these old coffee cans. Every baseball put in play for the past fifty years has been rubbed with mud from this one spot. Roger Maris's sixty-first home-run ball. Clemente's 3,000th hit. The ball that went through Bill Buckner's legs. They're all connected to this one little creek in New Jersey. All touched, in one way or another, by this same guy. How cool is that?"

"Pretty cool," I agreed.

But even more than the cool connective tissue Iona had discovered linking the last half-century or so of baseball history to some obscure guy with a flashlight crawling around in a thick of mud, there were also the separate astonishments that Major League Baseball teams continued to purchase buckets of mud collected from a secret New Jersey creek bed to be rubbed into baseballs before they are put into play, and that my adolescent daughter would know such a thing. And as I reconsider these, I think to myself, okay, Daddy-o, how cool is *that*?

◆

Funny, the way a racing imagination can go from sheer terror to slight anxiety to nothing much at all—all in the turn of a phrase or a shift in mood. Here I had steeled myself against a Stephen King novel about to happen right there on that Amtrak train, and at the now-familiar lilt of this man's voice and the gentle confidence of his manner I was suddenly, startlingly put at ease. How did that happen? I took time to wonder. What buttons were being pushed to turn me from dark to light in such a snap?

We caught each other's eyes—and in his I detected a warm smile. However, there was so much hair about this man's face, from muttonchops to handlebar, that there was no good view of his lips, and therefore no good way to discern a smile, but his eyes gave him away. This man meant me no harm.

"It used to be," he said, "you traveled by train, you felt every rock at your feet, every hillside." He offered a rickety-rackety pantomime meant to illustrate his point, although at the time his point was lost on me. I looked around and could summon up no great improvements in train travel in my lifetime, so I merely nodded.

He stood queerly before me for several beats more—making room in the exchange, I realize now, for me to offer him the vacant window seat to my left. I didn't pick up on this, and don't know that I would have wanted to ride with him if I had, and after a short, clumsy moment he simply claimed the empty seat directly across the aisle.

"You're headed to New York, Mr. Dunlap?" I said, not wanting to appear rude but unable to conceal my bewilderment at this latest turn.

"David, please," he said. "I thought we were beyond that."

"Fred. I'm sorry. It's just that you surprised me."

"I have that effect," he allowed. And then, after a beat: "New York sounds fine. It's been some time, you know."

No, I hadn't known. I hadn't the first idea. All I had were about a million questions, and for some unknowable reason the ones concerning this man's illogical reappearings were nowhere near the top of my list. First and foremost, I wanted to ask him for another calling card, to replace the one I had apparently mislaid, but I skipped past that question for the one next in line. "That ball," I finally asked, "from last night. What were you thinking?"

"Thinking?" he shot back as if I had suggested he'd poured ketchup over the thing and attempted a bite. "I'm afraid I don't understand."

"Throwing it back the way you did?"

"There was no thought in that, my good friend," he said, and he went into a long explanation of how in his day it was the custom for umpires to wait at least five minutes before declaring a ball lost or no longer suitable for game use and putting a new ball in play. He went on and on, with details and asides, and I wished I had a tape recorder to get it all down. Something about the players rustling under benches to root out foul balls. Another something about club owners safeguarding new balls like prized jewels. A final something about a game against a Washington nine, managed by a crazy Irishman named Corky Scanlon, stalled over an argument over whether a ball crushed off the bat of someone named Handsome Henry Boyle was too lopsided to be put back in play.

"He ended up forfeiting the game, that lunatic Scanlon," Dunlap concluded this particular aside. "He wouldn't send his players back onto the field. What few fans there were appeared about ready to hang that poor fellow by his fingernails."

As he spoke, I thought of the marked contrast between the way baseballs were hoarded in Dunlap's day and the way they're so casually discarded today, and how long Rolen's epic at-bat might have taken to play itself out if the players had to run down each and every one of those foul balls before the game could continue. I thought of the torn book pages at my left, of the life that lay between the stat lines in the Dunlap entry. I thought too of the man who sat across the aisle at my right, of the life that pulsed between the lines of his stories. Of all the things that now passed between us that were being left unspoken, unimagined. I was no longer afraid of this man, as I have stated, but I was plainly terrified of filling the spaces between this right here and that so long ago.

And then I surprised myself, for surely the thought of giving voice to this terror was unimaginable, but I imagine now the prospect of sitting on my hunches and not saying a damn thing was even less likely. "This game," I interrupted, "with the lopsided ball, it was a Union Association game?"

"Why, yes it was," he said, as if marveling. If the wrinkles about his eyes had suggested a smile a few moments before, they now registered a measure of pure delight I could not recall seeing in quite some time—not since Nellie first cradled our little Patsy. "You know of our Union Association?" he asked.

"Some," I allowed.

"You know of the St. Louis Maroons?"

"Some."

"And that glorious summer? Eighteen eighty-four? It was our season in the sun, you know. That was how we all thought of it."

I nodded.

The train rolled on for a while—and in the rumble we each seemed to lapse into our own thoughts. I couldn't begin to guess what was filling this man's head, but in mine I realized that we had just covered some deeply weird ground, that in the space between Princeton Junction and the stretch of track beneath my seat I had allowed myself to conclude that this man across the aisle to one side and this forgotten ballplayer immortalized in the torn pages of *The Baseball Encyclopedia* on the seat at my other side were somehow one and the same. It cut against every notion of time and space and spirituality I ever knew to be true—hell, it ran counter to life itself!—and yet I reached this conclusion without any thunderclap of realization.

It came upon me, is all, and I accepted it.

"You were the manager?" I asked. "You were on the other side of the argument with the Irishman?"

"How ever did you know?" Dunlap asked, and in his tone I got that it was he who was incredulous at this epiphany, not me.

"I don't know," I said. "I'm just asking."

Six
GONE

There was much talk of baseball over those next miles, and not much talk of anything else. No mention of the improbability that filled the aisle between us like a deployed air bag. No mention by me of Nellie or the girls back home in New York, and no mention by Dunlap of whatever family he may or may not have left behind. (Truly, behind!) No mention how this man might have raced ahead of my train in Philadelphia and beat me to Princeton Junction, or why he might have thought to attempt such a feat; I didn't ask, and he didn't offer.

It was just baseball, old time and new and in between, and as the industrial scenery clanked past our windows, the rest of the world melted away and I managed to lose what were left of my bearings.

I must confess, I was only too happy to shed the black terror of just a few moments earlier and throw in completely to the fantasy at hand. I could have done without the corresponding lack of focus, and the general fuzz of confusion that seemed now to follow me like the bowl of hot oatmeal from those ancient Maypo commercials, but at least the dread was (mostly) gone. Tell me I'm wrong in this: We build up all kinds of apprehensions over things we can't know or control, and the slightest pinprick can let all the air out of a looming worry and leave it seeming harmless. Here—at last, up close—I'd convinced myself there was nothing to be afraid of, except perhaps the fear of the unknown, but even this didn't register. It was all too much of a wonder. Suddenly, I was entirely prepared to sign on wholeheartedly to whatever adventure awaited me. If it was a delusion, it was such a comfortable delusion that every piece of implausibility made perfect sense; everything fit.

If I had somehow stepped onto some new substratum of reality that would now be my baseline going forward . . . well, then this was alright with me as well.

Dunlap, too, seemed happily oblivious to the century that might have separated us, and willfully uncertain of the gaps into which each of us had separately fallen, and focused instead on what we had both determined as common ground. Baseball. Just baseball. Our safe, certain harbor against a sea of confusion.

"The sacrifice," he said at one point, as if working off a list. "I will never understand it. To give up one out to merely advance one base. You only get but three, so what mudsill gives one away?"

In this, of course, he was deriding the prevailing practice of moving runners into scoring position by taking the bat from the hitter's hand, either by bunt or lazy fly ball or check-type swing to the right side of the diamond. You see it all the time, more and more, including four or five times during the previous night's doubleheader—and apparently our Dunlap had seen enough.

(Among those four or five instances, I recalled as I later consulted my scorecard, not a single one of those advanced runners came around to score, a fact Dunlap could not have failed to notice on his own.)

Next, I wondered if Dunlap didn't see the percentage in moving a runner to third with less than two outs so that the man might score on a passed ball, a sacrifice fly, a grounder to second or any number of means shy of a base hit, but he bristled at the move.

"Take your licks," he said, "or take your lumps. I'm all for improving your chances, but why give up a turn if you don't have to? The percentage move is to get the runner to third on his own steam."

"It's not so easy to steal third," I suggested.

"It's difficult to hit as well," he countered, "but we don't give up on the notion."

He had me there.

We went on in this way until Newark, which wasn't all that long a stretch from Princeton Junction, but while we were in its middle the time fairly flew. I could not have put a clock to it, for it seemed like all the time in the world and no time at all, both. It was like no other stretch of time I can remember—save for those long moments of Rolen's at-bat just the night before. *The longest stretch of time between a single happened thing and the next happened thing.* It was rather like that, and rather not. We covered great new territory, but at the same time we hardly moved. Those million questions I had queuing for attention were soon enough a couple million strong. I had only the time to follow Dunlap's lead. He had his theories on making a proper pivot when turning a double play, on playing outfielders deep to guard against the extra-base hit, on the overuse of relief pitchers—and, relatedly, the underuse of workhorse starters. He maintained that Big Dan Brouthers, one of the most storied hitters of his generation—a career .342 hitter, ninth best all time—was something of a lickfinger when it came to club management, but allowed that the man could whip his weight in wildcats. I didn't know what either of these expressions meant, but from Dunlap's tone I guessed the latter was a good thing, and the former decidedly less so. Also, Dunlap reported his deeply held conviction that there was never a good reason to walk a batter intentionally, which he took to be a kind of cowardly admission of defeat—or, at least, an unwillingness to engage. Somewhere in there he did manage to inadvertently confirm my theory regarding the Pittsburgh Nationals, to which he frequently referred in the kinds of terms usually reserved for difficult in-laws, but beyond such casually dropped details as these there was precious little to go on in terms of autobiographical information. There was the conversation we were actually having, and the conversation I was wishing we might have, and I hung somewhere in the rough middle, wanting to get through the one so I might be let in on the other.

Before I could pivot our talk onto a more satisfying line, we pulled into Newark. The station seemed to sneak up on us—on me, anyway. Dunlap was at some midpoint of a diatribe on the unmanliness of the platooning system that had its roots in his era but had recently become a kind of default strategy for contemporary managers. (For readers new to the sport, the practice refers to the time-sharing of a starting spot in the lineup, allowing left-handed hitters to face only right-handed pitchers, and right-handed hitters to face only left-handed pitchers, on the accepted notion that mediocre talent at the plate will have a greater advantage against his opposite number on the mound.) Dunlap had not quite made his case on this one point when the train pulled to a stop and the conductor called out the station.

At this, Dunlap stood hastily, reached for the bowler he had placed on the window seat alongside him, tipped it swiftly toward me in a gesture of leave-taking, placed the thing astride his head, and double-timed it to the double doors at the center of the car.

He turned back as he sped toward the front of the car. "I thank you for your company, David," he hollered past my welcoming coed and everyone else in the seats between. "There's a woman in Newark I once knew. She'd set her cap for me, not too long ago."

And then he was gone. He must have left the platform by a descending staircase at a right angle to our car, because I couldn't see him doubling back through the windows. I lurched across the aisle to the platform side of the train and tried to see down the length of platform stretching in front of me, my right cheek pressed to the grimy glass, but all I could see, once again, was a scattering of half-torsos and none belonged to my man Dunlap. He'd simply, swiftly disappeared.

It was the strangest thing—and I say this without qualification. Certainly, the very fact of this man's apparent existence was strange enough; his emergence the night before at Veterans Stadium, as if from the thin night air, was stranger still; his seeking me out on these two ensuing occasions had been the strangest piece to this whole puzzle. But to take such sudden leave! After such as this! Well, this was beyond strange. This was . . . well, who could say what this was? There weren't words for what this was, and yet as I returned to my seat and attempted to quantify the measure of oddity I had just experienced, the anomaly I had taken on faith, I found myself feeling deeply, profoundly disappointed. Whatever had just happened, however it happened, whatever it meant and wherever it might have led . . . it now appeared unlikely it would ever happen again, or that I would be led any old place but home.

I turned wistfully to the seat across the aisle, but there was no trace of the man. No dent in the seat cushion. No left-behind cane. No recent scent of must or mildew or chewing tobacco. No graffiti scratched into the underside of the seatback tray announcing that, indeed, *Fred Dunlap was here.*

There was nothing at all.

◆

One look at Nell early that afternoon in our apartment, dressed smartly in her nurse whites and tennis shoes, hair pulled tight into a bun, and I knew there wasn't a thesaurus or dictionary in the world to get me over this next hump. And forget the words! I didn't have the courage, the tools, the first idea where to begin. How could I tell her what had just happened? To get her to believe what I now believed? It was impossible, I felt sure, and yet it was also essential, for without Nell's ratification, the events of the past hours might have never unfolded. Who was I, to make a leap such as this, without my utterly sane wife along for the soaring? Where was the sense in it? The hope? What good could come if I remained alone in it?

She was cooking in our shotgun kitchen in need of a facelift when I spilled into the apartment with my news. She had her back to the kitchen doorway, and her ear to the powered microwave, so she didn't hear me come in. There was an open yellow tub of Polly-O ricotta cheese on the chipped mica countertop to her left, which meant she was laying in some stuffed shells for tonight's dinner. She'd leave a plateful in the fridge, along with the salad fixings and a fresh tumbler of her trademark vinaigrette, and I could pretend to cook. That was the routine.

I didn't want to startle her, so I jangled my keys.

"Hey," she said, turning around.

"Hey to you," I said back.

She spun and crossed to the doorway, planted a dry kiss on my mouth, and then she pulled back, startled. She indicated the gash over my eye and said, "What the hell happened to you?"

Instinctively, I touched my hand to the wound, as if to remind myself. "Oh," I said. "That. I tripped and fell, this morning at breakfast. It's nothing."

Nellie leaned in for a closer look. She said, "It's not nothing, Felb."

She has a way, my Nellie, of making her disappointment known, and here she made it clear that I was some kind of ass.

She said, "Did you even clean it?"

It hadn't occurred to me, I can freely admit in this account—only to admit it just then to my doting, judging nurse of a wife would have been a sign of defeat. And so, instead, I tried feebly to dismiss her concern. "It's fine," I said.

"It's not fine," she said, and then she spun on her heels and crossed to the medicine cupboard and pulled down a bottle of hydrogen peroxide and a fistful of cotton balls, which she placed on the counter. Then she continued about the kitchen, and after another while she crossed back to me for another inspection of my face and forehead. She lifted my hair and noticed the marble that had grown beneath my skin. She smelled of pasta dough and dishwashing soap and the starch from her nurse whites.

"Ice," she said, looking at my scalp. "Twenty minutes now, twenty minutes later."

"Got it," I said.

"Good."

"Got time for lunch?" I wondered.

"Can't. I'm out the door."

Only she wasn't, not just yet. There was still some kitchen business to be gotten through, so she leaned into the refrigerator to situate dinner. She had the choreography down. The dirty dishes sinked, the counter wiped close to clean. "Nomi's got the shift in front," Nell continued, "needs me to cover her last hour." (Nomi was one of Nell's nurse friends.)

"Bummer," I said, and it was. I hadn't realized how much I'd been longing to soak in the sureness of my unshakably rational wife until she announced she had to go. Granted, I still had no idea what I would say to her, or where I might begin, but the idea of being alone in our apartment was a deep disappointment.

"There's lo mein in the fridge from last night," Nell hollered from the front closet where she kept her bag.

"Great," I said.

"And Ralph's Ices," she said, stepping back into the kitchen, sidling up to me from behind, cupping my butt with her free hand.

"Rainbow. That should cheer up my baby doughboy PR guy."

I spun to face her and collect her in my arms. "Jeez," I managed, "I'm gone one night and you girls go wild. Chinese and Ralph's."

"Joy in Mudville," she said beneath an exaggerated shrug, and she leaned in for another kiss, this one noticeably less dry. Like she'd missed me. Or worried over me. Or suddenly couldn't figure me out. She pulled back from our embrace. "You look like shit, Felb," she assessed.

"Ice, I know," I said. "Peroxide, I know."

"No, not that. Just, you know, shit in general. Tired."

"Long trip."

"The spats guy?" she wondered, worried.

"Not just the spats guy, but yeah, the spats guy."

She considered this for a beat, like she was making another diagnosis. She touched my forehead with her open palm and then with her lips. "Girls won't be home for a couple hours," she said. "Maybe you should lie down."

Maybe, I thought. Wouldn't kill me to lie down, middle of the day, the apartment quiet.

"What about work?" I said out loud. I had been meaning to stop in at the office before the end of the day, just to be seen. There wasn't really anything to do—there was hardly ever *really* anything to do—but it was the being seen that mattered.

"You were out of town with an author," she said. "Pulled from hearth and home by your heartless superiors. You're entitled to an afternoon off."

Now that Nell had put the idea in my head, home sounded good. "You'll write me a note?" I said.

"I'll write you a note."

"Then maybe I will lie down," I said. Sleep sounded good, too.

"I'll check in," she said, making for the door.

I held up my right hand in a still wave as Nell started to pull the door shut behind her and then quickly pushed it back open. She curled her head around the door, and then the rest of her.

"Almost forgot," she said, reaching into her bag for what it took me a beat or two to recognize as a baseball, which she abruptly and crisply tossed to my right hand, still up in its still wave. I caught it like I would have received a yo-yo. "To make up for yesterday," she said.

Then she blew a kiss and left.

I looked at the pristine ball—an official Rawlings National League model, stamp-signed by National League president Leonard S. Coleman, without a trace of Lena Blackburne's rubbing mud or any other soil-based smirch. Leave it to Nell to race out first thing in the morning, before the girls left for school, to find a neighborhood store with a sporting-goods section deep enough to stock official Rawlings baseballs (probably Lambert's Hardware on Columbus), and to know that a generic or Little League model just wouldn't do. Also, leave it to Nell to bring the thing back in time for the girls to sign it—apparently with a Sharpie, the way a baseball is meant to be signed.

I twirled the thing from inscription to inscription, considering my good fortune:

Better luck next time. I.

Best wishes, Sally Felb. (She'd been working on her autograph, my Sally, thinking she might someday be an Olympic gymnast, or an actress, or someone in need of a practiced signature.)

I love you, Daddy! xxx Patsy.

I guess you only get to make one great catch per lifetime. Yours, Nell.

I rubbed my fingers gently across the smooth cowhide surface of the ball, along the waxed red thread at the seams. I tossed it up and down a few times and read the inscriptions once more.

I could have cried.

◆

For all my exposure to the written word, and to some of the greatest novelists, biographers and historians of our time, I couldn't navigate my way out of a library if I had a map. Understand, if they didn't also lend out videos at my local branch, or occasionally host one of my authors, I don't think I'd ever go inside. And you can just forget about me and the Internet, which our Elder & Gold authors variously insist is the single greatest research tool in recorded human history. I certainly haven't noticed. Yes, it's a great time-saver, even I can realize that, but if I can't find it on the navigation bar of my America Online home page, it will remain forever lost to me. As far as I'm concerned, a search engine is a directive, instructing me what to do when I lift the hood of a car and pretend to know what I'm looking at.

All of which goes to my inability to discover all that much about Frederick C. Dunlap, the once-great but now relatively obscure ballplayer from the 1880s about whom precious little had been written. (Or, more likely, about whom a great deal had been written in his day, even as precious little of this material seemed to have survived into mine.) His life and times might as well have been reduced to the stat lines in his official *Baseball Encyclopedia* entry; that's how bare the cupboard seemed to be on this guy.

And yet with a shade more persistence than I'd been accustomed to claiming, the big picture of Dunlap's life came slowly into focus—and I began to rework some of that picture that very afternoon. Sleep may have sounded good, but that notion passed. I wasn't about to lie down. I couldn't. I needed silent fuel to keep my eerie fantasy going. I had those loose pages from the *Encyclopedia*, but the information begged for adornment.

Over time, I should mention, I developed some trouble over the details of Dunlap's life, the day-to-day, the failed relationships, how he liked his coffee . . . that sort of thing. (Did they even have coffee back then?) My halfhearted attempts at scholarship left me wondering how historians ever get the goods on subjects long gone. They recreate entire conversations, put thoughts in people's heads, dress them in favorite clothes, craft fully realized lives from dashed-off notes in the public record. The only way to do this, I determined, was to make it up, but even here I was stymied, coming up half-empty in the imagination department. Those who know me will jump to confirm that I'm rarely one to embellish—not because I'm too scrupled, but because I can't always think how. Those who don't know me, I'm afraid, will figure this out soon enough.

The facts, then, near as I could figure, hastily as I could figure, were these: A second baseman by principle trade, Fred Dunlap had an arm stuffed with legend. He was a demon base-runner, a pesky hitter, and a peerless fielder, but it was his arm that made his name. Actually, it was his arm and his business acumen, bundled together, but I'll address his physical gifts first, because it was in the game that he put himself in a position to out-think his contemporaries. Therefore, his arm. According to one turn-of-the-century sportswriter, the ball seemed to sing as it flew from Dunlap's hand—actually sing!—which it did courtesy of a trademark swinging motion, as opposed to a more conventional over-the-top toss. It was, I gathered, more slingshot than throw, but it was tough to be sure without corresponding images on which to pin the colorful descriptions. I tried duplicating Dunlap's throwing motion in the full-length mirror bracketed to the back of Nellie's closet, based on the vivid accounts pulled from old newspapers. I tried closing my eyes and imagining it. I tried matching what I was reading to what I had seen the night before in Philadelphia, although I couldn't honestly say I had been paying the same kind of attention to the manner of the throw as I was to the mere fact of it. I tried grafting Dunlap's mysterious style to the familiar styles I knew from my own growing up, and where I was with all this was that Dunlap had an unorthodox sidearm, or submarine delivery—not so unusual today, but as if from another planet at one time. I recalled a relief pitcher named Ted Abernathy who used to pitch for the Senators and the Indians and the Cubs and the Reds with such a low-slung underarm motion it left me thinking he might scrape his knuckles against the dirt. It was positively Cro-Magnon!

Back to Dunlap: He was a short, powerful man, built low to the ground, and when he moved to his right to retrieve a mean-spirited ground ball up the middle, his throws to first skimmed the top of the short infield grass, as if skipping stones across a glassy lake. It was much the same to his left, because Dunlap was also ambidextrous; he could barehand a low liner as easily with his left as with his right, and pivot to throw with as much hop on one hand as on the other. He was his own mirror image.

And it wasn't just Dunlap's style of throwing that so captivated the fans, or that he could come at you from both sides; it was the terrible speed, the killing accuracy. The man could send it, to co-opt a phrase from a slightly later era. Dunlap had a throw like a rifle shot, it was reported in more than one account, and he was famous for the way he audaciously taunted his foes, holding the ball until the last possible second before rifling a dead-on bullet a half-beat ahead of the runner. Naturally, there was no showcase in throwing out a base-runner by ten or twenty feet, but to best him by a hair was a crowd-pleaser, and Dunlap surely relished the hat-tippings in his direction. No less an authority than King Kelly, the Hall of Fame jack-of-all-positions who tore up National League basepaths during Dunlap's career, dubbed his worthy opponent "Sure Shot" Fred, and the name stuck as sure and true as one of Dunlap's peas to home from deep in the hole. As late as the 1920s, long after Johnny Evers, Napolean Lajoie and Eddie Collins had left their own marks on the position, old-time scribes who had seen Dunlap play still called him the greatest second baseman of all time.

And yet, despite his fleeting fame, Fred "Sure Shot" Dunlap managed to die penniless at the age of 42, and virtually friendless, to where the Philadelphia funeral home that handled his burial—in December, 1902—had to first wait several days to find a former teammate to identify the body, and then to pull strangers off the street to act as pallbearers.

This much came to me without significant effort. A couple keystrokes online that even I could manage that afternoon, alone in our apartment, and I was on my way. Over the next weeks I discovered a page in an oversized paperback entitled *Nineteenth Century Stars*, and found time to initiate a correspondence with a curator at the Baseball Hall of Fame in Cooperstown, New York, and before too terribly long I had enough to know the rest would not come so easy. Indeed, in my inexperienced, ordinary hands, it was entirely possible the rest would not come at all. What did I know from original source material? Who was I to be entrusted with a life story other than my own? Were it not for the strange, uncertain man who alighted in my view that night in Veterans Stadium—the original source material to end all original source material?—I would have gone to my grave not knowing any more of Fred Dunlap's life and career than I knew of, say, Cap Anson's, to name a more heralded star of the period. For all my knowledge of the game and the kinship I felt with its names and numbers, my interest seemed to stop short when I reached past my grandfather's era. Before this Dunlap business, those old-time statistics had been an amusement, a way to place more recent feats in context. What could be more forgettable, I used to think, than a forgotten game of baseball, played out on a years-ago and now overgrown field, beneath a different set of rules, with players long dead and long-before-that overlooked? Without film footage, or even still images, where would be the validation?

I tended to date my own baseball lifetime to Bill Mazeroski's World Series-winning home run off Ralph Terry in 1960, my first true baseball memory—and even this, I'm afraid, was a memory once removed, relegated to the black-and-white newsreel recesses of imagination. Still, it marked a kind of turning point, a coming to awareness. I could know a thing, but if I didn't see it, or experience it, or have it wash over me in full force, or meted out by neighborhood kids schooled in big-footed tyranny against an adolescent's passion for the New York Yankees, it was as unreachable to me as starlight. There was what you knew, and what you *know*, and here, with this sudden downloading of Fred Dunlap's world into mine, I was inclined to set off the whole of my existence in italics.

Now, to the out-thinking, for which I soon learned our Fred Dunlap was also well regarded. His baseball savvy was such that he managed for all or parts of four seasons—as early as 1882! Dunlap was a keen student of the game, a master of its many nuances, one of the first to observe an opponent's tendencies and play the percentages— and, apparently, the first to do it effectively. I thought back to those tossed-off observations on our mystery train ride to Newark, and I realized there had been some bluster to them, some pride. It was one thing to play the game to advantage, he seemed to have been saying, and quite another to give in too easily, and it came to make perfect sense to me that a man who could see the odds shift in his favor by advancing a runner into scoring position might also see a kind of shame in doing so by dint of some sacrifice. Between the lines of these accounts there lurked a bull-headed arrogance, a determination to approach the game and the life it supported with the kind of all-out audacity that was inevitably doomed. The man's luck couldn't help but run out.

Before it did, Dunlap was said to have been one of the shrewdest ballplayers of the day, and upon his retirement, hastened by a broken leg just eight games into the 1891 season, he had accumulated a reported $100,000 in salaries and bonuses and endorsements over his eleven-year professional career. And this was just his *savings*! What he actually earned, and spent, is forever lost to time, or to some biographer's too-rich imagination. Dunlap couldn't read, or write his own name, but what's been recorded of his actions suggests a keen business instinct, a dogged perseverance, and a fairly sophisticated sense of justice—sophisticated, that is, for an uneducated ballplayer orphaned before his tenth birthday. He also had timing, and profited from having played during a period of tremendous uncertainty in our national game, which in turn saw the formation of three professional leagues to rival the senior National League circuit. The American Association in 1882, the Union Association in 1884, and the Players' League in 1890 each came into existence during Dunlap's playing days, and like many of his colleagues, Dunlap left the established confines of the National League to try his hand in all three. His forays into the Union Association and the Players' League (sometimes referred to as the Brotherhood, a distinction that cost me several hours in Periodicals) proved especially lucrative, because these new leagues did not honor baseball's basic reserve clause agreement binding players to their teams, and encouraged reserved players to "hurdle" to the new league with the promise of outlandish salaries and bonuses.

That Dunlap capitalized on such circumstances, in retrospect, was not surprising, for just as he shone on the field of play, he lit his own path off the field with his outspoken positions against the established practices of the game. He lashed out at club owners who treated players like chattel. He wanted to be able to cut his own deal, as he would undoubtedly have done in virtually any other trade. He was tired, he said, of being sold around from one club to another, and damned if he would continue to allow the League to tell him where he could play, and when, and for how much money. He didn't see how such arbitrary constraints could be applied to him—or to his teammates and opponents, for that matter, although he wasn't about to make a test case out of his teammates and opponents. He was, to marry a true memory from my baseball awareness to the dusty archives of history, the Curt Flood of his day. (Ah, now there's a firsthand memory from a baseball-rich childhood: the 1967 World Series, St. Louis Cardinals against the Boston Red Sox, an afternoon contest taken in during Mr. McCormick's social studies class on one of those wheeled-in black-and-white consoles from the audio-visual department.) Curt Flood, in challenging the dreaded reserve clause, was responding to Fred Dunlap's cry. So, too, was Andy Messersmith. And Catfish Hunter. And, in other venues, Rick Barry, and Paul Warfield, and Derek Sanderson. Each of them, and each of them who followed, appeared to owe a giant debt to Dunlap—and not a single one of them, I'm betting, had ever even heard of the man, a depressing turn considering what he had set in motion.

Let me pull back a bit. After establishing himself as a .300 hitter and bona fide star with the Cleveland Blues of the National League in the early 1880s, Dunlap helped to anchor (along with Pebbly Jack Glasscock at short and Big Bill Phillips at first) the legendary nineteenth-century infield known as the "Stonewall Infield," so named, presumably, for its impenetrability. In so doing, he emerged a fan favorite and was named team manager, and during the off-season of 1883–1884, he was arguably the best second baseman in the game. He might have come out on the short side of any such argument, but he would have been included in the debate just the same, and he knew enough to play his reputation to advantage. He let it be known he was in the game for the money, and prepared to sell his services to the highest bidder. Against the advice and what may or may not have been the better judgment of his peers, he bolted Cleveland for the upstart St. Louis Maroons of the Union Association for the staggering salary of $3,400, plus an unspecified signing bonus. To put this in perspective, top salaries of National League ballplayers circa 1884 were less than half Dunlap's take. Babe Ruth himself managed to match Dunlap's salary thirty-five years later in his final season with the Red Sox. Average salaries in 1884 were far less than Dunlap's stupendous fee, but such were the persuasive charms of St. Louis shipping and real estate magnate Henry V. Lucas that Sure Shot threw in with a mostly amateur group of renegades, outcasts and louts for the Maroons' inaugural—and, as it turned out, final—Union Association season.

But let the record show, it was quite a season, both for Dunlap and his new mates. He was joined around the league by a couple dozen defectors from the professional ranks, including Emil Gross and Bill Harbidge of the Philadelphia Quakers, Dupee Shaw and Dick Burns of the Detroit Wolverines, Charlie Hodnett and Jack Gleason of the St. Louis Browns, Bill Sweeney of the Philadelphia Athletics, and Dunlap's old partner up the middle in Cleveland, Jack Glasscock.

(See what riches a little time in the reference stacks can yield!)

He was joined, too, by Mike Scanlon, possibly the first native of Cork, Ireland, to skipper a professional baseball team, and a pitcher named Henry Boyle, who tallied a league-leading 1.74 earned-run average for the Maroons when he wasn't flattening baseballs in his own turns at bat.

The St. Louis Maroons of 1884 were not only the class of the Union Association; they were the single most dominant team in the history of professional baseball. It's right there in the record books. You can have your 1954 Indians, your Big Red Machine, your Murderer's Row. Keep 'dem Bums and the Gashouse Gang. I'll take the St. Louis "Onions," as they were derided by headline writers thick with disdain for the Union Association and its kind. Granted, the Maroons played a good portion of their 113-game schedule against ragtag teams from Altoona, Wilmington, and St. Paul, whose somewhat less-than-deep-pocketed owners were forced to fold their franchises before the end of the season; but they also competed against well-stocked and well-run teams from Major League cities. And they finished with a record of 94—19.

Ninety-four victories, in just 113 games! That's an astonishing .832 winning percentage. The 1998 Yankees, the most dominant team of the moment, would barely manage a .700 winning percentage in the regular season, and here Dunlap's Maroons (which he also managed for most of the 1884 season) were on a pace that would have left Joe Torre's Yanks more than twenty-one games back in the standings.

Man!

And what of Dunlap's contribution to such a standard? Well, he was nothing less than dominant himself, leading the league in hits, runs scored, home runs, total bases and batting average, as we have seen—for the most part by the kinds of wide margins rarely seen outside lopsided presidential contests. I know I repeat myself here, but I also know there's no overstating this man's running of the table during that 1884 campaign. He was all that, as my kids like to say. All that, and far more besides. Take the team home run total for the starting nine from second-place Cincinnati, stack it against Dunlap's total and he still would have led the league. If the official scorers had bothered to track runs batted in, "Dunny" would have likely come out ahead in that measure as well, despite his position at the top of the Maroons' lineup. His .412 batting average still ranks in the all-time top ten, and his 160 runs scored in only 106 games is also up there. (At such a phenomenal clip, over a 154-game season, Dunlap would annihilate Babe Ruth's modern-day record by more than 50 runs!)

So, clearly, Dunlap was something, and his St. Louis Maroons were something else again. But none of this explained what the mess of them were doing in my limited view, going forward, what they'd been doing tooling around in my recent past, where they might be lurking in my plain present. And Dunlap himself? What was I to make of this well-dressed, muttonchopped, waistcoated man who appeared to me on a wet August night as in an apparition? Who snatched away the one foul ball in a lifetime of ballgames that was headed my way? Who studied the bright lights overhead, the pierced eyebrow of the barely dressed young woman in our vicinity, the faux green of the stadium carpet as if he had never seen such things? Who lingered long enough and near enough to track me down, twice, only to set me back down at my plain station with nothing to show for it but a change in scenery?

Truth was, I didn't have the first idea what to make of any of it—except to suppose it was a good thing that Dunlap had apparently come and gone. Who would have believed me, anyway, if I'd attempted to explain myself?

Some of these revelations came to me later, as my interest developed into a fascination and from there to an obsession—yes, I'll admit it!—and some of them were helped along by various electronic assists from my computer-savvy, baseball-obsessed daughter Iona, but I learned enough that very first afternoon on the computer to know that this guy was now a part of me, that our lives were now interwoven, like the dovetailing waxed red threads stitched into the baseball Nell had tossed to me some hours earlier.

◆

Patsy came home first, reeking of paint. It's a nursery-school smell that lingers into kindergarten—and, summers, spills over into day camp as well. It permeates her clothes, her hair, her fingernails. Whenever I collect this child in a great hug at the end of her day I am put in mind of peeling primary colors. She'd been playing at a friend's apartment in the building across the street since camp had ended at four o'clock, and Nell had arranged for the child's caregiver to walk Patsy home in time for dinner. I'd left the apartment door open, so Patsy tumbled in like a latchkey kid.

"Hello, somebody!" she yelled from the entryway.

"Hello, somebody!" I hollered back. "I'm on the computer."

Patsy could navigate the 1,200 square feet of our cramped three-bedroom apartment in just under a heartbeat, and she was upon me before I finished my hollering.

"We watched you on television, Daddy," she yelled, bounding into my lap, smelling wonderfully like a too-brown sunset slathered thickly enough to crinkle contact paper. I breathed her in and thought of my four girls huddled around the countertop television over breakfast, sitting patiently through *SportsCenter*, wondering where I was. It was a gladdening image, even if they'd never shown my near-catch on the air.

"And what did you see, Pattycakes?" I tried.

"You looked funny," she said. "Not like Daddy."

"Like what?" I asked.

"Like, funny."

"Funny, this?" I made a scrunched-up face, tongue curled and punching through puckered lips.

"No, silly," she laughed.

"Funny, this?" I pushed up the bridge of my nose to make a snout.

She laughed again, and in her laughter I could hear the innocent delight I might have felt at discovering myself huddled in conversation with one of the game's long-dead greats, if I'd been prepared for the encounter. If these Dunlap exchanges had been some sort of thrill ride at Disney World, some "Hall of Presidents" recreation, and I had paid my money and stood in wait and expected to be blown away by the connecting line between present and past. If I had only known.

PART TWO

APRIL–OCTOBER 1999

Seven
PLAIN AS DAY

It had been the better part of a year—anyway, an off-season.

Whatever ordinary holes I had dug for myself, whatever sense of complacency I had cloaked around my routines, whatever failures I had long since embraced as my due, these had now blossomed into a new brand of disillusion. I found myself looking endlessly over my shoulder, anticipating the surprising specter of Frederick C. Dunlap at every turn. He had become forever just out of reach, and yet I kept reaching.

Imagine a constant series of small regrets—of the kind, say, you might experience on a crowded street, at an appointed meeting place, when from a distance you might spy the familiar face you are seeking only to recognize a perfect stranger upon approach. You know the feeling, yes? The gentle leap of the heart in anticipation, followed by its soft fall back into place? On an isolated basis, from time to time, these half-sightings are hardly worth noting, but the cumulative effect of such small disappointments can be wearying, almost debilitating. To look around *every* corner, to spin toward *every* sudden noise or movement, to approach *every* gathering of people with the certainty that the person you're looking for will somehow emerge from within is to lose a piece of yourself each time out. It changes you in fundamental ways. At least, it has me. At some point I realized I'd started looking out at the world somewhat differently than I used to, back before what I've taken to calling "the Rolen incident," and that the world was looking back with a new set of dubious eyes. The incident itself, this entire Dunlap business, became a millstone around my neck. I wouldn't have thought it, but it's enormously draining, to be so certain of a thing and at the same time so desperately unable to substantiate that certainty. For yourself, for others. Who wouldn't be changed by such as this? Who wouldn't move about waiting to discover some new and impossible reality? And, underneath that waiting, who wouldn't be fearful of being found out, of being discovered as he must appear?

My near-year had been marked by a series of comedowns wrapped inside a larger, more sustained meltdown—emphasis in each case on the *down*. Also, and perhaps more precisely, there was a constant whiplashing of the spirit, and if the Rite Aid drug store around the corner stocked an appropriate brace or restorative balm for such as this I would have cleaned out its shelves a couple months back.

Shrinks have a term for my new, somewhat altered reality—*hypervigilance*—only to hear it from clinical lips is to consider it a failing, a negative. I know, because I had lately heard the term applied to me and my recent behaviors in just this way, and yet I could not shake thinking it was an attribute. To be so abundantly aware of your surroundings, of each and every tic and movement and possibility, at all times, in all settings . . . it's like a superpower; wouldn't you agree? A *sixth* sense? And yet if you joined me in this opinion, we would be off on our own, at least within the mental-health community, into which I had been ineluctably drawn.

Nellie was no help. She meant to help, don't misunderstand, and she's still working on it, but she could not get past the fact that her lowly book publicist of a husband was holding to his story. That he had come across some ghostly apparition in decidedly human form purporting to have once been a Major League ballplayer. A spirit seen by no one but him, containing a life lived long ago and remembered only in the dusty archives of baseball history. It had, she said, become one of the great nagging aches of her life to have been asked to make sense of her baby doughboy PR guy husband who made no sense at all.

Of course she couldn't believe me, my Nellie. How could she? The story to which I'd been holding (like a lifeline!) defied all reason, and science, and every other damn thing—and yet there it was.

Still.

She hadn't said as much, but I believed Nellie would have much preferred if I had come to her as some born-again Jew for Jesus, announcing I had decided to accept Christ as my lord and savior and arbiter of my comings and goings. It is an easy line, and yet I'm afraid it only touches on how deeply troubled she had been by my deep troubles. There was that firewall between us, and we were stuck on either side, separated from how things were. From each other. From time to time, I caught her looking at me while we were watching television, or crossing the threshold of the girls' bedroom while I was reading to Patsy or Sally, her eyes laden with worry. And there I would be, on the receiving end of these looks, worrying in turn that I had put my plu-patient wife into such a pucker—to borrow a phrase from my new old friend.

Why is it, I took time to wonder early on in this sustained creepiness, that we are so quick to endorse such delusions and leaps of faith in our fictions and so reluctant to accept them as part of our reality? Why do we offer our cursory attentions to paranormalists and mediums and palm readers when we come across their accounts in newspapers and magazines, only to reject such claims when they've been superimposed onto our own lives? UFOs. Crop patterns. Images of the Virgin Mary or Abraham Lincoln in a wisp of cloud or a slice of burnt toast. Everything is fair game but ourselves, our husbands, our neighbors. Why is it that when it hits close to home, whatever the *it* happens to be, we look away? We might not mean to, and we might work against it, but we look away. We do. We put another hash mark in the crazy column and seek the haven of our safe, certain lives. But what about that ultimate leap of faith, organized religion? Stigmata? Noah and his ark? The parting of the Red Sea? Heaven and hell and points in between? How do we make sense of all that? We recognize that there is no sense in it, that's how, and that the common denominators in all of our lives are faith and acceptance. Beyond that it's all guesswork. We are not a deeply religious pair, Nellie and me, and outside of our obligatory High Holiday appearances at synagogue we are no closer to any concept of God than Nellie is to my concept of Fred Dunlap, and yet we make room in our shared landscape of acceptable beliefs and behaviors for those who sign on wholeheartedly to one faith or another. Anyway, we always had. Faith, we were told, is one of the base ingredients of a life well lived, so long as that faith has been ratified by a couple million other also-ordinary followers.

But what of Nellie's faith in *me*? Less than a year ago, it had seemed unshakable, unassailable—and after all this it had been shaken and assailed all over the damn place. By now, it was a crapshoot. Really, I could not imagine what I'd put my Nellie through, how things must have looked from her end, how I'd yanked at the stitches in the quilt of our lives. We tried to be quiet about it outside the apartment, among our few friends, but I refused to budge from my account, or accept any of Nellie's quite reasonable explanations for those inexplicable encounters in and around Philadelphia that August day not too terribly long ago. I wasn't quite myself, she suggested. I'd become so shaken by that hard-to-grasp experience in that baseball stadium that I was momentarily drunk with confusion. I'd chanced upon a series of admittedly odd coincidences that left me putting two and two together in entirely new ways. I'd hit my head (which, of course, I had). Or suffered a small stroke (which, who knows, is as good an explanation as any). Something. Anything but the truth. Or, as Nellie would insist I add, my *interpretation* of the truth. Her most reasonable explanation, even I'll allow, was that I was momentarily stalked by some type of borderline delusional outpatient—a flesh-and-bone turn-of-the-century baseball fanatic so obsessed with that bygone era that he now lived and breathed and dressed the part.

To these and other of her entreaties for sanity, I referred back to Dunlap's fancily frayed calling card, as if the small piece of linen paper could by itself justify my ramblings. It didn't help my cause that I'd misplaced it, but in my mind I waved the thing like a "Get out of jail free!" card. It is small proof, this, indicative merely of someone's ability to craft a prop to support a claim, but it's all I have and so I hold onto it like it's some pass to reason.

I indulged Nellie by agreeing to be seen by one of her psychiatric nurse friends from the hospital—and, further, by beginning regular therapy with the staff psychiatrist to whom I was referred. I went twice a week, but my heart was not in it—and, resultantly, my head was often someplace else as well. I let the man sift through the details of my life as if they might mean something, as if together they might yield a precious clue. I would not take any medication.

He recommended, of all things, an antidepressant, and on this Nellie concurred, but I would not accept that I was depressed. And I would not be talked down from my position. This was what happened. I was sure of it. And, I was equally sure that this encounter had nothing to do with whether I was breast-fed as a child, or whether I resented the birth of my younger sister, Marsha, or whether I still retain trace elements of my childhood fear of death.

(Who *wouldn't* fear death? That, to me, is crazy.)

At home, reaching for what remained of our familiar routines, there was a script we usually followed. Twice a week, Nellie would wait until the girls were asleep or tucked into their room doing homework and ask me about my session with my psychiatrist.

I'd answer by pretending to be surprised by her question and say something like, "Oh, you mean my shrink?" I was not being difficult, I don't think, but this was me being impish, playful.

She'd say, "That's not a helpful term."

I'd say, "We have a lot of friends in therapy. A lot of friends who are therapists. There's nothing wrong with 'shrink.' It's not a negative."

She'd say, "It's just not helpful, is all."

On and on we'd go, around and around.

And yet I'd cling to the language—perhaps because it was a way to reduce this psychiatrist's hold on my marriage. Perhaps because if I called him a *shrink* it would make him somewhat *less than*. It would undermine whatever authority my Nell had placed in his ability to judge my behavior, my experience. In his *assignment* to judge my behavior, my experience. I was not the world's most willing patient, I'll admit, but it's not like I was dragged kicking and screaming to these sessions. My mind was open—at least as far as Nellie and her psychiatric nurse friends and this staff psychiatrist had opened theirs. But Nellie would have liked it to be opened further still.

I'd say, "What do you want to hear, Nell?"

She'd say, "I want to hear that you are getting better."

I'd say, "Better than what?"

She'd say, "Felb." Admonishing me. Imploring me. Willing me back to whole.

I'd say, "Nell, I'm fine."

Again and again, this was how it went. Perhaps because if I kept saying I was fine it would make it so.

◆

About my only supporter over those difficult months was my Iona. She was fourteen, looking ahead to high school, one foot in adolescence and the other in young adulthood, assaulted by all kinds of uncertainties and indecisions in her own life, and the last thing she needed was a certifiable father, but she understood. She did; she truly did. Without hesitation. And she bought into it, too. She believed. She'd listened in on enough hushed late-night conversations between me and her mother to put together what was going on and determined that it was indeed some kind of ghost of Fred Dunlap that appeared before me, as surely as Fred Dunlap used to turn the pivot on a double play and fire the ball to first in his distinct slingshot motion.

Of course, I realize full well that what Iona believed in, truly, was me. She could not accept that I was delusional. I am her father, after all. I am her father, *most* of all. But even more than that, she could not accept that her mother and I had been at cross-purposes for the past several months—Nellie, determined to prove that my "vision" was brought about by stress, or fatigue, or depression; and me, determined to prove myself sane, and merely caught on the receiving end of one of the strangest interactions in recorded human history.

Sally and Patsy, in their own sweet ways, sought out some of the same common ground as their older sister, but they were too young to be throwing in with me for any reasons other than their love for me, and that I somehow loomed larger than their little lives for the time being. Iona, though, she was a different story. She had that gothic/grunge thing going on, my Iona. All along, she could likely be found dressed entirely in black, hair dyed some alarming shade of purple, nose ring daintily affixed over her left nostril, room in her baggy carpenter pants for Sally and Patsy besides. And yet there was not a stitch of anger in these affectations, no whiff of antidisestablishmentarianism or whatever was ailing the youth of America at those particular crossroads. No. With Iona, best as Nellie and I could figure, it seemed to be a form of entertainment, this outward tweaking of convention. She still pulled straight As in school, still slept with the stuffed monkey she won at a local fair when she was two years old, still accepted the wet kisses of her grandparents without complaint, still crawled into our bed at eleven most school nights to watch *Cheers* before turning in. She was, simply, a good kid who happened to delight in pissing off her teachers and her grandparents and her softball coach and the witless parents of her headed-for-trouble friends, who took one look at I and thought how difficult it would be to have their phone numbers unlisted.

Meanwhile, I could only look on and wish I'd had some of the same tools when I was a kid—and here she had chosen to deploy those tools in support of my story.

"Mom's such a coward," Iona would say when it was just the two of us washing and drying the dishes after dinner.

"Meaning?" I'd prompt, knowing there'd been some new aspect of the Rolen incident to catch Iona's attention, some conversation with her mother that had not included me.

"Nothing," she'd say, unwilling to give up her mother's confidence but at the same time unable to keep from venting. "It's just, I think she's afraid of what it might mean."

"Of what might mean?"

"Dunlap. If it's really him. She'd rather be afraid of you going completely nut job than all this cosmic stuff. Weirds her out."

Yes, I suppose it did. It must have. Weirded me out, too. But Iona took it on faith. In me. In the world her mother and I had made for her. In *baseball*, even. Or, at least, in a need to sometimes let loose her grip on logic and reason in order to hold fast to something bigger, something she could not yet know. She accepted my story for what it was, and the account muscled its way alongside everything else. Indeed, over the course of her young life, she had been asked to imagine all manner of unimaginable things. Saddam Hussein. The dot-com explosion. The presidential stains on the off-the-rack dresses of White House interns. It was no wonder she could take such as this into consideration. It fit right in. What didn't fit, and what kept me up nights, was the way this aberration unsettled our household. Left Nellie and me on a knife edge, and the girls to wonder in age-appropriate ways whether their parents could ride out the confusion, but children are a resilient subspecies, don't you think? They can take in a twist or turn and somehow manage to find their way.

For good or ill, my obsession became Iona's. She dug up more on Fred Dunlap than I could have ever managed with a roomful of computers and ancient periodicals. She even wrote a comprehensive survey of the man's life and hard times to fulfill a school assignment on the Industrial Revolution, and even though she was somewhat off point, it was an impressive effort. She learned more about the Union Association than I ever knew about the hapless Mets of the early 1960s and cobbled together enough information on shipping magnate Henry Lucas, owner of the St. Louis Maroons and a driving force behind the outlaw league, to run his category on *Jeopardy!* should it ever come up. All this beneath a curious façade of gothic/grunge chic that leaves her looking like the love child of Marilyn Manson and Morticia Addams. Oh, and there is also her theme song, the bass line to which she had taken to chanting loudly every time she entered a room: "My Sharona," power-pop tripe from a group of essentially one-hit late-1970s wonders known as The Knack, which Iona had co-opted with her syllabically correct name. No doubt you've heard it, and I'll put it into your head as Iona put it into mine: *Da-DEH, da-dum-DEH, dum-DEH, da-da-da-DEH, da-DEH, da-dum-DEH . . . MY IONA!*

It was into this package that Iona placed her latest theory, which had to do with the supposition that our Fred Dunlap had died such a miserable, lonely death that his spirit was somehow left restless by his circumstance. If you believe in such things (and I and I were prepared to do just this), it seems reasonable to conclude that a desperate man who gambles and drinks away his considerable fame and fortune might also be the sort whose restless soul can never find peace. In fact, it's more than reasonable—it's patently obvious. Hello? We've all sat through movies built on lesser premises than this, and here Iona had it figured. Consider: Dunlap died in Philadelphia on December 1, 1902, at the age of 42, estranged from friends and family and every nickel he'd ever earned. Philadelphia, the site of that fateful hand-holding, where our paths may or may not have met in those upper reaches of Veterans Stadium. Dunlap's last days were so unsettled he could never hope to find peace, just as my recent days may or may not have been unsettled, stuck in the unrelenting sameness of my plain existence. Accept the notions of heaven and hell and you can also make room for the prospect of a spiritual disconnect of the kind considered here. In Iona's imaginings, the man was so hopelessly, desperately lost and without tether that his soul was too restless to put down in any one realm, leaving his spirit to flit about the cosmos like an unreceived radio transmission.

He was *out there*, for eternity—and I was nearby, in Philadelphia, for the time being.

"Like a limbo," is how Iona explained it to me one Saturday afternoon in a taxi down to Chelsea Piers, where we were meaning to watch one of her sister's soccer games. "That must be it."

At this, goofily, I pressed my hands against the roof of the cab and started shaking my upper body like a party facilitator at a bad wedding reception. "How low can you go?" I sing-songed. "How low can you go?"

"Limbo, Dad," Iona said flatly. "I get it. Funny."

I guessed it wasn't, and I also guessed that if I had made such a goofy gesture in front of anyone else I would have been shamed into regretting it for a good several years, but Iona cared only that I wasn't taking her seriously. "Sorry," I said, giving her theory some thought of my own. "It's as good an explanation as any."

And it is. Or, it was. I was disinclined to invest this phantom with any more of a backstory than he himself placed before me, on the possibly confused notion that if he or it had any sort of agenda, even an otherworldly agenda, he or it might have made that agenda known, although at this point I was also unable to offer any other explanations for his or its appearance.

(*He* or *it*! Goodness, what was I into?)

There was no logic here—at least, none that I could see. But there was *something* here. Of that, I was certain. It was in my bones. Something I could not understand, should not understand, would never understand. And yet, however inexplicable, I could not look away from it. I could only accept it. I had no choice. Why? Well, I had been so thoroughly beaten down by the never-ending, not-yet-realized expectation of another encounter with this Dunlap visage that I was powerless against it. In my hypervigilance, I remained just that. Hyper . . . and vigilant. Ever alert, ever mindful. It was coming, I knew, as certainly as I knew the sun would rise over my building each day and cast long shadows against the funeral home across the street. *He* was coming, returning, reaching out to me. Trust in this, I told myself each morning as I stared into the shower mirror for a shave, and the image that came back—magnified, fogless—suggested that somewhere beneath my muddle I might find a surety that belied my otherwise ordinary circumstance.

Plain as day, I'd tell myself. Here it is. Here it comes again. Plain as day. For all the world to ratify. And throw into question.

Is it possible I imagined the entire Rolen incident, as Nellie sometimes suggested? Is it possible I'd connected the dots on what happened after I'd been outmaneuvered on that foul ball to form a picture that never quite took shape in the form I'd processed? I supposed it was, but how did that explain these various tributaries flowing from that single fantasy? The very real life I had tapped into? The resonant chord I seemed to have struck in my own life? The tug and pull of past and present? The deepening bond it had helped me to form with Iona? There was no explaining it, but there was acceptance. Faith and acceptance, just.

And there was also Iona, along for the ride.

◆

Work.

Through it all, there was my something-less-than-brilliant career at Elder & Gold, my going through the motions on behalf of someone else's bottom line and better judgment. It was not the career I imagined for myself when I started out. Back then, the thought was to work in publishing for a while, to learn the lay of the land, and then to splinter off and find a way to write for a living—on the back of whatever insights and connections I'd managed to build at the publishing house. But things didn't quite work out in this way. One thing led to another, and then another, and then another after that, and one day I looked up and realized to my very real surprise that I had been toiling in the Elder & Gold publicity department for twenty years. Twenty! There was even a cake, brought around by the folks in human resources, who rarely missed an opportunity to remind us that our lives were passing us by. And yet I had nothing to complain about, really. My job was secure. The benefits were good. And I was proficient enough at book publicity to be occasionally promoted, applauded, championed... as the situation warranted.

(At the same time, I should probably mention I was also insignificant enough at work to pass a good many days unnoticed in our Elder & Gold offices.)

Tellingly, amazingly, the combusting distractions that had overtaken the rest of my life since that August night in Philadelphia seemed to have had no impact at all on my job performance, even as they threatened what had become a finely balanced perspective. I could skate along on my own fine film of mediocrity, just under the radar of my boss down the hall, a disarmingly unattractive woman with the kind of thick, throaty voice that could sell cigarettes to falsettos and a fondness for fruit-flavored vodkas, all the while never fully realizing how insignificant my efforts were in any kind of larger scheme.

Ah, yes... work. *That*. This. What I'd become. The zero-sum of whatever dreams I'd allowed myself as a young man. Crafting predictable press releases to promote the going-through-the-motions of others. Distilling the essence of an obvious how-to book or a hardly thoughtful thinkpiece into cover letters and pitches that unavoidably did the job of the entire manuscript. Cajoling jaded talk-show producers for morsels of their precious airtime so that my authors might sit across the microphone from some too-gelled, too-collagened Ken or Barbie, who in turn would be too busy to even read the piece-of-shit title it was my job, in the first place, to promote.

As vicious cycles go, this one had teeth.

I had often thought I'd go home feeling better about myself at the end of a long, tedious day if I was an assembly-line worker of some kind, or a bricklayer, if I could have pointed to something I'd built or hauled or had a hand in, instead of merely pushing papers and coordinating mailings and updating our contacts and following through on all-but-scripted phone calls that on my worst days reeked of telemarketing. Put a thousand monkeys in a room with a thousand keyboards and before long one of them will type out a short story good enough to interest the fiction editor at *The New Yorker*, leaving the other 999 to figure a way to promote it.

But a job is a job, yes? And the longer you do a thing, the more difficult it is to do something else.

Lately, my front-burner attentions had been turned to exploiting the winsome account of a seventeen-year-old high school cheerleader who had had her right arm bitten off at the shoulder by a circus lion that had somehow gotten spooked by a misplaced spotlight—although *winsome* was not precisely the right adjective in this context, suggesting a too-easy jab regarding my author's now-missing limb (winsome, lose some), but I was inclined to leave it alone (despite the previous parenthetical aside). In any case, the poor girl was unfortunately seated in one of the front rows, hard by the lion tamer's prop cart, waving a smoked turkey leg of the kind concession operators will now think twice before serving at events featuring wild animals, and she had by now recovered sufficiently to authorize the writing of an unfortunately titled account of her ordeal and recovery: *Beauty and the Beast*. (What else?) Note that I do not mean to imply that the girl had actually written the book herself, merely that she had signed off on it, but she was poised to make the rounds of Katie and Jay and Oprah and every other one-named talk-show host or feel-reasonably-good journalist whose producer could be made to believe that a one-armed cheerleader in a sleeveless uniform top struggling to execute a one-handed cartwheel would invariably pass for powerful television.

Perhaps it would. Until then, though, it would keep me busily spinning my own wheels, suppressing the apparitional events of a year ago until I no longer knew what to make of them, if I was even meant to consider them at all.

It was underneath all of this wheel-spinning that I found my first significant development in the Rolen incident. Or, I should say, it found me. By way of Iona. She called upstairs from the Elder & Gold lobby one early evening, said she had to see me right away. She knew I'd be working late. The one-armed cheerleader was booked on Letterman, which even I knew taped in the late afternoon, and from there I had a few hours to kill until I (meaning, once again, me) had to escort my author and her mother to some silly music video countdown show on MTV.

"It's him, Dad," Iona said when she burst into my nothing-special windowless office. Her hair was dyed a softer shade of purple than usual, leaning toward lilac, close-cropped in the style of some reigning pop-music diva, a sequence of ever-larger zirconium studs arrayed in a kind of crescent around her left ear, the right one relatively unadorned save for a dangling plastic machete the size of a pinky.

If she didn't make me smile, the sight of her might have made me cry.

"It's who?" I said, knowing full well who, but not having any idea what, when, where, how or why and figuring I at least had to start somewhere. (*I* as in either one of us, in this instance.)

"Dunlap," she said excitedly. "At softball practice. After softball practice, actually. As I was climbing down from the roof."

"You're sure it was him?" I said, matching her excitement.

"Yeah," she said. "Pretty sure. I mean, who else could it have been?"

"Tell me everything."

And she did. She told me how she was one of the last to leave the turfed and all-but-caged practice field that sits atop an armory across the street from her school, how the coach had been working with her on her pitching, how it was nearly halfway through the preseason and the team still hadn't found a pitcher to master the unusual fast-pitch motion that some of the other girls at some of the other schools had mastered just fine. The coach was a mechanical engineering teacher who'd never played any kind of ball, and he didn't have the first idea about the mechanics of this distaff version of our national pastime. It was one of Iona's great frustrations to have to play softball for a man who couldn't even fungo flies to his outfielders. It was bad enough, she said, having to strip away her put-together look before each practice, and to shoulder the incredulous stares of her teammates as she stowed her costumed jewelry and wiped away her black lipstick, but to have to look like everyone else and at the same time run around the field in a state of shared cluelessness was an altogether different embarrassment. She told me how she'd spent another frustrating session wind-milling her arm to no great effect and with no great accuracy, and how she'd packed up her gear bag and headed for the stairwell and left the coach to clear the field.

"Same as every other day," she said, "only when I get to the stairs, there's this guy there, kinda waiting, kinda hanging out, looks at me kinda funny and says, 'Seems to me you could use some help.' Just like that. Not really asking. Not really offering. Just, you know, putting it out there."

"Moustache?" I tried, jumping to conclusions. "Strange sideburns?"

"No," she said. "That's the weird part. He was clean-shaven. Dressed, you know, normal. Like a Nike warm-up or something. Running shoes. Nothing like what he was wearing with you."

"But it was Dunlap?" I pushed, making sure. "You've seen pictures, right?"

"Well, that's the thing," she said. "Didn't look anything like his pictures. Clean-shaven, like I said. Regular hair. Talked normal too. None of that 'old wagon tongue' crap you talked about. Just, you know, like somebody's dad, some regular guy hanging around the field, completely normal, so that piece I'm not too clear on, but I haven't gotten to the best part."

I waited for it.

Iona reached into her gear bag and tossed me her first baseman's mitt. (When she's not struggling to pitch, she's guarding the line at third; or, over at first, struggling to dig errant throws from her teammates across the diamond.) She grabbed a fielder's mitt for herself and a scuffed ball that looked as if it had been left out in the sun for a couple weeks.

"Come on," she said, indicating the ball and the mitts. "Check out what this guy taught me."

She motioned me toward the corridor outside my office, bordered on one side by the half-walls of work stations that during normal business hours were occupied by our assistants and entry-level types, and on the other by a long stretch of badly framed Elder & Gold dust jackets commemorating our various trips to various bestseller lists over the years. My windowless office sat at some indistinct midpoint along this long stretch of corridor, and we only had to wander off a couple doorways in either direction until we could approximate the distance between home plate and pitching mound. Iona gestured at me with her glove, the way pitchers do whenever they mean for their catchers to take a crouch and await a pitch, so I did as gestured. It was a familiar routine, the back-and-forth of countless summer nights in Riverside Park, only here, in the corridors of my all-but-deserted place of business, it was bent a little out of shape. I planted both knees on the worn carpet by the copy machine closest to my office while Iona stood back by the office of my throaty-voiced superior. I was too old and creaky to crouch or squat or otherwise reduce myself to a comfortable catching position, and Iona had long since given up complaining about my something-less-than-graceful knees-to-the-ground stance, but in every other respect I was a serviceable catcher. Keep it straight down the middle, and up off the ground, and I did just fine.

The hallway was typically awash in high-hat lighting, but at this late hour most of the light came from the left-on desk lamps in the surrounding bullpen of work stations and from the ambient light that managed to spill from the open office doors. It was still bright outside, but the sunshine couldn't get much past the outer offices into this bullpen area.

Next, Iona unleashed a herky-jerky sequence of movements, the likes of which I had not seen from anyone, let alone my own child. If you didn't know what she was up to, you might have thought she was having a seizure. She flung her pitching arm straight up into the air like she might take lopsided flight, and then she uncoiled, whipping her arm down alongside her hip in a way that seemed to oddly and effortlessly combine the act of bowling with the act of rock-skipping. It was fluid and erratic all at the same time. We were close enough that I could hear the hard brush of fabric as her arm swept past the sweatpants at her hip, and I took time to marvel at how such harsh, purposeful noises could be coming from my daughter. My much-earringed daughter! And then, just as I was deep into my marveling, Iona released the ball with such a profound snap I'd have thought her right hand might be rocketing toward me right behind it. I thought, my goodness! I thought, what the hell was that? I thought, that's my girl.

The ball found my glove like it had been there before, and I tossed it back in a tight arc to avoid the soundproof tiles on the ceiling. Hurt my gloved hand like crazy, that first pitch, but I wanted to see more. Hell, I *needed* to see more, and on this second pass I fixed on Iona's powerful stride as she pushed off her right foot and began her assault like someone who'd been pitching this way her entire life instead of just a couple minutes. More to the point, like someone who had tapped fully into the torque her body could generate at a time in her life when such a thing might have been irrelevant.

I've since wondered if the appearance of speed on Iona's ball wasn't somehow exaggerated by the close confines of that hallway. The low ceiling. The bad lighting. The feeling that one of Iona's throws might somehow spin loose and take out a couple shelves of books or one of the exit signs pointing toward the elevators. It's possible, but that wouldn't explain the sting in my left hand or the hop on the ball.

Yee-hah, this girl could throw. All of a sudden. Like a slingshot.

"You weren't kidding," I said, my voice equal parts pride and confusion. "Goodness, gracious, me-oh-my!"

Like a slingshot. The phrase repeated itself in my head, and I realized it was a line from a yellowed newspaper clipping we'd dug up a couple months back, an eyewitness account of Dunlap's distinctive throwing style.

"Thank the Nike guy," she said. "He was in the stairwell. Came out and worked with me on the field for about ten minutes, and I had it down."

"Dunlap?" I tried.

"Who else?" she said, quite reasonably. "Come on, Dad. Who the fuck else?"

"Language, I," I parented.

She shrugged her shoulders and rolled her eyes and all but flipped me off with her body language. "Mom's not here," she said.

"Iona!" I said, trying to sound firm without scolding.

"Sorry," she allowed. "I'll try not to say fuck."

"Again, I!" I said, knowing she was pushing my buttons.

"Can we just get back to Dunlap?" she said.

"But he didn't look like Dunlap," I reminded her. "He didn't talk like Dunlap. He didn't dress like Dunlap."

"Agreed," she said, winding up for another pitch and sending a bullet to my glove like there was a six-shooter at her hip. "But he sure did throw like him."

◆

Iona's visit left me agitated, exhilarated, disoriented. I put her in a cab, called Nellie to tell her she was on her way, and said a silent prayer that we could all stay at just this age, at just this time and place, for just about forever and ever. Time was running away from us, even as it seemed with this Dunlap business to be catching us from behind.

I didn't let on to Nell about the nature of Iona's visit because there was no sense in setting her off. I just told her she'd stopped by after practice and hoped it wasn't such an unusual thing that Nell could leave it at that. Then I rode the elevator back up to my office to wait on my lion-tamed author, who had gone to dinner with her mother at a Jewish Italian restaurant they had read about in one of their guidebooks, the mother thinking this was likely the most incongruous combination of cuisines in culinary history and certainly something she had to try. ("What, they serve matzah balls and spaghetti?" she'd joked when she'd been put on hold attempting to make a reservation. "Cabbage-stuffed shells?") I didn't care about the food so much as the location. It was within walking distance of Letterman and just a few blocks from the MTV studios in Times Square. I wouldn't have to worry about them getting lost or stuck in traffic.

I turned down the lights in my office after Iona left and waited in the relative darkness for my author and her mother to call me to meet them at MTV. It turned out I had forgotten to return Iona's first baseman's mitt to her gear bag, subconsciously or no, and her softball was still wedged in the pocket, so I fitted the glove back on my left hand and idly tossed the ball in the air a couple hundred times with my right. And then a couple hundred times more. It was something to do to fill the waiting, and in the easy rhythm I soon developed—me, leaned back on my desk chair, feet propped on an open desk drawer, sending I's sunsplashed softball ceilingward, over and over and over again—I lost myself once more in the stuffings of these past months. This was how things were with me. This was what I'd become. A middle-aged man, now forty-seven, sitting in the near dark, playing catch with myself and waiting like some flunky to escort a disabled high school cheerleader and her mother to a cable television interview where they might draw down the account on the child's fifteen-minute allotment of fame before the public's attention was diverted by the fighting in the Middle East, the frenzied trading in the stock market, or some new obloquy of President Clinton. Mindlessly tossing a ball in the air, over and over and over, like I used to do when I was a kid, when there was nothing else to do and all the time in the world in which to not do it. Dwelling on an improbable sequence of unbelievable events that left me questioning my sanity and my place in the cosmos and my curious ability to hold down a job and maintain appearances while all around there was unknowable chaos and confusion.

I thought of Iona, with her crazy cartoon hair and her hellish new fast-pitch delivery. I thought of Sally and Patsy, cocooned from their father's craziness by a mother who refused to let our lives unravel on the back of my story. I thought of Nellie—dear, sweetsuffering Nellie—no doubt scared out of her head that I was coming unglued or unhinged or otherwise undone. Worried how the rest of our lives might look on the back of this Dunlap business. I thought of my sister, Marsha, out in Jersey in one of the Oranges, probably putting the finishing touches at just that moment on a macaroni-noodle map of the original thirteen colonies with one of her four kids, everything neat and ordinary and completely opposed to the extraordinary disorder surrounding her big brother. And I thought of Dunlap, imagined what he might look like in a Nike training suit, clean-shaven, with none of the quirks and affectations that had set him apart on our previous meetings. I wondered where he had been the past year or so, if he had been anyplace at all or no place I could imagine. If he had even *been* at all. I wondered, too, if Iona had been a quick study, mimicking his motions as effortlessly as she used to copy the batting stances of our favorite players, or if she had labored under his tutelage in some of the same ways she used to labor under mine. When she was a small girl, I remembered, we used to toss a tennis ball beneath a sorry-looking elm in Riverside Park for hours at a time, during which I made the repeated mistake of reminding her to keep her right foot planted as she threw and to step with her left. She was a natural athlete, but she got so caught up in her footing that she kept pushing off the wrong foot, or throwing flat-footed to avoid the confusion entirely, until I finally learned to let her alone and she managed to come to it on her own. Was Dunlap the same kind of impatient teacher I had been? Was it even Dunlap at all doing the teaching, or some well-meaning softballer who had settled on the armory roof to see what he could see?

I continued to toss the ball in the air as my mind raced—or, more accurately, as it *wandered*—and at some point I moved with it out into the hallway, lost in the repetitive motion, in endless waiting on my one-armed author and her mother, in never knowing where I stood alongside everyone else. The monotony of the game was a soothing distraction. I moved as I tossed, and tossed as I paced, and after a too-long while of this I looked up and realized I had drifted all the way to our bank of elevators. There were mirrors along one entire wall in the central space—on the elevator doors, even!—with the Elder & Gold logo stenciled in gold every here and there. I took a step back and tried to mirror the fast-pitch motion I had just seen from Iona, and to marry this onto the image I kept in my head from old newspaper accounts. Together, Iona and I had fashioned our own impression of Dunlap's distinctive throwing technique, but now that Iona may or may not have received some firsthand instruction from the specter-legend himself, I felt the need to make some modifications. My stride, for one thing. I had figured Dunlap deployed a quick-step sort of motion, which seemed to fit comfortably beneath the low-slung throw, especially when turning a double play, but now it occurred to me that he must have achieved at least some of his celebrated velocity from his legs. If that's where power pitchers lived, in the legs, then surely second basemen with powerful throwing arms must reside somewhere in the same neighborhood.

I turned to face the wall of mirrors and pantomimed a few throws without much satisfaction. I'd fallen into an unnatural motion that could hardly have been Dunlap's. There was too much awkwardness about it, too much effort, and as I tinkered with it I realized I still had Iona's ball, which I had set down inside her first baseman's mitt on the knee-high ashtray between the elevator doors. I reached for it yet again and tried a few more ways, slapping the ball into the glove each time on the follow-through. Finally, when I thought I had it down, I walked back to the hallway outside my office and claimed an orthopedic cushion from the chair of one of the publicity assistants and set it up against the plaster wall at the end of the hall as a target. Then I stepped back until I was about fifty feet from the target, never thinking I would hit anything but the sweet spot on the orthopedic cushion. As targets go, it was actually pretty big, about the size of an umpire's chest protector, and I had always had an accurate arm. And so, borrowing pieces of Iona's herky-jerky motion and grafting them onto the fluid, low-slung delivery I had long imagined, I went for it... and in so doing sailed the ball about six feet high of the mark and wide right, where there happened to be a shelf of empty vases collecting dust and waiting for the next happy occasion. I took out two green vases that had apparently arrived from the same 1-800-FLOWERS dispatcher, sending one of them to the carpet where it landed and bounced and came to rest without breaking, and the other to the wall holding the shelf, against which the vase shattered into a couple dozen pieces, and as the ball thudded to the carpet amidst the fat shards of broken glass, it occurred to me I might need to tinker with Dunlap's motion a little bit. After all, I thought, they didn't call this guy Sure Shot for nothing.

◆

Iona's column from the May 1999 edition of *The Meadowlark*, the Whedon Academy student newspaper that could probably use a more hands-on faculty advisor:

WHAT SUCKS ABOUT BASEBALL
By Iona Felb

What sucks about baseball is that the teams with the most money buy up the best players, and we fans are left to root for our favorite shipping magnate owners to have a good year in the shipping magnate business so we can afford to sign the top free agents. Or, we buy more toothpaste or personal pan pizzas or whatever else these owners *own* and feel in some small way like we are contributing to the success of our favorite teams so they can make enough to sign the next five-tool ballplayer to come out of Kansas City or Seattle or whatever small-market franchise can no longer afford his services.

What sucks about baseball is that you can go thirty-seven years without anyone really threatening one of the great all-time records like the single-season home-run mark, and then out of nowhere you get two players in the same season who shatter it by, like, fifteen percent, and a third who comes, like, ridiculously close. And you wonder how with thirty teams these journeyman middle relievers who wouldn't have even made a Triple A roster thirty years ago can ever expect to get anyone out.

What sucks about baseball is that you can stick around long enough and never even be one of the top three or four players on your own team, but if you manage to string together ten or fifteen better-than-average seasons all of a sudden people start talking about you like one of the game's greats. Harold Baines, a future Hall of Famer? Yeah, and while we're at it, let's add a new wing to honor all the number-one draft choices who never amounted to a wad of chewing tobacco.

What sucks about baseball is that you can be having a crappy season, and the guy who runs the centerfield scoreboard will still have to come up with something positive to post about you on the big screen every time you step to the plate, which is how you get lame stat lines like, "So-and-so is 6—21 in day games against left-handed pitching." Like it would be such a terrible thing if it said, "So-and-so has been a tremendous disappointment this year to teammates and fans alike, but also to himself."

What sucks about baseball is that a guy can hit .400 one season and score a sick amount of runs and lead his team to a league title and set all these great records, and a couple generations later no one has any idea who he is or what the hell happened to him. One of the top ten seasons of all time, maybe even top five, and he barely rates a footnote. Like it would be such a terrible thing if it said, "After such a tremendous season, so-and-so has been a tremendous disappointment to teammates and fans alike, but also to himself."

What doesn't suck about baseball is that, hey, it's baseball, and you can be a shipping magnate and spend boatloads of money on players and still finish second, or you can come from out of nowhere and win it all. Or you can hit .400 one year and .250 the next. You can thrill, or disappoint, or be slightly better than average over a slightly better-than-average stretch. You can be remembered and forgotten and remembered again. Everything is up for grabs, even your legacy. That's why they keep playing, to be remembered; and that's why we keep watching, to remember; and that's why we keep thinking, one of these days, it's gonna get interesting.

Because, hey, it usually does.

Eight
CALLING

Nellie and I were never quite sure what to make of Iona other than the best of it. From the very beginning, there was enough mule to our otherwise sweet-seeming daughter to suggest trouble of the kind that keeps parents of teenage girls at considerable remove from a good night's sleep, but our Iona managed to counter each piece of stubbornness with healthy dollops of kindness and insight and whimsy. We could only wonder at the strange mix. To my thinking, the mulishness was part of the deal, and maybe even charming; it was the darkness about Iona that had me worried. Where other little girls were all sweetness and light, she sometimes cloaked herself in shadow. Once, as an eight-year-old, she took the drill from our kitchen hardware drawer and attempted to pierce the exposed navel of one of her plastic dolls—Ariel, I think, from *The Little Mermaid*—only to drive straight through the doll's hollow stomach and directly into the floorboards below her bedroom carpet. Nellie pulled me out of a pitch meeting with the talent coordinator at *Live with Regis and Kathie Lee* to discuss the matter, and by the time I'd rushed home, Iona had turned her miscalculations into performance art, fashioning a coffin from a clear shoebox and leaving the poor plastic mermaid-princess entombed on the floor at the center of her room, a too-large screw gutting the doll's midsection and eliminating any chance an onlooker might have stumbled on the scene and confused it with one from some Disney fairy tale.

It was disarming, to say the least, and now in adolescence Iona had blossomed into a full-fledged conundrum. And yet she was good to her little sisters, conscientious about her schoolwork, and respectful of the stymied adults who came across her admittedly strange doings and breathed lucky sighs that their own children fit more neatly into their hopes and dreams and reasonable expectations, which made her a delightful conundrum, the way I saw it. Like I said, possibly even charming. We'd all gotten used to I, by now, and to be completely honest I'd come to enjoy her element of black surprise, her unwillingness to conform, the sport she appeared to find in tweaking convention. All in good fun. I'd look on and think, good for her. Good for all of us. And, lately, good most of all for me.

The contrast between the punk-tough Iona pretended to be and the good-hearted tomboy she most probably was turned up most glaringly on the softball field, although to call the diamond across the street from the main Whedon Academy building a field was to invest it with a shade more haphazardness than it deserved. The "field" sat atop an otherwise unused armory beneath an immaculate carpet of turf, between DayGlo orange baselines and professional-caliber dugouts that featured heated benches and cable television, all of it hugged inside a neatly caged perimeter that will be replaced before it has a chance to rust or fall into disrepair. The centerfield scoreboard featured a too-large Pepsi logo, and the bunting around the waist-high outfield fence announced the display advertising of prominent Whedon alumni and parents who have donated generously to the development and upkeep of the facility, promoting big-city law firms, advertising agencies, real-estate companies, and financial institutions. There are even overhead lights, lovingly (and fittingly) gifted by the proud father of the Whedon Warriors current second base*person*, who happened to work in some vague executive capacity for General Electric and whose wife was kind enough to share this connection with anyone doomed to sit next to her on the cushioned bleachers.

Anyway, the field. That's where Iona had suddenly and alarmingly shined beneath the wide-eyed (and open-mouthed!) stares of the extended Whedon Academy family. And no one had been more wide-eyed than her own father! To watch her roam that carpet was to wipe clean the troubles of these past months, and so I found myself skipping out of work at every invented chance to take in what I could of Iona's softball doings—and, perhaps, to push myself even farther from the specter of Frederick C. Dunlap.

Iona washed off her makeup before games and practices, and carefully removed her ever-changing assortment of earrings and nose rings and this weird chained collar she wore that was somehow connected to one of her earlobes, but there was no mistaking her out there between those DayGlo orange lines. She was the one with the bright-purple hair—or red, or silver, or green, depending—ponytailed like every other girl on the team except that in Iona's case the hair spilling from her cap looked like it came out of a cartoon. There she'd be, taking infield, whiplashing the ball across the diamond in a manner not usually seen in middle-school softball games. There she'd be, warming up on the sidelines, perfecting her slingshot pitching delivery so that it suggested not a windmill so much as a windmill on tilt. There she'd be, running sprints across the immaculate outfield turf, cutting a fluid swath across the school emblem painted in dead center and leaving her teammates in what might have been her dust if this had been a more garden-variety softball field. There she'd be, accepting the high fives and back slaps of her friends and teammates as if she has them coming. And there I'd be, the ever-so-proud father, beaming like I didn't have a care in the world but for these proceedings, although in truth I was so racked with constant uncertainty it was a separate wonder I didn't take up drinking.

Here was the nut of I's season, to date: The Warriors were at the top of their division with a record of 9-4; interscholastic rules prohibited middle-school pitchers from throwing more than seven innings in a given week, so as a starter I was a remarkable 5-0, with thirty innings pitched and only one base hit allowed, and an almost unknowable seventy-seven strikeouts. She'd hit a fair number of batters, and once even loaded the bases as a result of her wildness, but midway through the season, an opposing runner had yet to come around to score. Hell, opposing batters had yet to hit one of her pitches out of the infield. At the plate, she'd become a consistent spray hitter whose goal it was to jack one out of the park with the game on the line but whose lot it was to stroke clean singles to right and advance the base-runners ahead of her from first to third. And in the field, whenever she wasn't pitching, she stood confidently at third base, moved there on account of her suddenly strong arm, poised in the ready position to plant her body fearlessly in front of the occasional hardliners that came her way, and to put her gun of an arm to mostly good and effective use, although here too her wildness came into play. One of her great frustrations, she often said, was that third basepersons are charged with errors when they make errant throws, while there is no such denigration when pitchers miss their mark, and so she was sometimes tentative with her throws to first, which of course contributed to her wildness.

But it was on the mound that Iona earned her reputation, such as it was. She was virtually untouchable, and a balm for her confounded father. Her herky-jerky slingshot motion had changed her from a nothing-special eighth-grade pitcher to a bona fide phenom, so much that we Felbs were even fielding phone calls from opposing coaches inquiring about I's high-school plans and suggesting there might be room for her in their varsity programs, and some scholarship monies besides. We tried not to let all the fuss go to I's head, but she appeared to have a handle on it. Nothing seemed to rattle my Iona, even as everything continued to rattle me—and even as she rattled her opponents. In an early-season game against Nutley Day, she managed to record six strikeouts in a single inning, sending Whedon's athletic director to the record books to determine if such a feat had ever been duplicated at any level of organized softball.

(A refresher and some perspective for readers who don't follow our national pastime and its kissing cousin, softball, and who therefore might not grasp the sense of moment at such an accomplishment. Each team is granted three outs per inning, which typically means that the most opposing batters a pitcher can strike out in an inning is also three. However, if a catcher drops a called third strike or misplays the ball after the batter has swung and missed for the third strike, or if the ball sails all the way to the backstop without being touched at all by the catcher even though the batter swung and missed anyway, then the batter is allowed to run to first base. If she reaches safely before the catcher recovers and sends the ball down the baseline to her teammate, she is awarded first base, just as she would if she had beaten out an infield hit. When this happens—and it does happen, from time to time, most especially at the middle-school level—a strikeout is charged against the batter's record, and a strikeout is awarded to the pitcher, but no out is charged to the team ledger. In the professional game, it happens every other game or so that a pitcher will strike out the side—meaning he will strike out three opposing batters in a single inning. Once or twice a season, it might happen that a catcher drops a third strike and a pitcher manages to strike out a *fourth* batter in a single inning. But that's about it. No one ever fills the bases on dropped or wild third strikes and manages to notch *six*!)

As it happened, the athletic director's search was inconclusive, but that did nothing to diminish Iona's accomplishment. Six strikeouts! Nellie and I flashed each other *pinch-me* looks and took turns marveling at the way those poor Nutley Day girls flailed at balls they couldn't even see, let alone hit. Iona's wildness of course contributed to her dominance; opposing batters had no idea what to expect at the plate, and therefore approached each turn at bat with equal parts fear and wonder.

"Wouldn't kill her to get it over the plate," mumbled the woman in the row in front of mine, who happened to be the mother of the Whedon catcher, who happened to look something less than ept trying to block some of Iona's pitches, particularly those that short-hopped the plate.

"Wouldn't kill your kid to catch one of 'em every once in a while," Nellie shot back.

(In case I haven't made myself clear on this one important point, Nellie is fiercely protective of her own. Impugn one of her girls over one thing or other and she'll return the insult ten times over. Suggest that her baby doughboy PR guy of a husband might need to adjust his medications in order to stop seeing "ghosts" and she'll cut you down to gherkin size.)

"Aw, Nell," the catcher's mother responded, somewhere between sheepish and feeble, "you mistook my meaning."

"Entirely possible," Nellie said, never taking her eyes off Iona. She wouldn't cede the moral victory of eye contact if the woman stripped naked and helped her ungainly catcher of a daughter learn the salsa at home plate. And then, under her breath but loud enough for all to hear, as in a stage whisper: "Not very likely, but entirely possible."

The thing about Iona's pitching prowess is that it all flowed from that one rooftop encounter at the start of the season, with that peculiar interloper who may or may not have resembled my man Dunlap. There's no other explanation for it. Ten years under my tutelage (for she was about four when we first started playing catch in Riverside Park), and she was a better-than-average player; ten minutes under this stranger's thumb and she was transformed. Unfortunately, Iona spent the balance of the first chunk of season waiting for the guy to reappear at the butt end of one of her practices, or to turn up after a game, which left her looking endlessly over her shoulder for more of the same, a hypervigilance of her very own, which in turn left me even more determined to get to the bottom of things—although of what, precisely, I still had no idea.

Shrinks have a term for this as well—*folie à deux*, a madness shared by two. Regrettably, I came to know of this phenomenon through my own therapy, which had lately been ratcheted up to three times per week, straining the parameters of my Elder & Gold health plan and thereby threatening the health and welfare of our modest savings. I'd graduated from Nell's psychiatric nurse friend, and then from the staff psychiatrist to whom I was assigned at the hospital, to a kindly psychotherapist in private practice who just so happened to be a woman, and who further just so happened to be a somewhat bitter Brooklyn Dodgers fan and an avid reader—this last, a welcome aspect of not-so-professional character that allowed me to barter current hardcovers from the supply closet at work in exchange for the thrice-weekly copays I could no longer afford to copay on any kind of ongoing basis.

Money, as ever, remained a worry and a tension in our small household. Our remodeling plans had been put on hold, in large part because of the Dunlap distraction that now seemed to hover over our every piece of indecision but also because of the costs attached to my suspect mental health. Of course, this last was on Nell, as far as I was concerned. She was the one who insisted I go into therapy, although if you'd have asked Nell (also, of course), she'd say it was on me, because I was the one who insisted on seeing ghosts. Ah, but I digress...

The concept of *folie à deux*, a kind of communal psychosis, dates to nineteenth-century France, and according to my avid-reading therapist, a good deal has been written about it in the intervening years. Unfortunately, I have been disinclined to read up on it, so it remains unclear to me whether it is a disorder or a syndrome or a phenomenon. Or, merely, an emotional contagion beyond classification. In any case, without the need to buttress my opinion with case studies and supporting research, I lean toward the emotional contagion. If indeed this is a thing, then it must be a thing a mope like me can understand, like an airborne virus that can somehow leapfrog several members of the same household while infecting just a few.

Still, *folie à deux* or no, it doesn't much matter what you call it, because I reject it by any name, by any label. Far be it from me to appear closed-minded on matters relating to that August night in Philadelphia, especially as I required the open-mindedness of those closest to me in order to keep even the slightest toehold on sanity.

As my Dr. Belasco from time to time explained, the common delusion can take many forms or come about in any number of ways. Here, she suggested, it's possible I had somehow imposed my notion of Fred "Sure Shot" Dunlap onto poor Iona in such a way that I (me *or* my daughter, take your pick) had no choice but to accept it. In this scenario, I am told, Iona would be considered the secondary or "acceptor" nut job, while I would be considered the primary or "inducer" nut job—a sub-syndrome known as *folie imposée*. Either way, we were screwed. Either way, we were powerless against it.

Whatever it was, whatever it remained, we were now joined at the hip on this thing. We were each of us overtaken by the presence of Dunlap—a presence real or imagined—each of us determined to be found right and sane, each of us lost in the life and lure of a faded baseball icon. And Iona, bless her thoroughgoing nature, she was all over the 1884 Union Association campaign as well. She put together a kind of game-by-game journal of the St. Louis Maroons' historic season, mounting old press accounts in chronological order on black construction paper like she was preparing one of her middle-school reports. Inevitably, there were holes in her account, but a lot of what she couldn't find in the electronic archives of the *St. Louis Post-Dispatch* she managed to glean from daily newspapers in Union Association towns like Cincinnati, Baltimore, Boston, and even Altoona. *The Sporting News*, long regarded as the bible of daily baseball reporting, didn't begin publication until 1886, so there were quite a few games that went unreported, but that didn't discourage my Iona. She took it as a windfall that beginning in 1886 she could at least chronicle the downward turn of Fred Dunlap's career. Even without any help from *The Sporting News*, she managed to button together an impressive document which when taken in all at once allowed us to reimagine the Maroons running away from the rest of the Union Association field in 1884, and Dunlap's role at the head of the pack. Indeed, it was I's dogged research that revealed the presence of well-known nineteenth-century baseball promoter Timothy Paul "Ted" Sullivan in Dunlap's path that season. Sullivan, the college roommate and lifelong friend of future Chicago White Sox owner Charlie Comiskey (who would eventually marry Sullivan's sister, for those of you keeping score at home!), was somehow dismissed as the Maroons' manager early on in the 1884 season, despite seeing the team off to a 28—3 start, including twenty consecutive wins to start the season. It was only then that our "Sure Shot" Fred stepped in to skipper the Maroons to an only slightly less spectacular 66—16 mark the rest of the way, and yet we could only imagine what strange turns might have led to Sullivan's dismissal, for Iona could find no record of it and I could not have guessed where to look for same.

And so there we were with our mounting pile of newspaper clippings and the best running tally of Dunlap's accomplishments Iona could manage, and together we would lose ourselves in what may or may not have happened all those years ago. We had our ideas. We had it in our heads that Sullivan took ill and personally recommended his star second baseman for his job as manager to team owner Henry Lucas. Or, it could have been that Sullivan was spread so thin by his double duties as the Union Association's public face and chief promoter that he could not pay sufficient attention to the league's juggernaut team. There was the documented story from later in Dunlap's career about how he again took over as manager in midseason, this time for the 1889 Pittsburgh Alleghenys' Horace Phillips, who suffered a breakdown midway in the campaign and was committed to an asylum. Perhaps a similar fate befell Ted Sullivan. Or maybe there was a showdown of some kind between the manager and his franchise player, and Lucas came down on Dunlap's side and gave him Sullivan's job.

We thought through the whole business like it was some kind of sporting soap opera.

And so the place Iona and I made in our lives for Fred "Sure Shot" Dunlap was not front and center—it couldn't be!—but we'd set it up in such a way that he could stand alongside everything else. A *folie à deux*? I much preferred to think of Dunlap as our mini-obsession—a mutual hobby. After all, there are a great many fathers and daughters who enjoy stamp-collecting, or Spike Jones records, or the search for the perfect farm-stand pie. With us, our point of connection was now Dunlap. Between the two of us, for a good long while, he was in, around, and underneath every shared moment, every glance, every exchange, and yet we knew enough to keep him between us, just. There was no reason to upset her mother any more than I (meaning, mostly, me) already had.

He was there and he was not there, present and glaringly absent. He filled the room like nothing at all.

In the end, we were all over the place and no place at all, and the real trick of that uncertain time was finding room in our ruminations for the rest of our lives. For Nellie. For I's sisters. For softball. For school and work and everything else besides. And we managed to make a better-than-decent effort in this regard, I must say. Reality muscled its way in and took hold. Iona continued her run of good grades and cemented her place in the middle-school firmament. (Apparently, in a city like New York, there are enough cartoon-haired and strangely pierced adolescent girls to keep each other company, which Nellie and I counted as a great good thing—although I'll confess here that Iona wasn't so much a collector of good and close friends as she was an assembler of likeminded social circles.) I continued to go through Nell's motions regarding therapy, now under Dr. Belasco's care, which ran frequently enough to talk of baseball and the fates and fortunes of our Mets and Dodgers to hold my interest, and to keep on top of whatever predictable nonsense my bosses at Elder & Gold threw my way. I was an available and attentive father to Sally and Patsy.

I wouldn't go so far as to say that life was good, given the black hole into which I had apparently fallen, but it was very nearly good enough.

(Not exactly the stuff of bumper stickers, but I'd learned to take my small satisfactions where I could find them.)

There was one Saturday in there, with Sally and Patsy off on separate sleepover dates and Iona attending an all-night Marx Brothers marathon at the Ninety-Second Street Y, staged by a film studies teacher whose class Iona seemed to be taking ironically, when Nellie and I found ourselves home alone, without a whole lot to say to each other. The open evening caught us both by surprise, so it didn't occur to either one of us to make the most of it—or, even, to make of it anything at all. There was no romantic dinner, no lights turned low, no candles, no mood music. There was just the two of us, bouncing off the walls of our small apartment, desperate to fill the time, the spaces where the ease between us had once been.

"Should we take our clothes off or something?" I said at one point, trying to pickaxe what I took to be the tension in the room.

In response, Nellie could only flash me this weird, worried look—a look that seemed to leave her momentarily unsure how to place me.

Still, I kept at it. "I can take that as a no then?" I said.

"Yes, Felb," she finally said, dismissing me like a child who had spoken out of turn. "You can take that as a no."

In the end, we played cribbage, our conversation limited to the counting of our hands, to pegging, to me foolishly thinking to correct Nellie when she turned over a jack on the common card and failed to claim her two points—*his nibs*, for those who might know the game.

"Technically, those two points should go to me," I stupidly said.

"Fine," Nellie said, like it didn't really matter to her either way. "Take them."

"No," I said. "It's just, you know, those are the rules. When you miss something, it should go to me."

We finished out the game without a whole lot of note and comment, but as I've replayed that otherwise uneventful evening in my mind over and over and over, I can't shake wondering if there was some sort of subtext at play as Nellie and I counted our hands and went through the motions of being with each other—meaning, the idea that what one of us might have missed the other was somehow entitled to. It goes to the very heart of a marriage; I have come to believe. Yes? Attach one life to another and inevitably, ineluctably, the stuff of one becomes the stuff of the other.

But in Nellie's mind at least, it didn't exactly work that way.

◆

Iona thought it would be like a séance. Reality was fine, she said, but she was tired of waiting for Dunlap to re-alight in our path and thought she'd try to summon him instead. Where she got this idea, I'll never know, but she put it in play one afternoon on the softball diamond. The Lady Warriors were facing Eastside Prep, who sat one game ahead of them atop the league standings. How it happened that Iona was ineligible to pitch against their league rivals in a game for first place, you'd have to ask her clueless coach, but she was playing third base and hoping to make the best of it. By the fifth inning, the Lady Warriors were up 5—4 behind I's bases-clearing double in the bottom of the third.

(She had also popped out to left field and grounded weakly to short, so there's no call to think she was any kind of one-girl show.)

On to I's proactive summoning. Top of the fifth, she took the infield with the rest of her team, and I saw she had borrowed a mitt from one of her left-handed teammates. I can't say for certain, but I don't think anyone else on that manicured armory rooftop noticed. Clearly, such an insight was beyond the limited powers of the Whedon Academy coach, and the few parents sprinkled throughout the bleachers were too busy eyeballing their own daughters or talking cellularly to their colleagues at work or not knowing the first thing about the game to pay such attention to detail. Nellie might have picked up on it, but she was covering at the hospital for her friend Nomi, who had stepped on a rusted screw while jogging in Central Park and was forced to miss a couple shifts.

Now, let me once again offer some perspective for the non-fan. In baseball and its derivative versions, left-handed fielders tend not to take up position on the left side of the infield, and on the right side they'll play only at first base. The reason? Left-handed throwers are at considerable disadvantage making the throw across the infield to first, because the dimensions of the game require them to throw away from their own momentum. You won't find too many left-handed throwing catchers, either, only here it's because the game is staffed predominantly by right-handed hitters, who tend to get in the way of left-handed throwing catchers attempting to throw out runners at second or third. At the major-league level, you'll almost never see a left-handed third baseman, second baseman, or shortstop, although of course there have been exceptions, usually in an extra-inning game when a manager's bench has been depleted and he has run out of other options. In my own rooting memory, I can recall that Yankee great Don Mattingly played parts of three games at third and part of another game at second—owing probably to some late-inning lineup maneuvering. In Fred Dunlap's day, there was a journeyman left-handed pitcher with the great baseball name of Cannonball Titcomb who logged a couple games at third base, and Hall-of-Famer George Sisler, another .400 hitter, appeared in two games at third during the 1916 season. There have been other less interesting exceptions, but for the most part left-handed ballplayers are stuck playing one of the outfield positions, first base or pitcher, which was why the sight of Iona out there at third with a left-handed mitt on her right hand struck me as so strange. I looked on and it was immediately clear that something was wrong with this picture, and then it took a couple beats to figure what it was, and after that I kicked myself for not noticing it right away. At the youth level, where pure athleticism is often enough to overcome such slight disadvantages as momentum and percentage plays, it's not so unusual to see a left-hander at third as it is in the professional ranks, but it was like looking at my daughter through a mirror. There was something *off* about it, although I didn't have to wonder on it for too terribly long. And I didn't have to worry what it might mean. I knew my Iona. I knew what she was up to.

Next, the Eastside Prep cleanup batter hit a slow-roller toward the hole between third and short, and Iona moved casually to her now-barehand side, scooped the ball across her body on a short hop, and fired across the diamond to first with her left hand for the third out of the inning. Iona made the play as if she had been throwing that way her entire life. It was the most astonishing thing. Nell has instructed me to never use the pejorative phrase *throws like a girl*, but I'm too lazy a writer to avoid it here—and no other phrase calls its contradiction so readily to mind. Surely, there was nothing *throws like a girl* about Iona's motion from the left side. It was the same practiced rifle shot she'd taken to throwing from the right, with the same easy grace and familiarity, and in this instance she might not have recorded the out at first if she had been throwing with her natural arm. She'd had to move across the infield in such a way that as a right-handed third baseman she would have been moving away from the momentum of the play; she might have made the throw to first, but there would have been nothing on it, and the Eastside Prep cleanup hitter would have legged out an infield hit.

Iona's effort was lost on everyone else on that armory rooftop save for her Daddy-o. She fielded the ball cleanly and made a good, crisp throw across the diamond, and as far as anyone else could tell it was business as usual, even as I knew it to be an anomaly. (Once again, "I" as in Iona *and* me.)

As it happened, that soft-grounder in the hole was Iona's only chance in the field that half-inning, and by the top of the sixth she had discarded the lefty mitt for her right-handed job. Apparently her great experiment was over. She had meant to lure the ghost of Fred Dunlap to the armory field by showing off her ability to throw from both sides (her *ambidextrosity*?) as he had famously done during his career, and I had to admire her approach even as I considered the flaws in her logic. How does a fourteen-year-old girl get to that place in her thinking where she expects to beckon some century-old spirit by mimicking his century-old behaviors? How does the one follow from the other? And, assuming she was successful in compelling our man back into our realm, I wondered, what did she mean to do with him once he arrived? Invite him back to the apartment for dinner? Bring him to school for show-and-tell?

Whatever she had in mind—a séance indeed!—Iona believed she had made her point, and she returned her full attention to the game and her left hand into the well-oiled leather of her own glove. And it was a good thing, too, as I will attempt to explain. See, the Whedon pitcher retired the side in order in the sixth inning on three pop-ups to the right side of the infield, so Iona didn't touch the ball again until the seventh, her team now up by two runs. The first two Eastside batters walked to start the seventh frame, putting the tying runs on base with nobody out. Then the next two Eastside batters struck out, only there was a wild pitch mixed in there that allowed the runners to advance to second and third. The fifth batter was hit in the helmet and awarded first, loading the bases with two outs.

As middle-school softball games went, this was edge-of-the-cushioned-bleachers stuff. Bases loaded. Two outs. Last chance for the visiting team to get back in the game.

Eastside's cleanup hitter stepped to the plate with the game on the line—and first place as well. The girl struck me as a little too tiny to be batting cleanup, but she had hit the ball hard her first two times up before that routine grounder to Iona at third in the top of the fifth. She struck me, too, as something of a free spirit—the Eastside version, say, of my Iona, although her affectations seemed somewhat more closely aligned with the social norms on display on that armory rooftop. Three long braids spilled from her batting helmet, leaving her looking like a miniature Pocahontas with an extra appendage, but the too-long hair was merely a reddish-brown instead of the fire-engine red it might have been beneath Iona's helmet on some other day. The girl worked the count to two balls and two strikes. Then she worked it some more. She fouled off two rising fastballs that looked well out of the strike zone, and then she stepped out of the batter's box and stared down to her third-base coach for instructions. The Eastside Prep coach, a big-bellied man of indeterminate middle age, traced a line along the bill of his cap with his forefinger. Then he touched his nose. Then he spit. Then he clapped his hands together. Twice.

In response, the pint-sized Pocahontas traced the bill of her helmet with her own forefinger, but she didn't touch her nose or spit or clap her hands together.

I thought, what in the world could they be signaling? There were two strikes on the batter, which made the prospect of a bunt unlikely.

(A further tutorial: A foul ball off an attempted bunt is held to a different standard than a foul ball off a full swing. You're entitled to as many of the latter as you'll need—up to thirty-eight and more, apparently!—but a ball that's bunted foul when there are already two strikes on the batter goes down as a strikeout.)

I thought, what coach would take the bat out of the hands of his cleanup hitter when he's down two runs with two outs in his last turn at bat? Conventional baseball (and, in turn, softball) wisdom holds that you let your big hitter swing away in situations like this. And with those same two strikes on the batter, there's no way the coach was flashing the "take" sign. Really, about the only thing that could be passing between player and coach was some sort of elaborate distraction to get in the heads of the opposing players. That, or a base-running play of some kind. Only trouble was, the Whedon Academy Lady Warriors didn't know the first thing about picking up another team's signs. Their own clueless coach didn't pay attention to that sort of thing, and the players didn't understand the game well enough to pick up on it themselves. Except of course for Iona, who had the game's nuances nailed. She caught the peculiar back-and-forth between the Eastside coach and his cleanup hitter and knew immediately that something was up, so she called time and signaled for the Whedon catcher to come out to the mound.

The Whedon coach—bless him!—sat confidently on the heated dugout bench, fairly oblivious to the team meeting taking place on the field without him, and so Iona took charge in the huddle on the mound and told the catcher to keep her eye on the base-runner on third. Then she told her pitcher to throw strikes. Then she held up her glove and waited while her teammates touched their gloves to hers, and they all held their gloved hands aloft for a beat while they made a whooping noise. Then the players returned to their positions and the game resumed.

On the very next pitch, another rising fastball out of the zone that Pocahontas managed to restrain from chasing, the runner on third danced down the line as if she might be coming home. Iona had called it, and I allowed myself a small fatherly smile for having raised a child so keen on the game and at the same time so sure in her skin that she could drag her peers along to where they might know what she knew, and see what she saw. The catcher, alerted to just this eventuality, threw off her mask and unleashed a throw to Iona at third, although of course the more experienced play would have been to run the opposing player back to the bag without risking a wild throw. Still, you couldn't fault the Whedon catcher for reacting so aggressively to the situation. Nellie might have faulted the poor child's mother for being such a blowhard in the stands, and for having the temerity to give birth to a child who couldn't help but fall short in her extra efforts to block some of I's erratic pitches, but the girl was simply doing her best. Her throw, however, was a little off-line. It was wide to the left of the third-base bag and tailed even further left on its way down the line.

On an impulse, Iona dove to her right to grab the errant throw, her bare right hand outreaching her gloved left hand by about a fist, and she somehow managed to snare the ball with her bare hand just before she hit the ground—a spectacular play, especially when you take into account the size of a softball (like a grapefruit!) against the size of Iona's small hands. Again, I indulged myself in one of those fatherly smiles, this one a little larger than the one just past, this one owing mostly to Iona's peerless, fearless gifts as an athlete.

The Eastside base-runner had been heading back to third, but she must have seen the ball sailing wide into foul territory, because she doubled back for home on the throw, which turned out to be a mistake. Iona, for her part, bounced from the turf like her bones were made of rubber and let fly with a slingshot that seemed to skim the artificial surface on its way to the plate. Had she been wearing her teammate's left-handed mitt as before, she might have had an easier time making the same catch, but she would have never had time to transfer the ball from her gloved hand to her bare hand and the runner would have beaten the throw home, but her right-handed throw beat the Eastside runner by a half-step, the Whedon catcher managed to hold onto it and make the tag, and the Lady Warriors held on for the win.

It really was a sensational play, but I don't set it out here to blow smoke in my daughter's direction. I don't wish to come off as one of those boastful parents whose children can do no wrong. No, I offer these details to show the lengths my Iona would go to return Fred "Sure Shot" Dunlap to our lives. Because that was what this was, really. Because the depth of her faith was a thing to see. Because she might have just won the game for her teammates with her barehanded grab and heads-up throw to the plate, and pushed her team into a tie for first place in the bargain, but these were lesser windfalls to Iona at just that moment. What really mattered to her was that she had put Dunlap's ghost on some kind of notice, playing the game as the man himself had once played it. What mattered was that she had been a ready student. That she had an open mind and an open heart. That he would notice these things and return to acknowledge them.

And speaking of noticing, I don't think there was an earthly soul on the rooftop that afternoon who'd taken full notice of the events I've just described, other than me and my daughter, my *folie à deux* partner. In the home-team bleachers, on our side of the field, I don't think anyone had even a whiff of a notion that the opposing coach had been signaling a play, although there was one horrified mother seated a couple rows down to my left who pointed toward third base and said for the benefit of the other soon-to-be-horrified mothers seated nearby, "Why does that terrible man have to spit like that?"

It took Iona almost twenty minutes to gather her things after the game, and to run the gauntlet of high-fives and whooping Lady Warrior war cries that seemed to follow her around the manicured field as she helped her teammates put away the equipment. I waited for her at the chain-link gate leading to the outdoor stairwell that would take us down from the roof.

"Nice throw," I said to her when she was finally through with her post-game responsibilities.

"Which one?" she wanted to know—meaning the left-handed surprise in the fifth inning or the game-saving throw to home in the seventh.

"You know which one," I said.

She smiled like it meant the world to her. "Pretty cool, huh?" she said.

"Pretty cool," I agreed. "Coach say anything?"

"What, you think he even noticed?"

"Nah. Probably not."

"What about him?" she said. "Do you think he noticed?"

"Who?"

"Dad," she reproved.

"Sorry, I. Him. Dunlap. My bad."

With this, she punched my arm. Hard. She didn't like it when I spoke like her friends.

I thought, sorry, I. My bad. "What makes you think he was watching?" I said.

"He's always watching," she said.

Nine
BEANEATER

There was another hoped-for séance—again choreographed by my Iona—and this one found us a couple weeks later, wrapped inside a hastily conceived father-daughter road trip which in turn had been soaked in improbability and wishful thinking.

To come completely clean, Nellie had an unwitting hand in this one as well. It was Nell who first suggested I take Iona on a long-discussed pilgrimage to Cooperstown, New York, home of the Baseball Hall of Fame and repository of the hopes and dreams of anyone who's ever cared a whit for our national pastime, and as soon as her mother put it out there Iona grabbed at the notion with both fists. Nellie had about run out of ideas on what to do with me, what to make of me, where to place this unexpected Dunlap detour on the path we were meant to travel together. She could not have guessed at Iona's fixation, I don't think. In fact, I'm sure of it. If Nellie had even a scent of a clue, she would have never brought up the idea of Cooperstown, never allowed such a trip if it had come up on its own. To throw our baby girl into the firestorm of my confusion, feet first . . . well, it would have been unthinkable. And yet, in a vacuum, on its face, not knowing in any kind of full-on way that our daughter had her own pieces of unfinished business with Fred "Sure Shot" Dunlap, real or imagined, Nell must have seen a road trip to Cooperstown as just the thing to shake me from the doldrums and delirium that had lately colored my world like a hallucinogen. It would be a salve, of a kind. A distraction. For her. For me. For our no-longer-ordinary family.

Anyway, Nellie knew Iona was mad for baseball and had by now accepted that I was probably just plain mad, and so she thought to fuse these two madnesses in a positive way. The idea appeared to flow naturally from how we were as a family. Such a trip had been talked about since Iona first showed an interest in the game, but it had never quite come around on our family calendar—meaning it had mostly been talked about by mostly me. Each time it came up,

I could never quite justify forcing such a trip on Sally and Patsy, who of course showed no such interest, and Nell herself, despite her adult-onset devotion to the New York Mets, could think of a couple dozen places she'd rather visit than the cradle of baseball history—like, say, the Museum of Questionable Medical Devices in Minneapolis.

Leave it to my longsuffering nurse of a wife to come up with such as this, and to thereby reduce the hallowed halls of our baseball shrine to a mere curiosity. And, now, leave it to my whirling dervish of a disaffected *tweenager* to find a through-line from Cooperstown to what remained of the Rolen incident, one that may or may not have stretched all the way to our man Dunlap. You see, after capping her Whedon Warrior softball career with a 15—7 record that included a glowing 8—0 won-loss mark for herself as a pitcher, and a first-place finish for her team that announced not so loudly to the Manhattan private-school community that Whedon Academy was not to be trifled with on the immaculately turfed fields on the rooftops of the Upper West Side, Iona returned her full attention yet again to our shared delusion. I could not bring myself to think of it as such—a delusion! hardly!—but this was how the incident had presented itself to Nellie, and how it was being actively considered by my thrice-weekly Dr. Belasco, and how it was sometimes discussed in hushed tones in our cramped household, or whispered into the cupped mouthpiece of our kitchen telephone late at night as Nell shared the latest details of my slow-going collapse with her long-distance friends. It followed soon enough, then, that I would use the word in my own thinking as a kind of shorthand.

A delusion? Well, if you insist . . .

It got right to the point—and even as it appeared to miss it entirely as far as I and I were concerned, it pretty much covered it for everybody else.

Whatever it was, whatever it wasn't, Iona was now committed unreservedly to it, same as me, and as we inched forward on our shared journey, her interest in all things baseball appeared to deepen—specifically, in all things *old-time* baseball. She had learned, either by osmosis or by some twist of preternatural determination, that the 1999 Hall of Fame induction ceremonies were that year to include one of Sure Shot's contemporaries—Frank Selee, the turn-of-the-century manager perhaps best known for converting a journeyman catcher named Frank Chance into a first baseman for the Chicago Cubs, laying the foundation for the famed Tinker-to-Evers-to-Chance infield combination.

It turned out there was a bumper crop of Hall of Famers that year—seven in all, the highest single-year total since 1972 when Sandy Koufax, Yogi Berra, and Josh Gibson led the way. Joining Selee on the honor roll were a collection of greats from my deepest and fondest baseball memories—Nolan Ryan, George Brett, Robin Yount, and Orlando Cepeda—together with the late umpire Nestor Chylak and Smokey Joe Williams, widely regarded as the greatest pitcher in Negro-league history.

Iona knew all of this, of course. She knew of Ryan's late-career dominance, Brett's unrivaled eye at the plate, Yount's versatility and consistency, and Cepeda's glory years in San Francisco alongside Mays and McCovey. The details of Selee's story she pieced together soon enough—highlighted by the fact that the man began his professional career as the manager of the Boston Beaneaters in 1890, the same year Dunlap signed off on his National League career by logging an unremarkable seventeen games for Pittsburgh before finishing out the string with the New York Giants of the Players League.

In Iona's mind, at least, this likely put the two men on the same field at the same time, and such a prospect set her mind to racing.

"Dad," she said, "we have to go."

And so it was decided, even though it was not entirely clear to me what Iona expected. Still, it was clear even to her unmoored dad that Iona had been swept up in some sort of siren pull and that she was fairly powerless against it. (*We* were fairly powerless against it!) Granted, I was not as quick to plot the points of connection as my whip-smart daughter, but I was plugged in enough to know that in Iona's oddly colored, multi-pierced head there was something to it, something worth exploring.

I could not imagine what Iona had in mind, and I did not think to ask, and it is only now in the setting down of this latest puzzle piece that it even occurs to me there was anything to question. What did she expect, after all? Selee himself was long dead. (He died in 1909 in Denver at the age of 49.) Even his children were dead, and possibly their children as well, which in turn made it all very unlikely that there'd be a single soul at the induction ceremony who'd been alive to know the man they would be honoring. The man we were after for reasons we could not even begin to put into words.

And yet there we were, careening toward Cooperstown as if the town itself might reveal an answer or a clue. Something.

Selee's Beaneaters, of course, were soon to be known as the Braves, after a brief stretch as the Doves and the Rustlers, offering Iona a baseball through-line that ran all the way to Ruth and Aaron, if she chose to follow it. For the time being, she did not. Her interest in Selee lay only in the man's long-ago proximity to Fred Dunlap, the man whose life and career had fairly bedeviled our little family for nearly a year and thrown my loose toe-hold on sanity and purpose into all kinds of question, and yet it was all we could think about as we set off.

There'd been a time not too long before when a road trip of this type would have been a welcome point of pause beneath the heat and haste of our big-city lives. An excuse to dial down the pace of our days and soak in the past. Cooperstown, New York, is a land-that-time-forgot sort of town tucked neatly into the middle of nowhere in the central part of the state. There are lush valleys and rolling hilltop peaks and quaint little barns and antique shops dotting the countryside, but none of the scenery seemed to register as we wheeled into town in our rented Chevy Cavalier—hunter green, for the record, I guess so that we might better blend into the scenery. We were each of us lost inside our own thinking instead of in what was passing outside our windows, and in this way we might have been driving against a blue screen upon which we might have superimposed a series of corresponding images.

As we drove, there were long patches of silence punctuated by a comment every here or there that must have sounded like a non sequitur to whichever one of us had failed to give it voice. It was as if I and I had each momentarily forgotten the other was alongside in the front seat of the Cavalier, and then we took turns remembering and forgetting. Back and forth and all over again.

Iona: "I don't think he ever used a glove. That's weird, right? I mean, players were wearing gloves all the way back in the 1870s. Not a lot, but some."

Or, me: "A *lickfinger*. What does that even mean?"

Iona: "Did they even have photographs back then? Like, cameras?"

Me: "Does he watch over us, do you think?"

And on and on, all the way to the Legend Valley Campground, the only place in town that could accommodate this father and daughter on such short notice during Hall of Fame induction weekend. There's not much in the way of hotel or motel rooms to begin with in Cooperstown and surrounding parts, but for this one weekend each July, there's a run on available beds. The finer establishments have been known to honor a standing room reservation for years and years for returning baseball royalty, but even the lesser joints are booked solid. We had no choice but to rough it, so I'd dug out an old tent from the storage shelves in the basement of our building, set it up in our living room to see if the thing could withstand the rain and the bugs we would likely encounter in the wilds of upstate New York, and figured we would manage.

Once the tent was up in our apartment, Sally and Patsy made an adventure of it, and after a halfhearted few moments of pretending to be too old for that sort of thing, Iona happily joined them. Nell, never one to let a memory pass unmade, suggested we roast marshmallows on our gas stove, which wasn't exactly roughing it, but the girls were delighted to be standing around our galley kitchen campfire. Nell discovered a never-opened set of fondue forks to stand in as sticks for the girls' marshmallows. There were a couple Hershey bars, too, which I always kept in the fridge, so they were well on their way to making s'mores—only they were more like s'lesses, because graham crackers had never been too high on Nell's shopping list. Instead, we improvised with a half-eaten sleeve of

Ritz crackers, thereby disproving the much-advertised notion that everything sits well on a Ritz.

Iona crinkled up her face at the odd combination, but Sally and Patsy didn't seem to care.

At some wee-hour point in the middle of that living room campout, I shuffled from our bedroom to look in on my sleeping darlings, and the sight of my three girls splayed alongside and across each other like a litter of puppies was enough to break my heart, only it would have been a breakage owing to a fullness I no longer recognized. Perhaps, then, it would be more accurate to suggest that my heart was about to burst rather than shatter. There had been a time, not too long before, when the picture of family had been enough to sustain me. It was all I had, really. It was all I deserved, certainly. It was, by extension, the picture I carried of myself, only now, beneath the specter of Fred Dunlap, it was a picture clouded with worry. I could not soak in this sweet scene without thinking also of the troubles I had visited upon my poor family. There was no looking away from the distance that had grown between me and Nell, who would have had an easier time of it if I had been diagnosed with prostate cancer. Or dementia. Or Lou Gehrig's disease, even. Anything but this slow creep of weirdness that had inserted itself into our simple lives and defied diagnosis. Ah, my stoic Nursenel! She could not look at me without also looking away, and as she did I would imagine her thinking I was now lost to her. I could not remember the last time we'd made love, the last time we'd shared an intimacy of any kind, and when we were alone together, our conversations had mostly to do with the maintenance of our little family. And, always, beneath the lines of what was spoken and unspoken between us, there was Nell's belief that I had gone off some deep end or other. (Once, I overheard her talking to one of her nurse friends and refer to my recent behaviors as "unhinged.") There had emerged between us a sense that we were going through the motions, just. That we were unraveling, all of us, on the back of this vision she could not accept.

My delusion.

I could not let go of it, and she could not accept it, and in the resulting tug and pull, we were losing each other.

And yet, to me, it was a simple truth: I had been visited by the specter of a man who had been dead for nearly a century. A man who had once graced the game of baseball with a level of play that had not been seen in his time and has rarely been seen since. A man who appeared to have chosen me for some ghostly business that had yet to be made clear.

To Nellie, the truth was not so simple: Her husband was losing it—and by extension, she was losing her husband.

The one truth could not survive the other.

◆

It's important to note here that Iona and I had done a fairly good job of stiff-arming her mother from Iona's own Dunlap obsession. This was not a duplicity so much as it was a convenient necessity, and it was somehow accomplished without the unhealthy bits of collusion such a statement suggests. Be assured, I did not come right out and ask Iona to keep her own Dunlap encounter to herself. I didn't have to. She knew intuitively what it would mean to her mother to see her daughter headed down the same wobbly road—and I saw no good reason to insist Iona come entirely clean. As to her sudden makeover on the softball diamond, which Iona believed had to do with a rooftop run-in with the ghost of Fred Dunlap, stripped of his nineteenth-century adornments and dressed in modern-day Nike gear, she'd merely told an astonished Nellie she'd been tutored by a man at the armory one afternoon.

"You mean, like, your coach?" her mother had quite reasonably asked, for clarification.

"No," Iona said, offering no such thing. "Just some guy."

"You mean, like, an assistant coach?" Nell tried.

"I guess. Just, you know, some guy. Like an alum or something. Hanging around watching us practice."

I cannot imagine that Nellie was all too pleased to learn there were strange unaccounted-for men hanging around on the roof of the armory while our budding-prospect middle-schooler practiced softball with her Lady Warrior teammates. Frankly, the words *just, you know, some guy* rank fairly high on the list of Top Ten Things a Father of a Teenage Girl Hopes Never to Hear—only my concern was mitigated by the thought that Iona's *some guy* and my own *some guy* were one and the same. In tentative truth, I had no idea if the man I knew as Dunlap was a danger to my daughter any more than if he might have been a danger to me, and yet I had spent the past year accepting on faith that he was not.

His presence, in a purely physical sense, was benign—it was in the metaphysical sense that we had some trouble.

And so, back to Cooperstown.

It became clear early on that we could have done with some more thorough planning. Camping was one thing—pulling into town past eight o'clock at night with hardly enough left-behind daylight to pitch our tent was quite another. After checking in at the Legend Valley front desk, which featured a low-hanging strip of ancient bug paper that seemed to have run out of room to accommodate any additional low-hanging bugs, it occurred to me that we would have some difficulty making camp in the dark. Iona had the same thought at about the same time.

"We should have probably left the city a little earlier," she said—graciously taking some of the blame.

"Probably," I said.

I considered our options for a too-long moment. There weren't many. We could get started on the tent and see how we might manage it—although to judge from the difficulties I'd had back in our well-lit apartment, this didn't seem like such a good idea. We could double back and see if any of the motels we'd passed on the way into town had miraculously developed a sudden vacancy. Or we could drive the car to our designated campsite, move our gear into the trunk and find a way to make comfortable beds out of the reclining bucket seats.

"Car camping," Iona said, not sounding too excited when it appeared this last was our best option. "Yay for us."

"It's called making the best of it, I," I said.

"No, Dad," she said back flatly. "It's called car camping."

But it wasn't so bad, even Iona had to admit. There was enough room in the back for Iona to stretch out, and I was able to get enough recline on the driver's seat to create a serviceable hammock. We would turn in early, we decided, and get a jump on things the next morning, but we got a little sidetracked by our neighbors. It turned out our campsite put us next to a battered old Volkswagen microbus with Wisconsin plates that seemed to have made the trip from America's heartland with a clown-car-full of Brewers fans—at least eleven I could count, in all shapes and sizes. Best I could tell, the VW carried three generations, all variously determined to pay tribute to Robin Yount. Iona was roped into a conversation with one of them as we stepped from our car to head to the showerhouse to wash up for the night—an overalled, over-eager girl who seemed to be about the same age. The family hailed from Whitefish Bay, Wisconsin, and they were dressed in all manner of Brewers gear. The oldest—the patriarch, presumably—wore an old-school Milwaukee Braves parka. The youngest—a boy of about five or six—wore a Gorman Thomas jersey, powder blue, three or four sizes too big, that probably could have fetched a nice number on eBay.

Curiously, the adult men of Whitefish Bay had all grown biker-type moustaches to match the one worn by Yount during most of his playing career—a style oddly reminiscent of the horseshoe moustaches that had been in favor during Dunlap's era, and very nearly like the one Dunlap himself had been sporting that day in the Philadelphias. It was disconcerting to have been surrounded by this happy band of menfolk whose faces called Dunlap to mind, and I caught myself in the middle of a double take or two after I'd organized our few things and wandered over to a spot by the campfire where Iona and her overeager friend were sitting.

One of the men offered me a beer. "Old Milwaukees," he announced. And then, sheepishly: "Like, what else, right?"

I did not quite know what to say to this, so I merely offered up the proffered can in a kind of toast. "To Robin Yount," I said. To forestall the awkward silence that would likely soon follow, I mentioned I had seen Yount play during his second season—at Shea Stadium, of all places, back when the Brewers were still an American League club, long before the advent of interleague play, when a visit to Shea might have made a little more sense. You see, the Yankees played their home games in Queens that year, owing to a season-long makeover of Yankee Stadium, and I'd gone to the game with a couple friends from St. John's hoping to see Hank Aaron pull off a heroic or two before calling it a career.

I hadn't thought about that game in years, hadn't even thought to mention it until my first sip of Old Milwaukee, when I just started talking without thinking—never a good combination in my experience, although here the effect was negligible. I was fixed on the idea of making meaningless chatter, of fitting in and passing the time in a pleasant-enough way, and so the details of that day came rushing back and pouring out. It was April, 1975, and as I remembered it a nineteen-year-old Robin Yount stroked one of the first triples of his career—off Yankee starter Doc Medich—and I thought at the time that we were all in on the ground floor of something worthwhile. One star on the way up—Yount. One star on the way down—Aaron. It's not often you get to see greatness coming and going like that, on the same field, and I must have made a couple mental notes and filed them away for a time almost a quarter century later when I could call them back to mind. When my world was coming queerly undone and I could no longer tell if I was coming or going myself.

I went on and on, and when I got to where I thought I was going, the one Whitefish Bay resident who still seemed to be listening seemed to want to change the subject. "So who you here to see, New York?" he said when I had reached the end of my account—when it appeared our introductory pleasantries were about to die down ahead of the fire, and that our names hadn't registered with these good people in quite the same way as where we were from. "Don't tell me it's Ryan. He wasn't shit for you. Wasn't anything 'til you traded him away."

This was true enough, but I hadn't really given Nolan Ryan a whole lot of thought these past couple days. "Nah," I said. "We're just baseball fans, me and my daughter. Just here to see what we can see."

"What are you talking about, Dad?" Iona chimed in from over a portable picnic table that had apparently spilled from the microbus with the rest of the family. She was being playfully argumentative—a practiced tone whenever we were out in public. "Tell 'em who we're here to see."

I knew Iona wasn't about to share our secret with these apparently God-fearing people who would no sooner have accepted that we were here in pursuit of some ghostly apparition than if we'd been seeking the Devil himself, but at the same time, I was anxious to see where she was going with this. The girl was up to . . . *something*.

"And who is that?" I shot back across the campsite, also playfully.

"We're Selee fans," she said beneath an inordinate amount of fervor and glee. For a moment, I thought she might punctuate her declaration with a wave of her hands, a loud clap . . . some flourish of some kind.

"Who the hell is Selee?" one of our hosts wanted to know.

"Frank Selee," Iona proudly announced. "Only the most influential manager of his time." And then she was off on a detailed account of the man's many accomplishments, including his career won-lost record, his titles, his philosophies on the game, his eye for talent, his redeploying of Frank Chance, and on and on. The Milwaukee folks couldn't quite believe that this girl with the fire-engine-red hair and a face chain was able to offer up the stuff of this man's life in such colorful detail. And not just his life—his death, too.

"He died of consumption," Iona declared, knotting the loose ends of Frank Selee's life at long last, and when she was through there was a kind of stunned, protracted silence about the campsite. She'd been at it a while. I couldn't tell if our new friends were merely at a loss for words or if they were perhaps second-guessing their decision to invite us to join them in the first place.

Finally, another one of our new friends stood—the fellow who'd offered me the beer—and he threw up his own hands as if to indicate that he couldn't quite think what to make of these two New Yorkers in his company. "What the hell is consumption?" he said.

◆

Next morning, we woke early and pitched our tent, careful not to wake the Robin Yount contingent. In the interest of full disclosure, I'll concede that our tent-building effort was more of a soft-toss than a pitch, because it is no easy thing to drive a stake into the hard earth while worrying about the resulting noise. Here, especially, it was just short of impossible. I did not think to bring a mallet or hammer (another disclosure: I have never in my life even swung a mallet, let alone had one in my possession), so I sent Iona off looking for a large rock to do the job, but then I could only press the rock against the stakes and lean my full weight into each one in turn, because the sound of stone against metal bounced among the trees and threatened the peace and quiet of the Milwaukee faithful. It was slow going there on in until Iona had the bright idea to merely press the stakes halfway in for now, and it followed that we worked our way around the tent in this manner and decided to come back and finish the job at a more reasonable hour.

It struck me, then and still, as a fine metaphor for a life halfheartedly lived—for doing just enough to get by and always meaning to return to a thing later.

The induction ceremony wasn't until the next afternoon, and the plan was to head back to the city immediately afterward, so this was our day to see the sights, tour the museum, soak up what we could. We got it in our heads that we were on a tight schedule, so we set about it.

First, I decided to take a fresh look around. By daylight, our Legend Valley digs struck me as threadbare, ramshackle. The shotgun cabins rimming the campground were rustic, thrown-together shacks that from the outside looking in appeared to have been thrown together in a previous century. There was electricity, judging from the naked yellow lightbulbs atop each doorway, but no running water, judging from the handful of bath-robed or sweat-panted "campers" spilling from their shacks and making for the showerhouses, getting started on their own busy schedules.

The campground itself looked like a mini-Woodstock—or, at least, how I imagined a mini-Woodstock might have looked—only instead of hippies and stoners there were baseball fans, young and old, determined to reach back over the years and celebrate the icons of their childhoods. They moved about as if their being here was ordained, as if they belonged no place else. It was all so very civilized as we claimed and lolled about our little parcels of land, huddled close to the here-and-there fire pits, to the iron grills slam-bolted into the ground far more enduringly than our tired old tent, which for all I knew would soon be collected by a stiff breeze and set down somewhere else in these upstate environs.

The tents, I and I now noticed, were loudly colored (lime green! slate blue!), leaving me to think there had been some innovations in the camping industry since Nell and I had purchased our olive drab canvas number back before we had children. If you stood back and squinted—which I actually did to verify the hunch—the tent field looked like the start screen from the full-color version of the Galaga arcade game to which I'd been obsessively devoted as a young man.

For the time being, our car was parked on the edge of a huge open field dotted with tents and pop-top vans and RVs. We'd been instructed the previous night on checking in to move the car to a nearby parking field after setting up camp in the morning, so I imagined we were now in violation of some campground policy, although I noticed that almost everyone else seemed to have left their cars parked alongside their campsite for easy access. It was astonishing, really, to look upon this small sea of tents and recreational vehicles and notice how far from home many of our sleeping neighbors had traveled, how elaborately, just to be here in these cleared woods. There were license plates announcing Wisconsin, Missouri, Kansas, Texas . . . all indicating their owners' allegiance to some new Hall of Famer or other. Inexplicably, there was also an Oregon plate two sites over, and a Volkswagen Bug that appeared to have made the trip from one of the Dakotas. And on the elaborate front, there were tents far nicer than any I had ever seen, including one that featured a small anteroom, full-height ceilings, an awning by the front door and two smaller sections fanning from the back wall that seemed to have been designed as separate bedrooms.

Our decidedly more modest tent appeared to be in good enough shape to survive the rest of the day. After Iona convinced me it would be waiting for us, pitched, when we returned to the campground later that afternoon, she went off to the women's showerhouse to brush her teeth, wash her face, do her thing. I went to the men's and attempted to shave. Anyway, I thought about it, but the small stream of water that managed to fall from the tap was hardly hot, so I gave up on this idea as well. Soon, we were careening in the Cavalier down a small hill on a dirt access road that spilled onto the main highway just outside of town—and, soon after that, easing into a perfect parking spot directly in front of a small coffee shop called The Dugout, just a couple blocks from the museum.

Like almost every other establishment in Cooperstown, The Dugout was careful to remind its customers that baseball was the order of the day. A single egg, sunny-side up, was billed on the menu as "The Seeing-Eye Single," which struck us as clever, while a salad bar that opened for lunch was known as "The Field of Greens," which struck us as . . . well, not.

The featured breakfast was a hardly good-for-me feast consisting of four eggs, any style, with four different meats and four silver-dollar pancakes. It was billed as "The Grand Salami," and as I read its description I realized I was hungry. (Must've been something about sleeping outdoors.) When I ordered it the waitress kindly informed me that the four meats on the menu that morning were bacon, ham, sausage, and fried bologna.

I said, "What, no salami?"

The waitress said, "No, 'fraid not."

"But it's the 'Grand Salami' breakfast. How can you serve a 'Grand Salami' breakfast with no salami?"

"Blame it on Denny's," the waitress said. "When we first opened, it was the 'Grand Slam' breakfast, which was, like, *so* obvious, right? But then some guy came in with his kid like six months later, turned out he managed a small chain of Denny's restaurants near Albany. Bound to happen, right? Turned out he went back to work the following week and alerted the Denny's lawyers. Like these people have nothing better to do than chase down some mom-and-pop coffee shop in the middle of nowhere for trademark infringement, or whatever they called it. They even sent us a cease-and-desist letter, which I didn't know was, like, a real thing." The waitress pointed it out to us—the owner of The Dugout had had the letter framed and hung it over the cash register.

Iona had been listening to this exchange, of course, and she went from being embarrassed that I was even talking to this waitress about such as this to being momentarily incensed that these big-time corporate lawyers would even give a plain shit about such a small—but, probably, inevitable—similarity. I mean, we were here in Cooperstown, after all. What the hell else were they supposed to call their top-of-the-line breakfast?

"What a dick," Iona said, oozing disregard, disdain for this Denny's character.

I'll admit, I was more than a little startled by Iona's coarse phrasing. It was the way precocious Manhattan middle-schoolers spoke, I knew full well, but nevertheless it threw me to have to hear it from the mouth of my own daughter in such a public, practiced way.

"Language, I," I sort of scolded, sort of not—a rebuke that had evidently seeped into the language of our little family.

"Oh, come on, Dad," she shot back. "What's the big deal? It's not like Mom's here or anything."

"Yeah, Dad," our waitress chimed in, overstepping her station in what I took to be a playful way. "What's the big deal?"

Iona smiled, happy to have an unexpected ally—and, immediately, momentarily, my concerns were diffused.

On the back of this exchange, I guessed we'd made a new friend, and our waitress let us linger at our table long after our plates had been cleared, long after the place had started to fill, nursing our cups of coffee and hot chocolate and waiting for the Hall of Fame to open its doors so we could get started on our adventure.

Now, I will not offer here a floor-by-floor, exhibit-by-exhibit breakdown of the National Baseball Hall of Fame and Museum, because I don't believe it belongs in this account. I had been there before—once with Nell, even, for an Elder & Gold publicity event timed to commemorate the 1991 induction of the late baseball promoter and team owner Bill Veeck, the subject of a subpar biography from a subpar *Sports Illustrated* writer who didn't fully appreciate the extra efforts we were making to call attention to his dashed-off tome.

(Reviewers, let the record show, weren't particularly kind to this volume—wondering, for example, how a book about a man who used his wooden leg for an ash tray could possibly be such a snore.)

Indeed, the Hall has its many charms for lifelong baseball fans like me and my daughter, and we went looking for every last one of them. However, I will share a happy discovery that seemed to find us on its own. We were wandering through the museum bookstore at the end of our visit, scouring the shelves for any under-published volumes on the Union Association, the St. Louis Maroons—or, dare we hope, on our man Dunlap himself. After much wandering and scouring, Iona had the presence of mind to flag a young bookstore employee and ask if there weren't some additional books in a back room that might get close to what we were looking for.

At this, the young bookstore employee kindly inquired what, specifically, we were looking for.

Iona said, "Something about the Union Association. Maybe some biographies about Union Association players. I don't know, something."

"I might have something better than a book," the young man said. And then, I can't be sure, but he might have winked.

I and I were intrigued, and we let ourselves be led through a set of nondescript double doors and into a large, brightly lit and industrially furnished back room, a semi-public space that fairly thrummed with activity. We had to be waved in by a sort-of security guard, who merely looked us up and down before sending us along. Inside, there were dozens of people moving earnestly about, each engaged in some furiously important task or other. Some were dressed in the same style of slacks and polo shirt as our possibly winking young guide—the uniform of the museum support staff, apparently. Others were dressed as we were in jeans and T-shirts and flip-flops, indicating at first that they had no more business in this curious back room than we did.

Our helpful employee friend, who at last introduced himself as Brad, walked us to a small table where there were a number of forms strewn about. Golf pencils, too. We were supposed to fill out a request for information, he said, and one of his similarly shirted colleagues would take over from there. Iona quickly filled out one of the forms and handed it back to Brad, saying, "Now what?"

At the same time, I was meticulously filling out my own request, stalled for the moment on whether to take the macro view and ask for information on 1880s baseball in general, on the 1884 season in particular, or on the rise and fall of the Union Association; or to take the micro view and ask for somewhat more specific information on the St. Louis Maroons or Fred "Sure Shot" Dunlap.

(Also, I spent more than a little time grappling over the proper use of the terms *macro* and *micro*, which I had never before considered despite the fact that I'd cut-and-pasted enough press releases announcing midlist books from any number of Elder & Gold economist-authors.)

I mention my tentative approach only to show how it is that I'd never managed to get anywhere in my life to that point, and also to highlight the differences between myself and my firstborn child. Iona had simply scribbled Dunlap's name without giving it a thought, while I was mired in enough second and third and subsequent thoughts to cushion a great fall from a great height. She was good to go while I was stuck at the gate—another serviceable metaphor, this one for what was missing in my makeup, a piece of useful genetic coding that had somehow reached my daughter while bypassing me.

By the time I'd settled on a course of action, which coincided with my realizing that I had in fact been communicating with a Hall of Fame curator who might in connecting fact have been toiling in this very research facility at this very time, another Brad-looking fellow was returning to Iona with a manila file folder and a pair of white cotton gloves. I set my own request form aside and wandered over to Iona to offer a small piece of parenting. I leaned in behind her and whispered, "Ask him what the gloves are for."

She turned and flashed me a look somewhere between exasperation and pretending to have no idea who I was or why I was talking to her. She did not ask, of course. Instead, she plucked the proffered gloves and began to fit her fingers into one and then the other as she turned to me and said playfully, teasingly, "They're for my elbows, Dad."

The Hall of Fame fellow, sensing my confusion and my apparent inability to express it clearly, seemed to want to help. He said, "Fingerprints." And then for my benefit, "We're dealing with original documents."

The original document that appeared to be the prize in Iona's folder was a handwritten letter drafted on onionskin paper, dated September 30, 1974.

Here's what it said:

Dear Mr. Simenic:

> You directed the enclosed questionnaire to my brother, Norbert A. Dundon, who died in 1962. His widow forwarded it to me and I am pleased to comply with your request to fill it out to the best of my ability.
>
> My father came to Pittsburgh as a young man and married my mother in 1898. They had two sons and two daughters; one daughter died in infancy and both my brothers passed away in the 1960s.
>
> Both my brothers played baseball in the minor leagues (which ones I do not recall). They were well known as good ballplayers on the north side of Pittsburgh. In fact, brother Norb coached the Little Leaguers for quite a few seasons.
>
> Hope the above will be of some assistance in compiling data on my father as a former Major Leaguer!

Sincerely,
Roma E. Anderson

Let us be clear: I am certainly no mystery writer, and I acknowledge that whatever storytelling gifts I might possess in terms of building suspense or developing plot points have not come into play in these pages. There has been no need, I do not believe, because I am only interested in offering a truthful report. I do not wish to embellish any of the details, or place false emphasis on one turn or another, or deploy any narrative tricks to foreshadow or back-peddle or otherwise highlight a significant turn of events, and so I must state straight off that this letter would very quickly prove to be a red herring.

There: I've given away the ending of this brief episode, but so be it; the letter added nothing to our search for Frederick C. Dunlap.

For a brief few moments, though, it pointed us in all kinds of wrong directions—endlessly interesting directions to us at the time, but hopelessly wrong in the end. The letter had simply been misfiled, we soon enough determined, which in retrospect made sense. The names Dundon and Dunlap were close enough alphabetically on the all-time list of former Major Leaguers to explain away such a small human error, even as the inadvertent appearance of this one letter in the manila file folder Iona held in her white-gloved hands set off a kind of frenzy.

Consider: For months now—nearly a year—we'd been grabbing at the specter of Frederick C. Dunlap as if our lives depended on it, hungry for whatever scraps of information we could attach to his life and times. We'd had little to go on, even with a small, months-ago assist from the curator whose name I had apparently forgotten, but had somehow patched together a story that seemed to correspond with our sense of the man sportswriters called Sure Shot and the reasons he might have alighted in our thinking. And now, possibly, there were whole new elements to layer in. A wife . . . four children, two who'd gone on to become ballplayers themselves . . . one who'd been alive as recently as 1974, just twenty-five years earlier! . . . it was all a bit breathtaking, and quite a lot for the two of us to contemplate just then.

Did Sure Shot have a daughter who might still be alive? Grandchildren? We were giddy with possibilities, although the giddiness fell away soon enough. All along, we'd been operating on the morsels of information we'd managed to collect on our own, which had left us thinking Dunlap had died alone in Philadelphia in 1902—hardly enough time to have met and married Roma E. Anderson's mother in Pittsburgh in 1898 and fathered four children and then to have been erased from their lives by the time of his death. The math, together with the sequence of events detailed in the letter, didn't correspond to what we already knew, but it didn't occur to us to question any of it. To question the Hall of Fame would have been to question baseball itself, so we had no choice but to take this onionskin document on faith.

I keep a clear memory of my Iona in that brightly lit back room, pointing a white cotton finger to the alarmingly red hair at her right temple and scratching, scratching, scratching—saying, "What the..." over and over, each time swallowing up the expletive she knew would coax another one of my chidings. It was enough to let it pass her lips unspoken, she must have thought.

And it was, it surely was.

Our confusion set in motion a slight scramble for corroborating bits and pieces from Dunlap's life once it occurred to us we might as well take full advantage of the resources at hand. Regrettably, there were none. The file folder contained original and Xeroxed copies of old-time newspapers, a death certificate, some badly photocopied pages from relevant reference manuals, but nothing to illuminate the connection our Sure Shot might have shared with Roma E. Anderson. The rest of the research library offered up no clues we could recognize.

It wasn't until we'd returned home from our adventure that the connection came clear—or, I should say, the *lack* of connection. Another few keystrokes online revealed that the letter in Dunlap's file had been sent to a man named Joe Simenic, an armchair baseball historian who at one point was trying to fill in the margins on the backstories of hundreds of obscure ballplayers. The Croatian-born Simenic, one of the founders of the Society for American Baseball

Research (SABR), was well-known among researchers of the game, but not at all to me, as he would have likely remained if Iona hadn't looked him up in the Hall of Fame database.

Still, even with this essential piece of information on Simenic, it did not occur to us that Roma E. Anderson's father and Frederick C. Dunlap were not one and the same—not yet, anyway, until we thought (somewhat belatedly, I'll admit) to see what we could find about Norbert A. Dundon. Here again, there wasn't much, but the effort did lead us to a couple other ballplayers with the same surname, and it was at these crossroads that our confusion finally fell away. There was an Ed Dundon who had played in Dunlap's era, and for a compelling while he emerged in our sleuthing as the likely subject of the misfiled letter. And Ed Dundon came with his own compelling story: He was deaf, and he carried the unfortunate but not uncommon nickname of "Dummy"—which was also alphabetically close to one of Dunlap's nicknames.

Dunny, if you'd prefer...

(Another fine side note: When his playing career ended, Ed Dundon worked for a time as an umpire. According to one account, he might have been the first deaf person to call a professional game, which these days would certainly bring forth an endless stream of taunts and name-calling if he happened to miss a call. I mean, it's one thing for an ump to be derided as blind as a bat, but to be deaf as a doorknob... well, that would be something.)

But then we noticed that the circumstances of Ed Dundon's death did not match what we could glean from the letter, so we set Dummy aside and turned instead to Gus Dundon, a middle infielder out of Columbus, Ohio, who played briefly for the Chicago White Sox in the early 1900s and who died—get this!—in Pittsburgh in 1940.

Surely, this was our man—which, of course, was neither here nor there nor anywhere in between, but it was in the going around and around on this that our man Dunlap managed once again to spring miraculously to life.

♦

One thing I learned on that trip to Cooperstown was that the Hall of Fame induction ceremony is not held on the grand steps leading to the museum, as I had long thought. For a time, this had indeed been the case, and the familiar threshold of baseball's shrine struck a fitting backdrop to the proceedings, but attendance had grown so significantly over the years the ceremony was moved to a large field a short walk from the Hall's main campus.

This was a slight inconvenience that nevertheless yielded a keepsake moment, and here it is—but first, a bit of setup. The small town of Cooperstown was choked with fans on the morning of the ceremony. Police estimates would later put the crowd total at approximately 50,000—a very large assemblage of people to somehow fit into the nooks and crannies of a quaint Adirondack village. We could only park on the way, way outskirts, where we were made to board a school shuttle bus for the short ride to the ceremony grounds. From there, we joined a sea of baseball fans marching along a wooded path. It was like a parade! An exodus! No, there weren't 50,000 of us on that path all at once, but it certainly felt that way when we were in its middle. People waved banners and placards, chanted hometown cheers, bumped and jostled each other in mostly pleasant ways. We were knitted together by the game. Every hundred yards or so, we'd pass a small table manned by memorabilia dealers selling souvenirs, local kids selling snacks and lemonade. In spots, there'd be lawn chairs set up on the sides of the path where folks would simply sit and take in the passing scene. Under one large oak tree, there were a couple dozen Red Sox fans handing out small bags of uncooked rice and encouraging those on the receiving end of the transaction to toss the rice into the air at some predetermined moment during the ceremony—an elaborate show of support for the disrespected candidacy of Boston slugger Jim Rice, who had repeatedly fallen short in the annual Hall of Fame voting. Music spilled from boom boxes—mostly "Centerfield," John Fogerty's "Put me in, coach!" anthem from a bunch of years ago. It was disorienting to walk along with this festive crowd and be met every few paces by the same damn song, coming in and out of our hearing at odd points in the refrain—as if the song were being broadcast on an endless loop with ticks and doo-dads built into the playback in such a way that the message of the song had somehow metastasized, folded in on itself.

We're born again, there's new grass on the field . . .

At some point on this lovely march (here's the keepsake moment!), Iona's hand slipped to her side in such a way that it brushed against mine, but instead of flinching or pulling away as any other pierced teenager might have done, she left our hands to linger and dwell and touch. Then—unaccountably, wonderfully—she took my hand and held it, and we continued to walk in this way for the next while, she without a thought (I imagined) and me with a big fat bunch of them, most having to do with the seepage of time and certainty from our lives. I must admit, this was a surprising turn, and even as I relished it I allowed myself to take it in from an outside perspective. The picture that came back was a kind of balm: a father and daughter, just, scratching at the edges of baseball history, stuck on a confusing piece of common ground, joined inextricably by a love of the game, a determination to hold fast to whatever it was we were leaving behind.

I cannot now recall the moment when we finally let go of each other. I cannot say if it was me who released Iona's hand or Iona who released mine, or if some sudden situation arose wherein one or the other of us required the use of two hands. It does not matter, I have at last decided. We could not hold hands forever. We could only come together for this short while and then continue. Here again, as I set these reminiscences to paper, I can see in our actions the stuff of our lives coming undone: We could walk the same path for a time, and then we could not, and this is just the way of things between a parent and a child.

Oh, and here is another small exchange I have banked to memory. At some point along our march to these proceedings, we happened past a vendor selling nuts. Two vendors, actually—a man and a woman who looked to be husband and wife, dressed in the heavy flannels of old-time ballplayers. He wore an old Chicago White Sox uniform that seemed to have been modeled on those from the Black Sox era; she wore a nondescript jersey atop a maroon skirt in the style I'd lately come to recognize as dating to the All-American Girls Professional Baseball League of the 1940s. And they weren't just selling peanuts, these two. No, there were nuts of every kind: chestnuts, walnuts, almonds, cashews—some of them glazed and sugared and warmed like we'd find them on the pushcarts of Manhattan during winter months.

For whatever reason, I was drawn to these vendors, so I wandered over to them, and Iona fell in step behind me. They were doing a brisk business, it turned out, so we were made to wait a few long moments, and in those few long moments I caught myself staring at Iona's reflection in the polished stainless steel of the vendor's cart. We did not speak, each of us lost in our own thoughts, and as far as I could tell (and near as I can determine looking back now on this small exchange), Iona had no way to know that I was watching her, considering her. And what I was watching, considering, was the way she was watching and considering me. For the first time since our little Rolen incident, I saw myself as I must have appeared. I caught a look of concern and devotion on my daughter's face that seemed to want to break my heart. All along, all this time, I'd allowed myself to move about in the disorienting place I'd made for myself knowing that whatever might fall apart or fall away on the back of this Dunlap delusion, there would be Iona at my side. It was as sure as sunlight. And here she was, at my side, with a look that suggested she could not think what to make of me . . . what to make of *this*. It's possible I was reading too much into it, this look. It's possible Iona's expression was distorted by the way her reflection bounced from the dinks and dents of the cart's steel edges. It's possible she wasn't even thinking of me as we stood there waiting our turn. But I don't think so. No. Instead, I've come to believe that this was the look of my Iona in full. This was my cartoon-haired tomboy baby girl at bottom. She was with me on this adventure—and yet somewhere deep down, in the places that only appear to us in reflection, the places we could not get to on our own, I stood beside her as a curiosity, a wonder, a worry. She was her mother's daughter after all.

These few long moments passed eventually, and yet they stayed with me. Iona, she stayed with me, and even though I never lost the weight of her resolve, her conviction, there was now a kind of fissure beneath it—a sure, certain crack in the rock-solid certainty of her days. It was as if she could not stand by and watch me come undone. She could only will me back to whole.

◆

The ceremony itself yielded nothing we could add to our Dunlap quest. The sun baked hot as we waited for the inductees to take their places on the stage. Patti LuPone sang the national anthem—and, in a nod to Orlando Cepeda, the Puerto Rican anthem was sung as well. Texas Governor George W. Bush was there. So were Ted Williams, Bob Feller, Hank Aaron, Willie Mays—thirty-nine Hall of Famers in all, the most ever gathered for one of these affairs, and Iona and I scanned the crowd for a man sporting a waistcoat or a dandy cane, for a wisp of moment that did not quite fit.

Frank Selee was appropriately honored and commemorated in turn, but as I'd suspected, there was not a single living soul among that throng of reverential baseball fans who'd ever met the man, let alone suited up with him on the same field of play—at least, not a one who took the moment to reveal himself, herself, itself. There was no ghost of Fred Dunlap. There was, however, one piece of connective tissue, which Iona fisted from the pockets of her too-tight, too-torn jeans—a career stat sheet belonging to an old-time ballplayer I'd never heard of named William Walter Veach, a first baseman and pitcher whose nothing-special career aligned with Fred Dunlap's on the 1890 Pittsburgh squad, where it might have aligned with Frank Selee's as well. Iona had apparently stumbled upon Veach's name in the Hall of Fame library the day before and made a photocopy of his entry in the record books, for reasons I could not at first understand. There was nothing in this guy's stat line to make him stand out in any way—a career .215 batting average, with three home runs, and a lifetime record on the mound of just 3—10 in 13 starts. And yet Iona unfolded this sheet and handed it over to me with grand importance, like it held some long-ago secret.

I looked it over and over, up and down, and could not see any relevance to our man Dunlap. There was nothing to it that I could see, and after looking and looking and considering and considering, I handed the sheet back to Iona with a puzzled look. I now knew Veach's percentages, the statistical droppings of his career. I knew that he stood over six feet tall and hailed from Indianapolis, but I could not attach any of these random details to the lives and legends we'd been seeking on this open pasture.

Iona read my confusion—in fact, she'd probably anticipated it, and in response she simply pointed to the heading on the stat sheet. "The name, Dad," she said. "Check out his name."

So I did—and, still, I had no idea.

"William Walter Veach," I said uselessly. Announcing the man's name did nothing to clear up the matter, so I shrugged.

"His *nick*name," Iona tried again. "Check it out."

Sure enough, the man's nickname smiled back at me: "Peek-A-Boo."

I did not yet know where Iona was going with this, but I had to smile at the name. It fit neatly beside a century of great baseball handles: Peanuts Lowrey, Buttercup Dickerson, Cool Papa Bell, Steamer Flanagan, Three Finger Brown, Catfish Hunter, Moonlight Graham, and on and on.

Peek-A-Boo Veach—what's not to like about *that*?

"Come on, Dad," Iona said. "Think!"

I tried to imagine the sequence of events Veach might have set in motion to have left the hanging of such as this on such as him, and then I tried to think how this minor old-time ballplayer from another century might have rubbed up against Dunlap—or Selee, for that matter.

"Sorry, I," I finally said, "but I think I need to buy a vowel."

(Ah, one small detail I've neglected to mention: Whenever Nell worked an evening shift, the girls and I would watch *Wheel of Fortune* over dinner, and so the need to buy a vowel had become acceptable shorthand in our house for utter, confounding confusion—a tamer version of the "What the . . ." Iona had uttered back in the Hall of Fame research library.)

"Peek-A-Boo," she said, emphatically. "Like how things are with Sure Shot. The guy's his teammate, right? Probably played against Selee, too. Here we are in Cooperstown looking for some sign, some vision, something, and the guy's name just breaks it down."

"Meaning?" I tried.

"Meaning, you know, peekaboo," she said. "Meaning, now you see him, now you don't."

Ten
GRAND SINGLE

This next turn was something.

To be clear, in purely baseball terms, it was something. In terms of everything else . . . well, I'll leave it to the reader to decide.

It was a Sunday night in mid-October, Shea Stadium, fifth game of the National League Championship Series. New York Mets versus the Atlanta Braves. Our Mets were trailing in the series, three games to one, after losing the first three to start things off, while Frank Selee's Braves (what was left of them, anyway, almost a full century after he'd managed his last game) were looking to avoid an epic collapse, since no team in the rich history of baseball had ever come back from a three-game deficit in a best-of-seven post-season series.

These details did not much matter—except, of course, to those of us who cared about such things, those of us who saw the very spine of baseball history in every season, every game, every pitch . . .

It was all connected, all of a piece, all at once.

Somehow, Nell had wrangled a set of four tickets from one of the doctors at the hospital—the chief of surgery, no less. The guy knew she was a Mets fan, and she'd performed some heroic deed or other above and beyond her already considerable call of duty, so he wanted to show his appreciation. (Plus, Nell surmised, the chief of surgery, himself a diehard, was away at a conference, and he must have wanted to put his tickets to good and cheerleading use.) The seats were in the upper reaches of the upper deck—but, as I have previously indicated, such ordinary seats were surely meant for us ordinary types. Nell was so grateful for the gesture she couldn't even bring herself to remind the doctor's administrative secretary who'd made the arrangements that we were a family of *five*—that she had three children and that there was no way she could take one or two without the other one or two. Nellie wasn't about to give up her own seat, of course, and despite the tensions and uncertainty between us she wasn't about to give up mine, either, which left us in the fat middle of a game of musical chairs.

"It won't be a problem," I announced the night before the game with a confidence I hardly recognized. Up until this point, the tickets had only been a prospect, but once the Mets squeezed out a 3—2 victory in game four, thereby forcing a game five, we were put on notice. In truth, I had no idea that finding an extra ticket would not be a problem, but it was something to say.

(Also in truth, I could not imagine a sequence of events to keep our little family from heading out to the stadium en masse, to reach back for something we had lost, something we had known all along, something we might know again. Would we find a way to make it work? Hell yes, we'd find a way to make it work.)

"What does that mean, Felb?" Nell quite reasonably wanted to know.

"It means we'll find another ticket," I said.

"Like, from a scalper?" Iona piped in.

"Maybe," I said. "Or maybe we'll find some big-hearted someone with an extra ticket."

"What, one of us will sit on the other side of the stadium?" Nell said.

"Doesn't matter where the extra seat is," I explained. "Sally and Patsy can take turns on our laps."

We went back and forth on this for longer than was probably necessary, but Nellie wanted to consider every contingency. She was a by-the-book sort of girl, my Nell, so she had a bunch of questions. How much were we prepared to pay for the extra ticket? (Two hundred dollars, I suggested, considering that the first four seats had been a gift and that this was not an unreasonable number for taking a family of five to a playoff game—more than we could afford, perhaps, but still not unreasonable.) What would happen if the ticket we bought turned out to be counterfeit? (Well, then we'd be right back where we started—less the two hundred dollars, of course.) What if we couldn't find an extra ticket, after all? (I would send Nellie and the girls inside, find a sports bar near the stadium and meet them afterward.)

And so on.

Realize, it never quite got to where Nell and I actually agreed that this was the course we would take, but once I set it out and she ran out of questions, the idea gained its own momentum, and so it was decided: We would go as a family and hope for the best.

Alongside this *hoping for the best* part, I lay awake most of the night before the game thinking how to reach past the gulf that now separated us and pull myself close to Nellie's sleeping form. She'd been a disagreeable, restless sleeper even when things had been strong between us, never one for an unsanctioned cuddle or spontaneous bit of spooning, but now with this Dunlap business I was ever more mindful of my place in our bed. On most nights, I found reasons to fall asleep on the couch or stayed up late in the living room pretending to watch some West Coast ball game or other, but on this night I'd taken my place before Nellie had finished up in the kitchen, in the bathroom, and as she slipped into bed she seemed not to mind. She turned her rump to me, stuffed one pillow beneath her head and flattened another on top of it—making herself what I used to call, in easier times, a fine Nellie sandwich.

I wanted desperately to say something, but I couldn't even buy a vowel.

Finally, after about a million years, Nellie said, "The girls are excited, Felb," in the thick, soft voice she used when she was falling off to sleep—a voice I'd once thought would be the last I'd hear on this earthly plane. And as she rustled her rump into place a final time, completing the nest she made each night, settling in, I knew there was nothing I could say in answer. She was gone to me—for this night, anyway. Just gone. And yet I lay there beside her, careful not to move or twitch or breathe too, too loudly, fearful that I would rouse my disagreeable, restless wife and upset this small détente, this sweet point of pause, reaching across our long history for another time when I might have moved to her in sleep with a happy result. Frankly, there weren't too many of those moments I could look back on for reference, for with Nellie it had always been an intimacy on her terms—here again, even in easier times. She did not like to be touched, unless she wanted to be touched.

In this way, we passed what might have been an interminable night, were it not for the endless loop of possibility it seemed to hold, if only for me. For Nellie, who'd drifted off straightaway, it was simply another stretch of hours to be gotten past. For me, it was the sum of what our lives had become, an agonizing crawl to no discernible end. I was caught between thinking these long hours would never pass—dreading them, even!—and hoping I might put off daylight just a little while longer.

In darkness, in bed, I could imagine the two of us careening through this messy life together, all over again.

◆

The morning of the game, I sat at the kitchen table with several sheets of oak tag and some colorful markers and wrote up a sign to help with our appeal. Sally and Patsy joined me, making signs of their own—Patsy's an image-driven effort that featured a one-eyed snowman wearing a ball cap. (Also a bright-yellow sun, dooming the one-eyed snowman). Sally's effort was a straightforward "Let's Go Mets!" bulletin with an adorably drawn baseball for an apostrophe, and a bubble-lettered exclamation point for emphasis. When we were finished I curled up these few sheets of oak tag in a long tube and slip-rolled a couple rubber bands around them.

Iona and Nell didn't participate in these preparations—Iona because she probably thought herself too old, too cool to make an art project with her sisters; Nellie because she had been disinclined of late to encourage me in any endeavor that wasn't rooted in deep, deep seriousness. Still, I remembered a time when all five of us would go through these motions together. We'd make a game of it. We'd spread out around the apartment and cover our work so no one could see, and then we'd surprise each other with our efforts when we got to the stadium.

Once, around the time of her third or fourth ear piercing, Iona sat with her poster rolled up at her feet for almost an entire game, waiting on some moment or other to justify its unfurling, and after the Mets held on to win by a run despite a shaky bullpen effort, that moment still had not come around.

"Your poster, I," I said as we stood to leave. "You didn't get to hold it up."

"No," she said. "But that's okay. We won, right?"

"Yes," I said. "We won."

What startled me about this one moment, and what's stayed with me enough to write about it here, was that Iona simply stabbed the rolled-up poster into the mouth of a garbage bin as she went to the bathroom with her mother and sisters on the way out of the stadium. I looked on and couldn't understand how this intriguing child could go to the trouble of decorating a piece of oak tag with a message to rally her favorite players without at least sharing it with the rest of us, without maybe holding onto it for some other game, and for a long beat I weighed the pros and cons of digging the thing from the trash and peeking at what my daughter had drawn against the notions of betraying Iona's trust and going against her apparent wishes. The former won out, I'm afraid, and I pulled the poster from the bin like some once and future king pulling a sword from a stone, slid the rubber band along its length and spread the poster out for a quick look.

Here's what Iona wrote—a message to Mets manager Bobby Valentine:

BOBBY V: THE FELB FAMILY UNDERSTANDS YOUR DECISION TO PINCH-HIT FOR OUR FAVORITE PLAYER. WE'RE SORRY IT DIDN'T WORK OUT.

It was a heart-melting moment—and now, just a few years later, Iona appeared to have set aside the innocence and sweetness of that not-too-long-ago afternoon in a way that left me thinking there would come a time not too long in the future when she would have no use for these aspects of character.

What I wouldn't have given to take that little girl to another ballgame.

◆

We piled onto the 7 train at Grand Central Station. Nellie and the girls were dressed smartly in the Rey Ordonez T-shirts I'd picked up that afternoon in the sale bin at Model's—confirming that the Cuban shortstop was perhaps more popular in our tiny household than he was in the New York metropolitan area. (I sported the Tom Seaver jersey I almost always wore to Mets games.) The idea was to head to the stadium early to give us plenty of time to scout for a ticket. Already, three hours before game time, the train was packed with Shea-goers, and as we disembarked in Flushing and pressed through the turnstiles by the caged subway rotunda in the right-field parking lot, we were swallowed up by a festive, boisterous crowd. If I hadn't been preoccupied with the thought of securing that fifth ticket, it would have been a festive, boisterous moment in my head as well.

I went to work at once. I lifted Patsy onto my shoulders—the bottom hem of her one-size-fits-most Ordonez T-shirt stretching all the way to her knees, making it somewhat difficult for her to wrap her little legs around the neck of her dear old dad—and unrolled the poster I'd made to advertise our plight. Then I told Patsy to hold it up over her head.

Here's what it said:

HELP! I PROMISED MY DADDY I'D TAKE HIM TO HIS FIRST PLAYOFF GAME.

Nellie took one look and tried not to smile, and as she did it occurred to me I hadn't seen that smile for most of the past year.

"Cute, Felb," she said.

And it was, I had to admit—once again, *I* as in Iona and me. "Irony, Dad," Iona said, also trying not to smile. "Nice."

Sally was probably too young to get the half-joke, and Patsy was just learning to read, so they had no opinion on it, except Patsy seemed to like that I'd used the Mets colors.

(Speaking of the Mets colors, I would be remiss as a reporter—

and, arguably, a shade self-serving as a parent—if I failed to mention that Iona had dyed the hair on each side of her head a hometown shade of blue and orange, which I supposed was her angsty teenage answer to making those oak tag posters with her sisters. She went with blue on one side, orange on the other, woven together in a braided ponytail that spilled from the opening of the by-now off-white Mr. Met ball cap she'd worn to Shea for as long as either one of us could remember—her sugary nod to tradition to match my well-worn Seaver jersey.)

Next, I found a large boulder that had been industrially landscaped into the pavement, on which Nellie and the older girls could sit while Patsy and I walked around to see if we could shake an extra ticket from the crowd.

"Wait here," I said to Nell. "We'll be right back."

Off we went against the moving current of fans heading for the stadium gates, so they could read our sign and take in the full effect. We collected a few smiles and stood on the receiving end of a good amount of pointing and cheerful noticing, and we even posed for a picture or two . . . and yet no one offered up a ticket. A few people shrugged and held out their hands, palms up, as if to indicate they would happily give up a ticket if they had one to spare. At one point, I realized we had circumnavigated the entire stadium and were about to start our second lap, but instead of despairing I was fueled by the looks of joyful surprise and the gladdened expressions that came back at us from the fans on their way in to the game. Plus, on each pass, the crowd seemed to thicken, so I made the calculation that our cute piece of begging was being seen by more and more people each time around—and that each time we were soliciting a whole new batch of people.

I kept telling myself something would turn up on the next pass.

I was caught between hoping for the best and bracing for the worst—the story of my life, it was now coming clear. The closer we got to game time, I realized, the more likely we'd encounter a late-arriving ticket-holder about to give up on a last-minute no-show. And yet I also realized that the closer we got to game time, the more likely time would run out on us.

Finally, at the end of our third time around the stadium's perimeter, we noticed Sally and Nellie standing on the boulder where we'd left them, waving their arms frantically. Iona, I saw as I approached, sat sullenly on the rock, facing away as if hoping no one would notice that she was wearing the same shirt and looking a whole lot like these other two. Nellie appeared to be motioning us over to them, so we cut through the crowd at a new angle and did just that.

"You'll never believe it," Nellie gasped when we finally reached her. I could not recall the last time I'd seen her so excited.

"Daddy, Daddy," Sally said, hop-skipping from the boulder to the ground at my feet. "There were these nice, nice people. The lady was sick but Mommy made her better."

Apparently, Nellie and the girls had shared their rock for a long few moments with an elderly woman who had begun to feel faint on her way into the stadium. The woman needed a place to sit, so Nellie shooed Iona and Sally away to make some room. Nellie also took it on herself to give the woman a bottle of water and to take her pulse. She didn't mention she was a nurse, I don't think, but she didn't have to, because if there's one thing I've learned about my Nursenel it's that she wears what she does on her sleeve. She takes care. And she puts it out there that she knows what she's doing when it comes to how the body works and how it sometimes doesn't.

Soon, the woman started to feel a little bit better, but together with her husband decided that it no longer made sense to go to the game, and once they stood and voiced their decision Nellie asked if she could buy one of their tickets at face value.

Well, these good people were so appreciative of the care and concern offered up by Nellie—and, to a lesser degree, by Iona and Sally—that they refused to take any money. In fact, they wanted to give Nellie *both* tickets, but Nellie insisted we were only in need of one.

"You can probably sell the other one for a lot of money," Iona offered, and then she backed into a half-joke of her own for her mother's benefit. She said, "There's this guy in a Seaver jersey walking around and around. He's like practically begging for a ticket."

Nell told me later that she thought for a moment this would cause the couple to rethink their impulsive kindness and make some excuse about deciding to keep their tickets after all, but they were good to their word—and just like that, our fifth ticket came to us on the back of yet another windfall, one kindness on top of another, so we collected our things and made our way inside.

◆

The Mets jumped out to an early lead on a two-run first-inning home run. The Braves tied the game in the top of the fourth with back-to-back doubles and a single. And that was that—in fact, for the longest while, for another *ten* innings, for a whole other game and a little bit more besides, that was that.

Patsy fell asleep around the top of the sixth inning as the Braves loaded the bases on an error and a couple of walks. Sally followed in the seventh when the Braves loaded the bases again—suggesting by this small statistical sampling that my younger daughters were allergic to opposing team rallies. By eleven o'clock, even Nellie was flagging. She had to get up early the next morning for work, and we'd eaten our way through our tote bag of sandwiches and snacks, and the kids of course had school, and we were perched so far away from the action, huddled together with the other *ordinaries* in the up-high right-field stands, so it was around this time Nell started making noises about heading home. She made these noises knowing it was unthinkable to someone like me to leave a ballgame early. This was true even in meaningless, one-side games in the heat of summer, but it was especially true in an extra-inning post-season duel that seemed to want to stretch on and on until morning. I cannot believe, therefore, that Nellie truly wanted me to leave with her and help put the girls to bed, but at the same time I knew I had to at least make the argument against.

It turned out I didn't have to, because Iona weighed in soon enough—in her own best interests as well as mine. She said, "Mom, you can take Sally and Patsy and I'll stay with Dad. This is, like, too good to miss." She wasn't asking so much as she was making a pronouncement, stating the obvious, and as a kind of exclamation point she waved her right hand in the direction of the field down far, far below like a hostess on a television game show presenting a prize.

"Yes," I said, joining in, offering a hostess-y wave of my own hand. "It's, like, too good to miss."

I had to think this was the way Nellie expected the conversation might go, but she offered me a look of disappointment just the same, and as she climbed gingerly from our seats trying not to disturb little Patsy sleeping on her shoulder, she turned to Iona and made a sweet, small effort to brighten the sour mood she surely hadn't meant to leave in her wake. She nodded in my direction and said, "Don't keep him out too late."

Iona smiled. "Tell that to the Mets."

But, alas, the Mets did nothing to hasten our departure—and neither did the Braves. The two teams traded punches for another few innings, past midnight and on into the wee small hours, and things went on in this way for what felt like the longest while—a while that began to remind me of that record-seeming stalemate, the Rolen incident that had set this whole Dunlap business in motion.

I'll confess here that I started to flag as well in these late innings. My therapist, Dr. Belasco, had finally prevailed in getting me to consider medication—but only after backing down on her insistence that I take an antidepressant. She had some help in this, I'll allow, as Nellie took every opportunity to reinforce Dr. Belasco's new diagnosis—that I was simply delusional. For some reason, this was more acceptable to me, delusion over depression, so I was started on an antipsychotic medication called Haldol, which had been used for years in the treatment of schizophrenia and had lately been found effective in curbing delusional disorders such as the one Nell and Dr. Belasco had seemed to identify in me. In my case, it turned out, the medication was merely effective in making me tired—an allover malaise I couldn't seem to shake—and here I caught myself thinking I might not make it to two o'clock, which was where this game appeared headed.

As ever, I kept score. Or, to be precise: As ever, I *meant* to keep score, only it was not so easy in the middle innings while I was trying to also amuse a restless Sally and Patsy, and these extra innings didn't exactly transpose themselves tidily onto the page. In truth, my scorecard was a disaster. Soon, there was no place to record all those zeroes, all those pitching changes, but I kept at it in what ways I could.

Finally, top of the fifteenth, the Braves got a rally going against Dotel, the *ninth* Mets pitcher. (Nine pitchers! Who even knew their bullpen was so deep?) Dotel had struggled in his first two innings without letting up a run, and his struggles continued here. A single to left, a stolen base, a triple to center.

Trouble all around.

The crowd, which had been beaten down by the late hour, was now beaten down further. It was like the air had been slowly let out of the stadium as the Braves pushed across the go-ahead run, which left the Mets to crawl to bat in the bottom of the fifteenth down by a run, their season on the line. But then, before we fans could feel too, too deflated, the shortstop-turned-centerfielder Dunston opened up our half of the inning with a single to center and promptly stole second—putting the tying run in scoring position with nobody out.

(Dunston, whose entry appeared on the same pages ripped from *The Baseball Encyclopedia* as our man Dunlap's—as did the entries for the misfiled Gus and Ed Dundon, who had earlier claimed their own separate links to "Sure Shot" Fred, however inadvertently.)

This Dunston single was a welcome turn, and on the back of it the mood of the ballpark lifted, and then it lifted further when the workmanlike pinch-hitter Franco walked on a full count.

First and second, nobody out.

That brought up the hard-hitting second baseman, Alfonzo, a fan favorite, who neatly sacrificed the runners to second and third—again calling to mind that doubleheader at Veterans Stadium, when I was similarly seated in a faraway, highaway row debating the merits of the sacrifice with the man I would come to know as Frederick C. Dunlap.

You only get but three outs. What mudsill gives one away?

Runners on second and third, one out.

Olerud, the sweet-fielding first baseman with the lovely arcing swing, was intentionally walked to fill the bases, at which point the speedster Cedeño came on to pinch-run for Franco on second, representing the winning run.

Bases loaded, one out.

Next, the Mets' thick-necked, thick-armed catcher, Pratt, strode to the plate and eked out a walk, tying the game in this tired, painstaking way which nevertheless sent the still-patient crowd into a brand of pandemonium I had never before seen. We were all jumping up and down like we had just invented the art of jumping up and down, and the stadium itself seemed to want to join in—oh, was that place pulsing!

I could not recall a moment when a base on balls had let loose such a wild rumpus among the Mets faithful, and yet I realize now that we'd been whipped into this sudden frenzy by the faintest whiff of a rally. A single, a walk, a sacrifice, a walk . . . it didn't exactly add up to a thundering display—and, indeed, once the initial excitement of the walk to Pratt began to ebb, I noticed yet another shift in the mood of the crowd. Where there was jubilation and chaos just a beat or so earlier, there was now also a vague feeling that we were on some new precipice or other. No, the game was no longer on the line, but there was a sense among those of us in the right-field upper deck, at least, that if our Mets left this one scoring threat to fizzle, we might never see another, and so we went from being up against it to breathing a shared sigh of relief to feeling an intense pressure to finish things off . . . all flowing from this one bases-loaded walk to force in the tying run.

The emotions of the crowd bounced and swayed on every turn and twist and slider just wide of the plate, and here we all leaned close as if we might will the game in our favor. I cannot overstate: There was a pulsating, undulating kind of excitement that seemed to wash over those of us still in the stands, and Iona and I were swept up in it. We were. It was a marvelous, transporting thing, but it was a *tension-filled* marvelous, transporting thing—of the sort that left me thinking these upper-right-field decks were not the best place to be at just this moment if you happened to be a Mets fan of a certain age with, say, a heart condition.

 We were standing, along with everyone else. We were holding out our caps, upside down, as if to catch the winning run as it fell from the night sky. We were shouting, almost in a primal way, without really having anything to contribute to the din but the sounds of our voices. It was a crazy, loopy chorus of *woo-hoos!* and *yee-hahs!* and *Let's go Metses!* and every last thing we could think to scream and whoop and holler, and as I screamed and whooped and hollered I caught a flash glimpse of my daughter—doing most of these same things, but in a completely unselfconscious way. Me, I was caught up in these celebratory rooting motions, but not so much that I lost sight of the context, the ways I was coaxed to behave. I saw myself as others must have seen me—as I wanted to be seen. Iona, though, her mad frenzy was pure, wild, total. She was outside herself, disconnected, and in that one flash moment I was filled with a kind of envy, jealousy, admiration . . . because underneath my jumping up and down and screaming and presenting to my Shea Stadium cohort in a manner consistent with my Shea Stadium cohort, there was some visceral adrenaline shot of emotion I suddenly realized I would never know.

 Whatever it was going on in those right-field stands, whatever it wasn't . . . I could only experience it in this once-removed way. I could only step outside myself and feel blessed that this—what?—this magical *something* had somehow found my daughter and spirited her away, away, away.

◆

 Robin Ventura was coming off his first season as the Mets third baseman. He'd joined the team as a free agent after establishing himself as a slick-fielding, clutch-hitting middle-of-the-lineup player with the Chicago White Sox—and to judge from his first-year numbers in New York, it had been a successful signing. He'd hit .301, with 32 homers and 120 runs batted in—in all, an MVP-type season that had helped to lift the Mets into the playoffs. He'd struggled so far in the post-season, but he wasn't a bad guy to send to the plate in this spot—still bases loaded, still one out.

And, in a nod to baseball symmetry, in an artless disassembling of the points of connection that simmer beneath this account, I cannot imagine a more fitting player to appear in just this way, in just this spot. Think of it, as I now thought of it: another Robin, attaching to our story a couple months after I'd toasted his semi-namesake, Robin Yount, at the Legend Valley Campground in Cooperstown. A second Boy Wonder, if you'll indulge this thread-tying narrator in a possibly meaningless Batman reference, however meaningful it might have appeared to me that night in Shea Stadium, as I noticed his name come around on my scorecard, announcing itself in my own hardly legible hand. Robin, the Boy Wonder . . . sidekick to the Dark Knight . . . keeper of his own uncertain flame . . . champion of all that is right and good and true . . .

For whatever reason—perhaps because I'd had a bit too much time on my hands as an unexceptionally introverted child, and because I'd chosen to spend a good deal of that time reading comic books and baseball novels—my mind leaped to this Batman connection the moment Ventura stepped from the on-deck circle.

The Boy Wonder: sideways, dyslexic, turned in on itself . . . twisted . . . it came out sounding like *Wonderboy*, the name of the prized bat swung by Roy Hobbs in "The Natural"—a dubious association I had made early on in these Dunlap musings. How about *that*? I thought. In my racing imagination, the pieces fit all too neatly, although in reality it was merely a series of coincidences that aligned themselves in just this fleeting moment, in just this way, offering a place to rest an idle mind—an idle mind, which as I have previously established, was already twisted and turned in on itself in ways I could not fathom.

Back to the game. A sacrifice fly, a seeing-eye single, a soft grounder to the right side, a suicide squeeze . . . there were any number of ways for Ventura to drive home the winning run, even as my racing imagination had me thinking he would end it with a gargantuan blast to the light stanchion in right field—a grand finale befitting this *supernatural* tale.

I was not alone in this melodramatic line of thought, it turned out, for as Ventura stepped from the on-deck circle and knocked the dirt from his cleats with the barrel of his bat, Iona turned to me and said, "This is it, Daddy-o."

Now, I don't mean to give the impression that my hard-to-figure daughter and I were so plugged in to this moment that we could predict what would happen next, that our *folie à deux* (if, indeed, that's what it was) had by now taken hold of our days, our dreams, because it took three more drumroll pronouncements from Iona's blue-and-orange-glossed lips before Ventura put the ball into play:

"This is it, Daddy-o."

"This is it, Daddy-o."

And finally, with the count at 2—1: "This is it, Daddy-o."

Yes, it was. *It*. All of *it*. Ventura got hold of a McGlinchy fastball and sent it soaring deep into the October night. The ball sailed past the fence in right center in the time it took for our hearts to fill our throats. We'd been standing and jumping up and down all along, and now we stood taller, jumped higher, clapped each other on the back with more reckless abandon than we might have thought possible.

Man, it was a thing to see!

The ball did not hit the light stanchion, of course. Ventura's bat did not burst into flames. There was no ominous-seeming background music to gather in richness and fullness as the ball cleared the fence, no slow-motion camera to record the flight of the ball as it pierced the night sky. No. But in my heart this was how it went. In my heart this was what the moment *weighed*, and as I let the full weight of it sink in and make a place for itself in my long-term memory, I reached for my scorecard to record it on the sheet as well.

Standing, cheering, I managed to trace a pencil line around the empty diamond along Ventura's box, but the standing and cheering got in the way soon enough. I'd hardly noticed this at the time, but I didn't finish the job. Normally, when a batter hits a home run, I fill in the diamond box with the edge of my pencil, indicating that he had come around to score. It's the way my father always kept score, the way I've always kept score, the way I've taught Iona to keep score, when she can be bothered, but here I dropped my pencil in the excitement. If I thought about it at all, just then, I must have figured I'd bend to retrieve the pencil once the excitement died down, once the moment had been shaded in for everyone else in the stadium. It was only a small piece of bookkeeping. It was not so important that it couldn't wait, so I turned my full attention to the standing and cheering all around.

Iona, having never before been so thoroughly surprised or delighted in her young life, did not quite know what to do with herself. At least, that's how it looked to me. The jumping up and down didn't quite do it, not for her. The screaming, I imagined, was only a small release. There were some random acts of hugging, too, but I didn't think Iona was too particular about this last. If you were close enough to touch, if you were overcome by the same set of emotions, you were entitled to a hug—but then so was the guy next to you in the Art Shamsky jersey, the lady two rows over with the clown wig, the couple on what looked to be a first date that would now be stitched to a lifelong memory if they found a way to stay together.

Even with these default stadium outlets for our bursting emotions, there was still an outpouring of energy about my delighted, transported daughter, and as I half-noticed the action on the field and half-noticed Iona rejoice at my side I saw her eyes brighten with a sudden, wonderful thought.

She acted on it straightaway. She reached exultantly for her baseball cap, the one she'd worn faithfully to every Mets game she'd been to since her first visit to Shea Stadium, and in one skillful sidearm motion she slung it by the brim across the railing two rows below us—a forearmed, Frisbee-type toss that called to mind the wind-milling artistry she'd shown on the mound for the Whedon Lady Warriors. I watched as the cap appeared to lift on a gust of wind and flutter off into the night sky, and at the same time I watched Iona, watching. I could not tell, just then, if Iona was bending some graduation-day ritual she might have seen in some coming-of-age movie or other, flinging her cap into the air as in a rite of passage, or if perhaps she'd been following hockey behind my back and had suddenly thought to mimic the tossing of hats onto the ice to commemorate a hat trick.

A relevant aside: One of the great mid-inning diversions at Shea had always been the crafting and launching of paper airplanes made from the torn pages of our official programs. At least, it was a favored pastime among a noticeable few. It was like a game within the game, the way upper-decked Mets fans chased the doldrums of a long season by sending paper airplanes across the vast expanse of stadium, and every few games there'd be a savvy paper-aeronautical engineer or origami whiz who could somehow fashion the perfectly weighted, perfectly designed vessel for a long and sustained journey, or another savvy someone who had mastered the fine art of the throw against just the right breath of wind and was able to get one to swirl and bow for hundreds of yards.

Something about Iona's flick-toss of her cherished Mr. Met cap left me thinking of these paper airplanes as the cheering lapsed into a kind of dull swath of white noise. It fell away into the deep background of what would happen next. My attention shifted to Iona's cap. Here again, it wasn't just me—it felt as if all eyes were now on this one white baseball cap, which sailed out across the sky above a section of airspace I took to correspond to the midpoint of the right-field foul line. Iona, too, seemed to stop with her jumping and clapping to watch the flight of her cap, which now dipped and spun like the feather bookmark from the credits of *Forrest Gump*. Remember? A gust of wind collects the feather and tosses it about while we're supposed to think about the arbitrary nature of things, the winds of change kicking up and sending our lives zigzagging in so many directions.

Now, thinking back on this long, sweet, weird moment, I cannot imagine it took more than a few seconds for the notion of tossing her hat to register in Iona's eyes, for her to grab it from her head and whip it like a slingshot into the air, for me to follow its harebrained flight— down, down, down toward the field. And in these same few seconds, I must confess, I completely forgot about the hero of this late hour, Ventura, who I learned later had been swept up in a giant bear hug by his teammate Pratt, who'd been just ahead of him on the base path, the two of them ending up in a pile of triumphant Mets—each with their own overflows of energy. I'd lost sight of them, lost all thought of them the moment Ventura touched the bag at first and made the turn toward second, the moment my own gaze shifted onto Iona and the setting free of her cap into the wilds of this baseball night.

Yes, it was only a few seconds, but in those few seconds I came to believe the rest of the world had fallen away and that I had only to follow the flight of this one baseball cap. And so I did. Iona did as well. All else was silent. All else was distant. Iona, though, she was quite near. Quiet, but near. She reached again for my hand—ah, how wonderful!—and together we held hands and watched as her cap was lifted and tossed out over the field, until it finally came to rest on a patch of infield dirt between first and second, just beyond the pile of Mets players who had swallowed up the Boy Wonder Ventura and kept him from rounding the bases. Cedeño and Olerud had come around to score, I now noticed as my eyes pulled back to take in the full picture, as the volume switched back on the scene, but Pratt and Ventura dusted themselves off and slapped at each other another time or two and left the field by way of first base.

None of the players on the field, none of the umpires, appeared to notice Iona's cap, which remained where it landed, and as the field slowly emptied of cameramen and umpires and grounds crew it made a curious tableau—an off-white cap, frayed by the years, resting in the kicked-around infield dirt like it belonged no place else.

There followed two significant developments—the first leading to a much-discussed ruling that would take its place in the chronicles of baseball history; the second, a hardly noticed grace note Iona and I took as a sign from Frederick C. Dunlap, who was surely with us on this grand night.

The first: It was determined after quite a lot of head-scratching and hand-wringing that Ventura would not be awarded a grand slam for his game-ending heroics. Already, the scoreboard had posted a final score of 7-3 and lit up in response to his bases-clearing blast. Already, old-time fans had begun to dutifully record the moment in their scorecards, shadowing the diamond alongside Ventura's name in pointless posterity. Already, the Shea Stadium organist had played a couple bars of the ubiquitous "Celebrate!"—sounding more like a parody of a church wedding than a tribute to KC and the Sunshine Band. But these turns had been premature. By rule, Ventura would have needed to complete his way around the bases for a home run to be properly recorded, so instead his game-winning hit went down as only a single. He had crossed first base, and pushed the winning run home, and this was where the game would end.

The scoreboard was corrected, the organist silenced—and, according to the official record, Ventura would remain stranded in the dirt between first and second for all of baseball eternity. He had ended the game with one swing, but he would never get the chance to finish his run around the bases, just as I would never get around to filling in the box on my scorecard, placing us yet again in a kind of fold on the continuum of our national pastime . . .

The longest stretch of time between a single happened thing and the next happened thing . . .

The news rained down on us by public address, and for a long few moments there was serious and sudden speculation among those of us remaining in our section of stands that Ventura and Pratt could return from the clubhouse and complete their turns around the bases and all would be right in our little baseball world, but then the chatter went another way entirely when it was reported on the portable radios in our vicinity that the ruling on the field would likely stand, and that it didn't much matter.

However, it mattered to me—and at first I could not think why. It was only a few beats later, following the *second* significant development, that it all came clear. And here it was: Off in the distance, flitting dreamily over the Mets bullpen in left field, there appeared another object in the night sky—out of nowhere, as if from the thin night air itself. Like Iona's cap, the object was slapped about by the wind, surfing the cross-currents of the stadium swirl. It made its way slowly across the outfield. I couldn't make it out at first, but as it approached, as it drifted, I raised my right hand to it—the hand that was still holding Iona's—and together we pointed and tried to follow the object's path. It was still unclear to either one of us what it was, exactly, just as it was unclear to either one of us if anyone else in the emptying stadium was seeing what we were seeing. Surely, no one was pointing. No one was staring. No one was tilting their eyes heavenward to follow the small, uncertain sweep of this small, uncertain thing.

And yet there it was.

It might have been a paper airplane, a wadded-up hot dog wrapper, another Mr. Met cap, a Gump-like feather . . . who could tell? Whatever it was, it held our gaze, and we followed its path as it appeared to spiral downward, as it hovered and shook and spun all the way to its soft fall onto the infield dirt. It might have taken a full minute for the object to be blown across the stadium and pressed to the ground, and it might have taken no time at all, but as it came to rest it revealed itself for what it was—a felt bowler, gray, looking unmistakably like the one Sure Shot had worn that night in the Philadelphias, that next afternoon on the train.

And—get this!—just as the man's hat seemed to settle itself into the dirt, there kicked up another firm gust of October wind, which in turn lifted the hat onto its brim and rolled it along in this way, like a dapper tumbleweed, until finally the hat was flipped over, right side up, and came to rest against the bill of Iona's Mr. Met cap.

◆

Iona's column from the Fall 1999 edition of *The Quartermaster*, the student newspaper of Hudson Preparatory, where Iona had started high school the previous month:

WHAT SUCKS ABOUT POST-SEASON BASEBALL
By Iona Felb

What sucks about post-season baseball is that it gets played on a knife edge. It doesn't forgive, it doesn't forget; it just hangs back and waits to see who screws up.

In post-season baseball, the margin for error is so paper-thin you might sneeze at just the wrong time, or forget to run the bases all the way around, and nobody will really care or even notice because everything is happening at, like, breakneck speed, and if you think to question it you might end up doing just that—breaking your neck.

What I mean by this is that your team can find a way to win in the most remarkable way, but there'll be no time for the remarkable stuff to register or sink in because you have to come right back out the next night and pull a whole other rabbit from a whole other hat. That's how it goes. If you don't find a new way to win, your season just might be over. Just like that, you could be done.

For some people, this is what post-season baseball is all about. I call these people *win-or-go-homers*, because those are pretty much your options. That's the knife edge part. It's one or the other, win or go home, but that's not the kind of baseball we're used to seeing. That's not the kind of baseball that gets you to the post-season in the first place—because, hey, over the course of a long season it's not so dramatic. You can stumble and there'll still be time to pick yourself up and go at it again. You can fall into a terrible slump and fight your way through it, and you can also go off on a tear and you'll still be far, far away from where you'll need to be at the end of the season. There are highs and lows but mostly it's a season of *in-betweens*.

What sucks about post-season baseball is that it stops rewarding the careful grind of forward progress. In the regular season, it's all about accumulating, building, growing. It's about getting it right more often than not. And if you can't quite get it right, you'll get another shot at it. And another. Things don't fall apart in any kind of sudden way, and they don't come together in any kind of sudden way, either. You can get lucky a time or two without having to feel like you need to stay lucky. You can win-or-keep-trying. That seems like a better deal, don't you think?

PART THREE

MARCH 2000

Eleven
TURN BACK THE CLOCK

Another winter, with nothing to show for it but a deepening chasm between the life I once knew and the one I was now living.

For some months, Nellie and I had been like strangers, although that word doesn't quite get to how things were with us. How could we be *strangers*, after all? We were connected, our lives everlastingly entangled, so it would be more accurate to call our state of affairs an estrangement, although even here we'd be off by a few shades. An estrangement suggests a mutual alienation, yes? A loss of affection, perhaps. A coming apart, certainly. Our arrangement felt to me somewhat *other*—like we had been sent off course and left longing for some slipstream to blow us back together.

If I had to bet my life on it, I would have stated with absolute faith and clarity that Nellie still loved me. Deep down, I knew she did. Oh yes, oh yes, oh yes she did. And yet the depths of her deep-down emotions had me worried. I'd piled on so many layers of strangeness and muddle she couldn't possibly burrow her way through to find the ways she once felt about me. How we were, what we might become ... it was all buried, pressed down by the heaviness of so much confusion and worry.

Essentially, we had been separated by my refusal to disavow or disremember or in any way distance myself from the specter of Frederick C. Dunlap, and by Nellie's refusal to accept it. This right here was the fault line of our cascading troubles. I might have been okay with this arrangement—to me, it was nothing more than an agreement to disagree, an instance to get past or set aside. Nellie, understandably, was not—to her, it was a kind of deal-breaker. Mostly, she was not okay with my sudden decision to stop taking my meds. I'd been on the antipsychotic Haldol and eventually an atypical antipsychotic known as Risperdal, which failed to shake me from my certainty regarding my admittedly odd encounter with this century-old ballplayer, succeeding only in making me logy and lethargic—

and, to be honest, resentful of Nellie and the social conventions that left me reaching for these medications in the first place.

As well, I started to think the meds were messing with my stomach in a big-time way, leaving me in a constant state of gastrointestinal agitation, bouncing back and forth between the shits and the plugs—Nellie's term for constipation. (For the record, Dr. Belasco insisted that my uncertain stomach had nothing at all to do with these medications—if anything, Risperdal was known to cause rapid weight gain in patients—but I was in and out of the bathroom so often during this period my colleagues at work must have assumed I had a coke problem, or a severe case of adult-onset lactose intolerance. Was there a connection here between my head and my gut? Who can say? But in my estimation, at least, the one followed from the other.)

It turned out that Risperdal left me feeling jittery and dry-mouthed and disoriented in entirely new ways. Also, *desultory*—a word I have just now looked up in my pocket dictionary to confirm it expresses my precise meaning. And so in my clearheaded moments, I allowed myself to rethink my position. Early on, as I have already stated, I had bent to Nellie's urging to consider therapy—and, soon after, to consider medication. Let me once again be clear on this: At the time, I would have agreed to anything Nellie asked of me regarding this Dunlap business; that's how eager I was to convince her I was sane and whole. The logic behind my acquiescence was soon lost on me, however, for who can lay any kind of reasonable claim to sanity and wholeness when they're pumped up on antipsychotics? When they're stuck seeing a shrink who treats them like an extra on the set of *One Flew Over the Cuckoo's Nest*? Alas, despite her affinity for the Brooklyn Dodgers and her willingness to accept the free books I collected for her from the Elder & Gold storeroom, Dr. Belasco had turned out to be rather unaccepting of my story—and not so subtly dismissive of my tale. But by this point I was so deeply committed to following Nellie's lead, I could see no way to re-establish control without sounding another set of alarms, so I couldn't step away from treatment entirely. I was caught. *Stuck*. Eventually, I persuaded Nellie to allow me to redirect my own care. I was aided in this last, in part, by a change in our health care coverage, which led me to an aggressively cheerful clinical psychologist who asked that I call him Dr. Steve, who didn't necessarily endorse my version of events on the night of the Rolen incident but at the same time didn't see the need to medicate me from my certainty.

This was a good and welcome thing—a chance for me to reclaim the aspects of character that had been flattened by my ever-changing antipsychotic cocktails. At long last.

With Dr. Steve, the goal of our therapy was to improve my general mood and outlook, to buttress my self-esteem, to refocus the quality of my relationships and help me to function as I had before this Dunlap business. Of course, if I can be completely honest with myself and my ordinary accomplishments, I must question just how well or fully or wholeheartedly I was functioning, but at least Dr. Steve was not out to disabuse me of what he continued to refer to as my delusion. Our goal, he said, was to help me find a place for it in my day-to-day—a far more agreeable outcome as far as this lowly middle-aged book publicist was concerned.

At some point, however, I began to tire of the tug and pull that passes between patient and therapist—specifically, the tug and pull between a patient dead-solid certain of his clear, sound mind and a therapist just as certain of the gaps in his patient's logic. I came to believe that Dr. Steve was humoring me, just. I came to see myself in his eyes, and to recognize that he was somehow sitting in judgment— and that I was somehow condensed in his estimation. And so, in a moment of what I took to be clear thinking and Nellie took to be another indication of my encroaching madness, I announced flatly that I was done with Dr. Steve—done with therapy or treatment of any kind.

Understand, I had been going through these motions to appease Nellie, who held to the belief that my Dunlap story could only be explained away as a mental-health issue. (Held to it like a lifeline!) And here I could no longer reduce myself in this way. In response, Nellie decided I was being stubborn, a petulant child clinging to a fantasy that had no place in our lives, and so for the next months we lived at cross purposes, in shifts. What Nellie could not make happen with reason and patience and pharmaceuticals, she instead hoped to achieve by shutting down. By pulling away. And it was not as if she was trying to freeze me out or force my hand. No. It was more likely that she could not think how to *be* around me, how to share a life with a man who insisted he was seeing ghosts. She arranged her schedule at work so that it no longer dovetailed with my own. We were rarely in the apartment together, with all three children. Our conversations were limited to logistics. We went through the motions of living together and nothing more. We were pleasant to each other, but only in a "please pass the butter" sort of way—meaning we only connected on the surface of things. As before, as ever, Nellie made most of the decisions regarding the comings and goings and doings of our daughters. She ran the household, even when I was the parent in charge. We continued to share the same bed, although Nellie's night shifts conspired to leave us sleeping separately more often than not. On school days, Nellie returned home in time to have breakfast with the girls, make their lunches, send them out the door. I was meant to follow, so I fell into the habit of walking Sally and Patsy to school after the three of us escorted Iona to the subway stop down the street for the short ride uptown to Hudson Prep.

Nellie would then crawl into our unmade bed and sleep until early afternoon, when she'd switch into after-school mode and get started on cleaning, shopping, homework . . . whatever needed to be done around the apartment.

She left instructions for dinner.

Weekends, we were scattered across the city. Between play dates and sleepovers and birthday parties and other choreographed activities, Nellie and I fetched and ferried our girls all over the damn place. We were in such constant agitated motion, there was hardly any time for us to even *think* about sitting still—all together, all at once—or pursuing some sort of family activity.

On Saturday nights, I usually fell asleep in front of the living room television, and then on Sundays we'd start the whole business back up again, our weeks going around and around in the tight circle Nellie had made for us—the ghost of Fred Dunlap continued to alight in my thinking, and I have to think that in some way my sweetsuffering wife was made to look upon him every time she caught herself looking at me, worrying over me, despite herself.

The cliché would be to write that we were like two ships passing in the night, only this does not get anywhere close to how things truly were. (How they *are*! Still!) And besides, there is room for only one ship in our relationship—our U.S.S. Nellie. I do not make this distinction with any rancor or regret. I am only stating the truth. In our household, in our marriage, Nellie is our mother ship. I am more like one of those lifeboats that travels along for the ride, suspended on board the main vessel by a crane, hovering above deck until needed. Probably, this was true even before my run-in with Sure Shot that summer in Philadelphia, but back then the differences in our roles had more to do with Nellie's strengths as a parent up against my relative shortcomings, while here it had mostly to do with the ways Nellie was keeping me from any of the heavy lifting. She could no longer trust me to advocate for my own children, she said, to consider their best interests, and yet we did not have the wherewithal for Nellie to run the show entirely, or for us to farm out any aspect of our parenting to some daycare provider or part-time nanny, all of which left Nellie believing she had no choice but to leave me alone with the children for these huge pockets of time and hope for the best. She'd say as much, and I'd take her point, but it killed me to have to see myself through Nellie's eyes. It killed me, what she thought I'd become.

And, mostly, it killed me that there was nothing left between us beyond the basic care and feeding of our children.

The silver lining to this setup was that Sally and Patsy were not plugged-in enough to register what it all might mean. At least, this was my hope. Oh, they noticed that things were different around the house, but only in their childish ways. Surely, they must have noticed how unlike myself I had been, flattened out by those medications. And yet there was no judgment attached to what they knew. They knew that Mommy worked—a lot, a lot—and that Daddy put them to bed, but this was where it ended for them. This was their new baseline. Iona, though, she got it. She got that her mother had set me aside—yes, that's probably the nicest, noblest way to put it. Like I'd been tucked away on a high shelf, a half-forgotten curio.

In this way, in my own home, I had become like Dunlap at the end of his days—overlooked.

Iona, my ghoulish poser, with more shock value to her wardrobe and demeanor than the entire freshman class at Hudson Prep, was in a difficult spot. She was caught between loving her delusional father so much that she had taken up my delusions as her own and siding with her stoic nurse of a mother, who only wanted to will her family back to whole. How does a child deal with such as this? For all her wiles and wisdom and weirdness, Iona was a child, after all, and here she'd been put on a kind of pivot point with no options but to lean one way or the other with the slightest turns in our broken household.

Through it all, Dunlap remained the elephant in the room. More so and ever more so. After a while, we no longer talked about him, much, although occasionally Iona and I would huddle to discuss some new tidbit she'd unearthed on the Union Association, or the Maroons, or the man himself. But even when his name wasn't on our lips, his spirit was in the air and all around. Despite our best efforts to set *him* aside as well, he was constantly considered—by Nellie, by me, by Iona. There was no overlooking him, I'm afraid. He followed me to work, even. Together with the various medications I'd been taking for the past year, and the nagging doubts I was made to shoulder at home, I had been left to tread water among my fellow publicists at Elder & Gold, to further distinguish myself by not distinguishing myself any further . . . as if I had ever really distinguished myself at all. Regrettably, I was passed over for a promotion within the publicity department that at another time might have been mine. There had been a few instances of me dropping some ball or other—missing a deadline on a press release, failing to arrange for a media escort to collect one of our brand-name novelists from the airport in Los Angeles and usher him to his interviews—but nothing so heinous or egregious that my job was ever in jeopardy, only my advancement. I was distracted in meetings, my head someplace else—or, more accurately, no place at all.

This was what my life looked like. This was what I'd become.

◆

Soon after I stopped seeing Dr. Steve, I found myself alone in the apartment with Iona. Sally and Patsy were off on play dates. Nellie was at the hospital. It was just the two of us for dinner. Nell had determined we were to eat leftovers—there was a slice of meatloaf and half a tin of her homemade spaghetti sauce we were meant to put to good use. But I had another idea. Nellie's meatloaf and spaghetti sauce are world-class, but I had my back up. As if from nowhere, I was come upon with the thought that I could take care of myself—at least when it came to my dinner plans. I had something to prove, I guess. Anyway, I'd decided I was tired of sleepwalking through the life I had made, doing what was expected of me, eating what I was told to eat, pushing the buttons I was expected to push. I hadn't realized I'd been thinking in this way, but here it was, and in this one small act of defiance—rejecting the meal Nellie had left for us—I suppose Iona saw something in me she couldn't quite place.

"Let's go a little crazy," I said to her as she peered into the fridge and began pulling the leftovers.

"Thought that's what you've been doing," she said back, deadpan—never missing a chance to needle me on the ways her mother had dismissed my behavior of the past year and more, on the ways the world looked back on my belief in all things Dunlap. On the ways, I sometimes feared, that Iona herself had been made to consider me.

"Good one, I," I said. "Put me in my place. Kick a Daddy-o when he's down." I was not so far gone—yet!—that I couldn't give as good as I was getting.

Iona re-fridged the meatloaf and turned to me and said, "Crazy, as in . . . ?"

And here is where I went off the rails a little bit. In just that moment, I couldn't think how to fill in the blanks, even over such a simple, nothing decision like what to have for dinner. Yes, it had been my idea to go rogue, to reject the plans Nellie had made for us and kick up a little dust, but now that I'd put it out there, I was without a next move. It was like a switch had been flipped and now for the life of me I could not have picked out my own clothes, parented my own children, chased my own dreams. I was paralyzed with indecision. There was spine enough for me to want to resist being told what to do, but not nearly enough for me to come up with something to do instead. And so I panicked—more accurately, I froze. I stood there in our shotgun kitchen unable to pull the trigger on a fully formed thought. My breathing became heavy. I started to sweat.

Iona could see I was struggling—and, of course, I could see how I must have appeared to her just then: lost . . . damaged . . . *off*. It tore at me to have to see myself reduced in this way in the eyes of my own child, and I suppose it must have torn at Iona too, to have to see me like this, and we stood there for an agonizing moment, neither one of us quite sure how to move past it.

Finally, Iona said, "Pizza? Chinese?" Our go-to takeout options when we ordered in.

Looking back, I cannot help but marvel at the composure my Iona put on display—here and all along—although I'm sure it was mostly a surface composure. It had to be, right? How does a child watch the unraveling of a parent and not become a little unraveled herself? Only I wasn't worrying over Iona's mind just then; I was too caught up in discovering my own. Oh, I was a hopeless, helpless wreck. Even when it was put to me plain, a multiple-choice quiz with no wrong answers, I couldn't say what it was I wanted, what it was I felt I was missing. Pizza or Chinese? How hard is *that*?

Iona couldn't begin to make sense of the way I'd seemed to come undone right there in the kitchen over nothing much at all. In the end, she found a way to steer me from the apartment to the street below. She grabbed my coat for me on the way out—there had been a dusting of snow the night before and the small, edged-in patches of dirt cut into the sidewalk every here and there were still dotted with white. The cragged sidewalks were slick with snowmelt. It was the time of year when people dressed their dogs in questionable cold-weather gear, and I remember stopping abruptly in a Columbus Avenue crosswalk to consider a peppy terrier wearing a Scotch plaid sweater vest as it approached, pulling on its leash.

"Come on, Dad," Iona said after a too-long beat. "You can't stand here in the middle of the street."

And with those words, whatever chokehold there had been on my ability to think clearly, to move about the planet as if I belonged here and no place else, to put one foot in front of the other with small steps that might take me somewhere worth going . . . it fell away.

I was myself again—close enough, anyway. And Iona, shaken finally, could only look on and wonder what the hell had just happened.

◆

Here is something: Despite the strain of these past months, despite the growing disconnect in our marriage, Nellie and I had never discussed the idea of divorce. Not with each other. Speaking personally, I'd never once considered it, although I could not be so sure the thought didn't cross Nellie's mind. A part of me—the biggest part!—hoped against hope that it did not, but surely, it had. Surely, it must have crossed back and forth and run all the way around through Nellie's thinking in one form or another, at one time or another, at all times and then some, and yet she refused to give it voice.

At least, not to me.

Why? Well, it was simply not a prospect; that's all. That is how I chose to see it. For all of her aching worry, for all of her doubts about my fitness as a parent and partner, Nellie could not bring herself to put an end to our time together. To *us*. Our marriage might have been on life support, barely ticking, but she would not pull the plug—and for this I was profoundly grateful. Oh, it was clear to me I'd been set aside, but not so way off to the side that I was out of the picture. Not to where Nellie could no longer see the points of connection linking me to Iona, to Sally, to Patsy. Still. Linking all of us together as a family. Still.

I belonged—as surely as I did not.

All along, Nellie might have been boundlessly confused, and worried sick, and all of that, but she was never ready to cut me loose. Set me aside, yes. Cut me loose, not so fast. Why? Perhaps because a part of her was clinging at first to the notion that the therapy might start to work, that the medications might kick in—and, later, that I might someday come around.

Basically, I'd gone from a front-row seat to a spot in the upper decks—far, far from home.

How's that for a dispiriting preamble to this next episode? Not exactly the most hopeful portrait, I'll admit, but I want to show how an unexpected turn—like, say, being visited by the ghost of an old-time ballplayer—can send a life spiraling in so many directions. And it's not just my life that was sent spiraling—it was the life of my family.

It was my entire world.

Still, I've just reread these past few paragraphs, and I feel I should apologize for setting such a *down* tone. From the opening pages, I've meant for this narrative to be an uplifting report of a transforming adventure, but as I reach this present juncture I see it has not come across this way at all. There has been little in the way of uplift that I can see, and the only transforming going on in these pages has been in the recounting of the changing shape of our family dynamic.

First I was plain, and then I was plain crazy.

And now? Oh, well . . . it is what it is, I suppose. And yet I believe it has been necessary for me to place these next moments in full and appropriate context, for as I set them to paper I start to think they might be the last such moments I'll share in this account.

Okay, then. Here is what may or may not have been the end to my Dunlap tale. It happened on a Saturday in Central Park—the first Saturday of spring, in fact. Nellie had assigned herself birthday duty, shuttling between a craft-painting party for one of Patsy's little friends on the Upper East Side and a somewhat more sophisticated bumper-bowling party—across town, off West 116th Street—for a boy in Sally's class who'd once bitten Sally on the arm so fiercely Nellie had to rush her to one of her emergency-room friends. This left me and Iona with a day to fill—our last Saturday before the Hudson Prep softball season kicked into full gear. Already, the coach had the girls to the field early that morning for some light stretching and soft tossing, but by the following week they'd be at it with two-a-day sessions and then doubleheaders on most weekend afternoons, so it occurred to me that my daughter and I should find something to do together.

Typically, Nellie would suggest impromptu outings for me and the girls. Street fairs, concerts, festivals, happenings . . . she'd clip articles or calendar announcements from *The New York Times* or *New York* magazine and set them on the mail table by the front door where she knew I'd see them. Or maybe there'd be an item circled on a folded-over newspaper she'd leave on the kitchen table, or a flier she might have collected on her travels . . . some bulletin she'd set out for me to discover on my own. But there were no prompts on this morning. There was nothing for us to go on but a whim, a bright sky and an empty chunk of hours before we were expected back at the other end of the afternoon, so I grabbed my mitt from the hall closet and suggested to Iona we head to the park for a catch.

One thing about my cartoon-haired, chain-festooned daughter: She was always up for a catch. Even at fifteen, figuring her way through the social minefield of her first year of high school, worrying where her cultivated affectations might fit among her new peer group, she'd drop whatever she was doing to toss the ball around. Nothing was more important, more pressing on her calendar. And so it was on this spring Saturday. Her face lit up with the idea—her sweet, sweet face, beneath all that Halloweenish makeup. She grabbed her gear bag by the front door and together we bounded the six flights of stairs to the lobby and broke toward the park.

To look at us gave no clue to the general state of unease that permeated our household: We were like any other father-daughter pair in upper Manhattan—well, any father and daughter who'd seen a ghost. We headed for a favorite spot in the North Meadow of Central Park that's always thrumming with activity—specifically, with *baseball*-related activity. There are a half-dozen softball fields, some in better shape than others, and another half-dozen full diamonds, with ninety-foot base paths and regulation mounds and rickety bleachers in assorted states of disrepair. We were in the habit of getting something to eat from one of the eclectic food trucks we'd pass along the way ("Gorilla Cheese!") and then scarfing down our lunch while watching a Media League softball game, or maybe a Broadway Show League game, and here we stumbled upon what was left of a late-morning contest between the casts of *The Lion King* and *Kiss Me, Kate*. The game was in its late stages when we arrived, and a young actor who was understudying the lead role of Simba had apparently put on a dazzling display at the plate for the *Lion King* side. It was something to see, we were told, and as the understudy took the field we could guess from the way he carried himself that he'd been a ballplayer once.

We finished our drinks and our grilled-cheese sandwiches just as this backup Simba managed to catch a soft liner to his glove side to end the game—an elegant, effortless stab!—and as the actors and stage hands gathered by home plate to congratulate each other and make their farewells before heading downtown to their respective matinees, Iona and I gathered our few things and continued on toward the northwest corner of the meadow, to a hardly used field we knew where we could stretch out our arms and really let fly. And, for a while, we did just that, but not before we kind of eased our way into it. Not before Iona pulled a cap from her gear bag and fitted it into place atop her head—in such a way that you could barely tell that the ponytail spilling from the back was an electric shade of green that would have looked more appropriate on a sucking candy. Not before she wiped some of the shock from the shocking pink lipstick she'd applied back in her room. Not before she carefully unplugged, unhinged, unspooled and variously undid her many bits and pieces of jewelry and accessories and placed them carefully in a small plastic case she carried just for this purpose.

(It used to be she'd leave her earrings in for a catch, but after she was clocked on the side of the head by an errant throw from one of her teammates, pressing a crescent-shaped scar to the cartilage above her left ear beneath the corresponding half-moon arc of costume studs she was in the habit of wearing at the time, she started taking these extra precautions. And yet, the wiping-away of her too-loud makeup wasn't a precaution so much as it was a preparation—a show of respect that had once been insisted upon by one of I's youth coaches and had since spilled into her own approach to the game. "There's no makeup in baseball," she used to say, bending the great Tom Hanks line from *A League of Their Own* to explain the shift in her presentation.)

Over the years, our father-daughter catches have developed their own rhythm, their own routine. We start about twenty feet apart, at conversation distance. We toss the ball back and forth for a while to loosen our arms, and after another while we take a step or two back, away from each other. The whole time, we're usually talking, talking, talking. Baseball, school, an adorable bit of something Sally or Patsy might have said or done or shared . . . whatever pops into our heads and rates a mention. Then another step back, and another, until we're maybe forty or fifty feet apart and really slinging it. The talking tends to fall away at this greater distance, which allows us to pick up the pace, and soon we're sixty feet apart and whipping our arms around in such a way that I can really get my heart rate going. In warm weather, we might break a sweat, only here on this Saturday afternoon in the park, the temperatures were a little too cool for perspiration. Too, there was enough of a chill in the air for the pocket of my glove to feel as if it had been painted on my palm—meaning it offered no cushion against the velocity of Iona's throws.

It had been some time since we'd tossed the ball around like this—not since the end of the previous season, I was now realizing—and in the intervening months, Iona had added considerable arm strength. She'd grown, too. (Our pediatrician said she still had another few inches to add to her frame, which would put her just shy of six feet, which in turn might put an end to these full-on, full-throttle catches, because I was already having trouble handling Iona's heat.) We used a hardball, which lent a little more weight to Iona's throws than a softball. She threw in a straightforward over-the-top motion instead of the slingshot delivery she'd modeled after our man Sure Shot, but there was enough hop on her balls to leave my hand stinging. However, after another while, I switched things up and started throwing Iona a series of hard grounders—to her left, to her right, up the gut—and as she picked each ball clean off the raked dirt of the infield she turned and fired it back to me with her by-now familiar sidearm delivery. And these came at me even harder. It was like she'd been putting all kinds of thought into her over-the-top tosses, but now that I had her moving and digging for tough hops she'd bounce up from her crouch and fire the ball across her body without thinking about it. The ball would leave her hand by some instinct, whip-sailing across the field to my outstretched glove like it belonged no place else.

Things went on in this way for a long few moments, until we were interrupted by a voice that found us through the rusted chain-link fence along the first-base side of the field.

"Jeez, where'd you learn to throw like *that*?" the voice said.

We turned and noticed a young man, thirty-something, dropping his gear bag on a bench behind the fence and beginning to sort through his things. Strangely, he wore what appeared to be a heavy-thick jersey made of wool flannel in a shade of gray the color of burnt charcoal. A large letter *N* was affixed in some way to one side of the jersey, and a large *Y* was affixed to the other. The buttons down the middle were open, revealing a Bart Simpson T-shirt underneath. Also strangely, he wore a pair of pastel-checked Bermuda shorts, which he began to slip out of as we turned to face him, revealing a pair of sliding shorts that appeared to hug his meaty thighs so tightly I worried for his circulation.

Iona spoke first. "Softball," she said. "Fast pitch."

The young man nodded. "Hmmm," he said, unfolding a pair of wool flannel pants to match his jersey and stepping into them as he leaned into the fence. "That explains it."

As he donned the rest of his uniform, he was joined by another few men of unfixed middle age, similarly dressed or half-dressed in wool flannel uniforms of their own. A few of them wore caps of the old-fashioned style once favored by the Willie Stargell-era Pirates, the ones that sat squarely atop the head. Some of these men sported fancy, meticulous moustaches—handlebars, horseshoes, walruses . . . the men emerged from the footpaths rimming the meadow, from beneath and around and alongside the occasional stand of trees, from every which direction, and in this way the benches along the first baseline were quickly filled with an odd collection of ballplayers looking as if from another time, waiting to take the field.

None of the players' jerseys appeared to match—some didn't even match their corresponding pants!—and as these men began to stretch and toss and sprint along the sidelines, I wondered just what they were doing here. Their uniforms were all of a similar style, from a time I now recognized as late-1800s, but the colors and shadings and stitching were all over the place, suggesting that someone had raided an old-time thrift store instead of planning ahead and ordering a proper set of color-coordinated uniforms.

After a while, Iona's thirty-something admirer approached. He said, "You guys almost done? We've booked the field."

I hadn't realized these men were waiting on us, so for a beat or two I was embarrassed. Inanely, beneath a small shrug, I said, "We're just having a catch."

By this point, Iona had crossed to where we were standing, and as she did the young man nodded in her direction and said, "I can see that. Quite an arm."

Iona smiled and did a small curtsy—a slightly sarcastic show of appreciation that left me hoping the slight sarcasm only registered with me.

I fumbled for something to say and settled on some slight sarcasm of my own. "Throws like a girl, huh?" I managed—tweaking Nellie's admonishment of a lifetime ago.

The gray-flannelled ballplayer laughed. "Hardly."

Iona, meanwhile, had been checking out the other players who had by now stepped all the way onto the field—as if the posted time on their permit had finally matched the times on their watches and cell phones and granted them access. She noticed them throwing the ball back and forth, barehanded—the balls like crabapples against their large hands. She noticed that even though the uniforms were mismatched, the caps were all the same color, the same design. She said, "What, you guys are in some league? Turn-of-the-century baseball? That the deal?"

"That's the deal," thirty-something said. "Nineteenth-century rules. Every tournament, it's different."

He saw that we were interested, so he explained that there were a series of tournaments run by a local baseball historian who used to play himself before a hip replacement forced him to the sidelines. Apparently, the guy was a well-known Civil War scholar, on the faculty at Fordham, and he took this kind of thing seriously. He'd research a set of rules from different periods and then set up these tournaments, and the players were meant to dress the part and take the whole thing just as seriously.

"The guys who play," our guide explained, "they get into it. You see the same group, over and over. Their wives and girlfriends, some of them, they'll come out in period clothes. Bloomers, bonnets, the whole deal."

"Cool," Iona said, taking it all in.

I could tell from the sparkle in my daughter's eyes she wanted in, only it wasn't just the sparkle that tipped me off. It was the way she started tugging at my sleeve—softly, so that the young man would somehow not notice. It was the way she positioned herself slightly behind him, so that his back was to her when she looked me full in the face and mouthed the name, "Dunlap!" (Letting me in on some secret!) And it was the way she did these things beneath a smile so wide it could have held a banana, sideways.

I thought it best to sidestep Iona's transparent enthusiasm and turn the conversation onto more assured ground. I held out my hand to this younger man and introduced myself. "David," I said, and then pointed to Iona. "This is my daughter, Iona. Okay if we stick around and watch?"

"Okay by me," the young man said, collecting my hand in his fat grip for a shake. "I'm a David as well. Friends call me Davey."

"Quite a handshake, Davey," I said, indicating his right hand, which I now saw was just shy of enormous.

"It's this damn game," Davey said, looking at his own hand as if for the first time. "They didn't believe in baseball gloves back then. Mitts, they were like, way in the future. You play a couple games, you've got meat hooks for hands."

Here again, Davey held out his hands for inspection, this time toward me and Iona, palms up, to prove his point. His left hand was worse than his right. It looked like it had been inflated with air and then flattened and steamed with an iron.

He must have caught me staring. "I'm a catcher," he said. "We get the worst of it. Catchers weren't allowed to wear gloves until, I think, 1870-something."

"Actually, 1875," Iona said.

Davey looked at her like she'd sprouted horns. "The young lady knows her stuff," he said, and then he pointed to his teammates. "Most of these guys, they're way into it. But some, they come out to one of these turn-back-the-clock games, they don't know what the hell is going on." And then, to Iona: "But not you, huh?"

I smiled, happy to play the role of proud papa, even for just this while. "You'd be amazed what the young lady knows," I said.

"Today's tournament," Iona said, moving things along. "What are the rules?"

"Runs all spring, this tournament," Davey said. "Today's just the first game, so I'm not really sure. Rules are from 1882, I think. Pitching rubber is fifty feet from home plate. Seven balls for a walk. A foul ball caught on a bounce goes for an out. Plus, a bunch of other rules, can't keep 'em all straight."

In the middle of Davey's explanation, a ball skittered past my feet and came to rest against the fence at my back. Iona moved to pick it up, and as she turned with it she noticed a handlebarred fellow in the outfield, waving his arms to signal it was his wayward throw that had come our way and that he would appreciate it if we could send the ball back out to him, thank you very much. He stood a couple hundred feet from Iona, and without a thought she let fly with the herky-jerky submarine delivery that had become her accustomed throwing motion. The ball vanished from her hand and cut a clean, crisp line through the air toward the man in the outfield. Such a rope! I can't be sure, but I think I heard the ball hiss and whistle as it passed, and others must have heard it too because you could see a half-dozen heads snapping in the direction of the ball as it made its way to the outfield.

It was as if all of that stretching and loosening and mingling had been stilled so these variously committed old-time ballplayers could watch the flight of this one ball.

The ball got to where it was going in like, nothing flat, and as soon as it did I could see those same half-dozen heads snap back to face Iona, each sporting its own curious, crinkled-up look. Clearly, these good people—athletes, all—had never seen such a bullet thrown over such a distance, and it made no sense to them that a mere schoolgirl could have unleashed such a rifle shot.

And then, as if to ensure that it made sense to me, Iona spun on her sneakered heels and mouthed Dunlap's name again.

Davey turned back to face Iona. He took his cap from his head, scratched briefly at what was left of his hairline, and seemed to just now take notice of her. "Seriously," he said. "Where'd you learn to throw like that?"

◆

Iona and I walked back to the bench on the third-base side of the field where we'd left our gear, talking conspiratorially along the way. Iona wanted to know if I thought these guys would let her join in. If *I* would let her join in—because, after all, a game of barehanded hardball with grown men who could clearly play was not at all the sort of activity Iona's mother would have suggested with one of her left-behind fliers or newspaper guides. Already, our new pal Davey had let slip that his team would be down a man, and that they'd have to play with two outfielders and a skip-spot in the lineup—meaning, when the empty position came around in the order, the team would be charged with an automatic out.

I did not think such a decision was within my purview as a second-class parent, so I moved to avoid it. I said, "Might be against the rules, I. Far as I know, there were no women in 1882."

"Ha," Iona said. "Funny."

I kept at it: "You might have to wear a petticoat or something."

"Once again," Iona said. "Funny."

"We could always ask," I said. "Our new pal Davey, all he can do is tell us no. If it's yes, maybe we can call your mother, see what she thinks."

"What about you?"

"You mean, what do I think?" I said.

"No," she said. "I know what you think. Duh. You think it'd be fine. Probably, you think it'd be amazing. You just don't want to get into any trouble with Mom if I get hurt."

She was right about that. (Duh!) "What about me, then?"

"Playing," she said. "What about you playing, too?"

I thought it was sweet that she didn't want to leave me out. Here these turn-back-the-clock fellows hadn't even invited I to join their game, and she wanted to include me in the mix as well, but before we could drift too far along in our reverie, she heard her name being called from across the field. Twice. My eyes followed the voices and landed on two kids who appeared to be about Iona's age. Two kids I'd never seen before. A boy and a girl. On bicycles.

Iona turned to me and said, "Be right back, okay?"

I nodded, and Iona skipped off in the direction of the bicycles, leaving me to wonder when it was that my baby girl had built a life of her own, when it was that there could be a pressing encounter to supersede whatever we were doing, just the two of us. When it was that baseball had taken a back seat to . . . well, to pretty much anything. I watched her talk animatedly with her friends from this safe distance, trying to imagine what was passing between them, among them. It occurred to me as I was trying to read I's lips that I'd never seen my daughter interact in such an easygoing manner with a boy her own age—at least, not since elementary school. Come to think of it, which I had now come to do, I could not recall seeing her so relaxed, so naturally at ease with *anyone* her own age for the longest time. At one point, she tipped her head back and laughed—an actual full-bodied, unselfconscious laugh that quickly ran through this small group like an infection.

Whatever it was, surely it must have been the funniest something in recorded human history, judging from their doubled-up howling. I guessed you had to be there.

After a while, the boy sat down on a bench beneath the tree by where they'd all been standing. He let his bicycle drop to the dirt. The girl and *her* bicycle dropped to the ground alongside them, and then Iona followed, too.

I must tell you—to just me, just then—this was about as startling a turn of events as any I have recounted to this point in my clumsy narrative, for I had never before seen my winningly antisocial child relate in such an easy, appropriate manner to kids her own age. Once again, I repeat myself, I know, but I do so for emphasis. It was as if she'd been sent by Central Casting to play the part of a carefree teen, if you could look past the sucking-candy hair.

I wished like crazy I could call Nellie and fill her in.

As Iona sat and chatted, the old-timers took the field and began to play. Iona had apparently given up on the idea of joining in and positioned herself so she could follow the action. It was only the top of the first inning, but I imagined she was torn. A game like this, I would have guessed it had landed in her thinking as another one of her séances, another chance to summon the ghost of Frederick C. Dunlap, and yet she remained on its periphery. She had wanted in just a few moments earlier, and now she appeared as content to chatter meaninglessly with her friends as she would have been to coax Dunlap from the thin air.

Meanwhile, in these same few moments, I could see that the caliber of ball among these old-timers would run good to high. These wool-flannelled men had likely been college ballplayers, American Legionnaires, low-level minor leaguers . . . they played the game at a level well beyond my reach. Even with their bare hands, they could make plays. They could move. They could hit. And Davey, squatting behind the plate with little in the way of protective gear and a glove that looked like a child's oven mitt, was getting banged up pretty good, especially with a hard-throwing pitcher standing just fifty feet away.

I wondered if Iona was feeling for him the same way I was feeling for him. I wondered if she was taking it all in the way I was taking it all in.

I wondered a whole lot of things, actually—but then, suddenly, I wondered no more as a left-handed batter stepped to the plate and sliced a looping liner down the third baseline. The ball wasn't hit particularly hard. It sailed foul by about thirty feet and took a big hop-bounce off the bike path that had just been traveled by Iona's friends. I'd been distracted by the crack of the bat, the flight of the ball, and so hadn't noticed Iona leap to her feet from her Indian-style sitting position—legs akimbo!—and move to make some kind of play on it. Somehow, she managed to anticipate the skip of the ball off the concrete and leap to her right to snatch it with her right hand, just behind her right ear.

It was a remarkable grab—and then, even more remarkable, she planted her right foot in a continuation of her leaping motion and slung an absolute pea homeward. The ball *plunk-slapped* the waiting oven mitt of an astonished Davey, who quickly pulled his bare hand from his glove and shook it out exaggeratedly—the pantomime of the weekend ballplayer chasing the sting.

"Jeez!" he cried, looking down the third baseline toward Iona, who offered another mock-curtsy in receipt of his stare.

"That's supposed to be an out," she called back across the field toward a decidedly too-well-dressed man in a top hat and Prince Albert frock coat, sitting majestically astride a stool positioned along the first baseline—the umpire, apparently. *A gentleman arbiter*, in the parlance of the day.

Then she pointed to Davey behind the plate. "Caught it off one bounce," she hollered. "Like you said. Those are the rules, right?"

◆

Now, alongside these few astonishments I must tack on another—a final astonishment, if you will.

As you might imagine, Iona's display caused a good deal of rumbling and gesticulating among the few fans who had gathered to watch the game. Among the players, certainly, it was a bit of a spectacle, and it took a good few moments for the fuss to fade and the game to resume. During that time, Iona went back to huddling with her friends for another beat and then crossed from the tree where she'd been sitting to our spot on the bench along the third baseline. As she did, an older man walking with a pronounced limp strode from his seat on the first-base side to intercept her. I could only assume this was the Fordham professor with the fake hip.

The professor reached first. He stopped at Iona's gear bag and turned to me and said, "Some throw."

I said, "Catch wasn't too bad either."

He gave me his name. I gave him mine just as Iona sat down beside me. He reached for her hand, shook it, and said, "I gather you play a little baseball."

"Softball, mostly," Iona said.

"You know of our old-time game?" he asked, pointing to the field with a measure of pride.

"I know the Union Association," Iona offered with a measure of her own. She pointed to Davey behind the plate. "Catcher over there said you do a lot of research. Turn-of-the-century-type stuff. Ever come across anything on the St. Louis Maroons?"

"Only the most dominant team in baseball history," the professor said.

"And their star player?" Iona said. "Fred Dunlap?"

"Only the most dominant player over a single season," the man replied. "One of the greatest seasons in the history of the game. Sure Shot, they called him. Did you know that? Because of his arm. The man hit .400 and that's what people remember, his arm."

"I know, right?" Iona said. Like she was talking to one her friends on their bicycles.

We exchanged another few pleasantries, another few details of Dunlap's life and career, but after a while the professor said he had to return to the official scorer's table on the other side of the field. As he did so, Iona took her spot next to me on the bench, and we sat in this way for the next while. The whole time, I noticed her friends, right where she'd left them. Too, I noticed Iona noticing them in a way that had me thinking she probably wanted to join them back under their tree.

"Kids from school?" I asked, looking their way.

"Yeah. Probably I should have introduced you. Like, why didn't I introduce you?"

"That's fine," I said. And it was.

"They're the twins," Iona said.

"Ah. That answers every question I could possibly have. The twins. Good to know."

"Mom's heard me talk about them," Iona replied. "Everyone knows the twins."

"Not me. I don't know the twins." Beat. Then: "These twins have names?"

"Kelly and Casey."

"Kelly and Casey," I said back, turning my head again to face these well-known twins. "Which one is which?"

"Ha," she barked. "You are just so very funny." In a way that left me thinking I was so very . . . *not*.

"No," I said. "Really. Could go either way."

"The boy," Iona said. "He's Kelly."

"See, I would have guessed he was his sister."

She punched my arm softly and turned her attention back to the game, and we sat in this way for the next while. For the rest of the half-inning, we didn't say anything. I kept hearing Iona's voice from just before. *Mom's heard me talk about them* . . . over and over. *Mom's heard me talk about them* . . . this, alone, had been enough.

Finally, Iona spoke. She said, "D'you think he saw?"

At first, I thought she meant the boy, but then I thought again. "Dunlap?"

She nodded.

"I don't know, I . . ." I started. And, really, I didn't. Really, I didn't have the first idea.

There was another long silence neither of us could quite think how to fill, so Iona changed the subject. She tilted her head toward the twins beneath the tree and said, "There's this kid, Stacey. They're going to hang out."

"And?" I said, not sure what this kid Stacey had to do with anything.

"And they asked me to come with," Iona said.

I gave this some thought. "This kid, Stacey," I eventually said. "That a boy or a girl?"

She punched me again. "Dad!" she said admonishingly.

"Dad!" I mimicked.

"Would that be okay, do you think?" she said.

I turned, punched her back—softly, sweetly. I said, "Okay with me."

She leaned in to plant a hot-pink kiss on my cheek, but as she stood to join her friends her face abruptly filled with second thoughts. "What about Dunlap?" she said.

"What about him?" I asked.

"What if he's here? What if he's coming?"

I pulled her in close for a hug, which she didn't seem to mind. "He's not here, I. He's not coming."

It tore at me to have to say it, but I believed I had no choice. Already, I'd dragged Iona all the way into this Dunlap craziness. For a year and a half, we'd been searching, searching, searching for this man's spirit, and now as I watched her interact so genuinely, so guilelessly with these two kids from school, these *twins*, I wondered if maybe Iona wasn't just holding on to me the whole time. If maybe I wasn't holding on to her, on a kind of carom.

When she pulled away, I could see she was crying. Not a lot, but her eyes had started to mist, so I tried to react like an attentive parent instead of the hopelessly confused, romantic, tentative, medication-resistant mess I had apparently become. I reached into Iona's gear bag for the plastic container that held her makeup, her jewelry, her accessories . . . her *stuff*. I held it out. "Here," I said. "Might want to freshen up before you run off with your friends."

"Nah," she said, dabbing at her eyes with the pinched sleeves of her sweatshirt. "I'm good."

"You sure?" I pressed, holding out the case to make sure I had the parenting piece covered. I didn't want Iona getting all the way to this Stacey person's apartment and figuring out she wasn't wearing her jewelry. "Your little nose-chain loop thing," I said. "I'm certainly not planning to wear it."

"Nah, Dad," she said. "Take it home for me, 'kay? I'm good."

And she was. Truly, she was.

◆

Iona's column from the Spring 2000 edition of *The Quartermaster*:

WHAT SUCKS ABOUT GROWING UP
By Iona Felb

What sucks about growing up is that you start to see yourself as you really are. You, your family, your place in the world . . . it begins to come clear. You carry this picture in your head of your little-kid self, and nothing really seems to matter except what seems interesting in that moment, whatever's caught your attention, but then there's this burst, like a giant wave of knowing, and it starts to roll in and then it just kind of washes over you, collects you in its swell, and sets you down on a whole other shore.

For a while, you might have no idea where you are, how you got there, where to go next.

Here's what I mean: When you're a kid, your parents are just your parents, these giant, safe-seeming monoliths. They are all-knowing, all-seeing, all-comforting. They feed you, bathe you, hold you close, tell you what to think. But then you learn to take care of yourself, think for yourself. You figure a few things out. You understand how your mom is when she gets a certain way, how your dad is when he gets a certain way, how they are when the rest of the world isn't looking. And underneath this understanding, you might get that one parent appears to the whole rest of the world to really have it together, while the other parent can appear to be falling apart, but at home it might be flipped. At home, behind the scenes, the one who's a little off out in the world is completely sane, while the one who's a little sane out in the world is completely off.

Anyway, you start to notice things—things that had probably been there all along but you're now seeing for the first time.

What sucks about growing up is that now you have to acknowledge these things and set them right. For the first time, there's a weight attached to your days. There's responsibility. You can't just chill and do whatever you want, whatever seems interesting in that moment. You have to do things that matter. You have to take care of the people close to you. You're no longer a kid, just, but now you're something else. Maybe you still feel like a kid, a little bit, but now you're also on the way to something. Now you're next in line, so it's up to you to know if whatever's broken between two people can be fixed. You go from nothing really mattering to everything mattering most of all, and suddenly it's on you.

Whatever it is, it's on you.

It's like how it is in those Disney movies, the way the wise-beyond-their-years kids know how to push just the right buttons at just the right time to get their parents back together, but only if they truly believe this is how things should go. Only if they know in their hearts that they hold some secret piece of some secret puzzle that can put back the picture of their family. Only if they go from being wise beyond their years to where the wisdom kind of catches up and they're exactly as wise as they're supposed to be.

What, did you honestly believe that some blowhard Hollywood executive came up with the idea for *The Parent Trap*? No way. Just, no way.

What sucks about growing up is that you're forced to choose sides. Like, if you're used to having a parent tell you what to do, what's best, you have to look at what's in front of you and make sense of it. You become aware of a time not too, too far off when you'll get to drive, to vote, to pay taxes, to pick a path and follow it, to maybe pick a partner and follow each other. And at the same time you become aware of the people around you—your parents, say—and the choices they've made in their lives, the paths and partners they've meant to follow.

Sometimes, it works out that the choices we make don't take us where we thought they might. Sometimes, there are twists and turns, or we veer off course, or maybe it's just that people change. They do. *We* do. Yep, that's probably it. All of the problems in the grown-up world, it's just a simple matter of people not being how they were or who they were when they first met. That's all. You decide to spend your life with someone, to start a family with someone, you think of them in a certain way. Or maybe you're born into a family, and you have these set ideas of how people are. You expect them to be that certain way the whole rest of the time you're together, and if it works out that they're no longer able to be who they were or how they were, it's all messed up. People change. Things happen to them and they have to figure out a way to deal with these things, and it doesn't always go the way you think it will go.

Mostly, what sucks about growing up is that it changes how you see yourself. All along, you have this certain frame of reference. You know how things are. You look out at the world in this certain way. And then, you start high school and it's like you're looking in a funhouse mirror. What you get back looks like nothing you've ever seen.

ACKNOWLEDGMENTS

A grateful tip of the pen to David Buss, John Marx, Dona Chernoff Eichner, Jonathan Paisner, Jeff Stern, Ron Darling, Matthew Benjamin, Michael Homler, Nichole Argyres, Dan Strone, John Silbersack, Greg Aretakis, and my own sweetsuffering wife, Leslie. Thanks as well to Mel Berger, who found enough things to like in this story to want to help me put it out into the world, and his former assistant, Katie Breaux, who carried the torch for a good long while. And, most of all, to Dallas Hudgens and the enormously talented team of publishing professionals at Relegation Books—Jules Hucke, Zach Dodson, and Lauren Cerand.

"Impressive."
—TOBIAS CARROLL, THE FORWARD

On Bittersweet Place

A novel by
RONNA WINEBERG

$13.95, now at your favorite independent bookstore

Coming October 2016:

The Loved Ones
by Sonya Chung

RELEGATIONBOOKS
www.relegationbooks.com